CONIMICUT HURRICANE!

The Exciting Adventure Novel of Two Lonely Kids...Trapped by Deadly Hurricane Glenna!

All orphaned Tommy desperately wanted was a home, someone to love, and to love him. He hoped this summertime foster home would be it. But all he found in seaside Conimicut Village was crusty old Granny Parker, back-breaking work and even greater loneliness. But then he met lovely, tomboyish Kathy, wild adventures, ghosts and crooks, terror, tears and triumphs.

Conimicut Hurricane is the exciting, captivating adventure story of Tommy and Kathy as they grow together, and find a dream...of wise, old Ben Brown who saves their lives—twice!...only to realize they are all trapped in a doomed house on Conimicut Point, directly in the path of the century's most vicious hurricane!

Conimicut Hurricane is the story of four new friends—many generations apart—who brave the terrors, raging 156-Mph winds, and two massive tidal waves of Hurricane Glenna which devastate seaside Conimicut Village and the entire Rhode Island coastline.

One Summer in late August...

Happy Reading!

Don Vieweg

12/98

CONIMICUT
HURRICANE!

**The Exciting Adventure Novel of Two Lonely
Kids...Trapped by Deadly Hurricane Glenna!**

By Don Vieweg

A Bellman Publishing Co. Book
P.O. Box 9118
Warwich, RI 02889-0118

CONIMICUT HURRICANE!

Cover Art and Maps by Tommy Wayne and Don Vieweg

Cover Photo by Ted Pickering

Published by:
Bellman Publishing Company
P.O. Box 9118
Warwick, RI 02889-0118 USA
(401) 737-2058

ISBN 1-884487-05-X
Printed in the United States of America
10 9 8 7 6 5 4 3 2 1

Books by Don Vieweg:

Conimicut Hurricane! (The Adventure Novel)

Motivational Lessons My Dog Skipper Taught Me!

(A Humor, Self-Help, Doggie Book to Remind You That YOU Are in Charge of Your Life.)

Dedication

To Dorothy, my wife, who rowed a skiff, and to Shirley, Judy and Donnie, our children...and to all the other Narragansett Bay and Conimicut Village kids who are the real Kathys and Tommys in these exciting adventures.

Enjoy!

***

Special Notice

All people and events in this work of fiction are products of the author's imagination. Hurricane Glenna is fictional also, but is based on the unnamed 1938 hurricane, and Hurricanes Carol and Edna, 1954, Gloria, 1985, and, of course, Bob, 1991, all who chose—unwanted—to visit Conimicut Village, Rhode Island and New England.

CONIMICUT HURRICANE!

Table of Contents

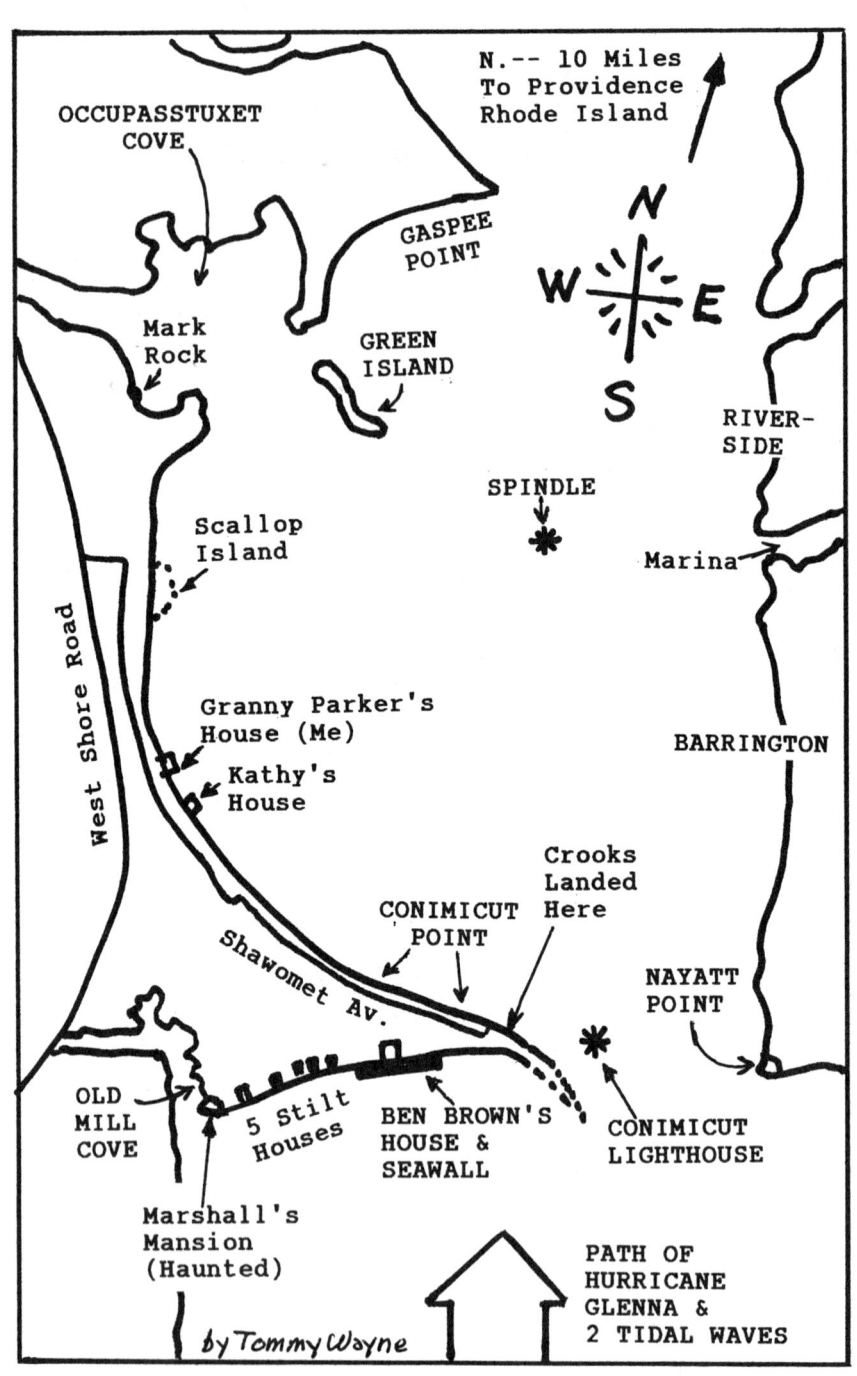

Conimicut Point Area: Narragansett Bay, Warwick, Rhode Island

CONIMICUT HURRICANE

by Don Vieweg

Chapter 1

The Wave And The Wall

Young Tommy Wayne struggled fiercely to peer into the black rain slashing horizontally into his worried face.

Yes, he was sure he had seen it coming...but he dared not tell Kathy. She was already terrified of the increasing hurricane winds and raging seas slamming their tiny outboard skiff.

"Please, God, help us!" Tommy prayed again. "None of this was supposed to happen."

Again he stole a glance at Kathy huddled in a ball in the bow of their tiny fourteen-foot boat. He felt the slamming and tugging of Kathy's half-sunken sailing pram in tow behind them.

"What a wonderful, brave girl," he thought. For several hours Kathy had fought her fears so bravely. Now she was too dazed with terror and exhaustion to even realize what was happening to them. Perhaps that was better, after all.

Kathy had risked her own young life to courageously sail her tiny eight-foot pram sailboat all the way from Conimicut Village to Prudence Island in the middle of Narragansett Bay, a distance of over seven, terrifying, full gale miles—just to warn him of the coming hurricane. She had braved four hours of slashing winds, huge waves, and her own fears, just because she cared for him and wanted him to be safe.

No, it wasn't supposed to have happened this way...

All Tommy had wanted was a home! Just a home of his own, someone to love him and whom he could love, a feeling of belonging to someone! That wasn't too much to ask for, was it?

And he had worked so hard, so very, very hard, to be accommodating and cooperative to Granny Parker. And to be loved by her...

But Granny Parker was still sending him back to the orphanage.

So he had run away to Prudence Island to think and form plans: How could he stay in Conimicut Village on lovely Narragansett Bay? How could he stay here with Kathy and old Ben Brown?

"Oh, God, I really messed things up!" Tommy cried out loud, but only the screaming winds heard him.

It was *his fault* that he and Kathy Turner were trapped in a sinking skiff in the middle of Narragansett Bay with Hurricane Glenna bearing down upon them. It was his fault!

Again Tommy prayed the small ten-horsepower outboard motor pushing his skiff would not fail. It was a good motor, his very own, really. Just like the used skiff was actually his own possession.

All Summer, after his hard work for Granny Parker, he had earned the money to buy it. And Granny Parker had—amazingly— given him permission to do so.

Kathy's father had helped him pick out a good second-hand Johnson outboard motor in Providence, and Tommy was extremely proud of it. The dealer had said it was a strong, dependable motor.

Now if it would only continue to work, and, somehow, miraculously, get them five more miles to land and safety...

Tommy heard Kathy moaning. The rain and salt water in the boat was getting deeper. He'd have to bail out again. If he could. He knew Kathy couldn't bail any more. She was too exhausted.

As he thought of his wonderful, new friend, a great warmth filled him. But only for a moment. Again he was seized with bitter anger at himself.

"It's all my fault," he choked. "If only I hadn't run away! Then Kathy would be home, and safe, and old Granny Parker wouldn't be worried about me—if she was worried."

Maybe the grouchy old lady didn't even know he had gone. Oh, she must know by now, he thought. It had been over twelve hours since he had run away from Granny Parker's tumbled-down house on Bellman Avenue in Conimicut Village. Besides, Kathy had told him she had checked with Granny Parker...

Actually, the old lady wasn't really his grandmother at all. No relation, just another temporary foster-mother who needed a strong back and capable working hands for the summer. Yes, Granny Parker was another of dozens of foster parents in his young, orphaned life.

But the past three months living, working and boating on beautiful Narragansett Bay more than made up for all the blisters and aching muscles from working on the old house and seawall. Besides, there was Kathy in his life now, and—

The tiny skiff suddenly lunged bow down. Its stern leaped high so the outboard propeller screamed as it knifed the air. The skiff suddenly slammed down again, the propeller biting solid black water, shoving the skiff sharply to the right—starboard.

To compensate, Tommy fought with the controls, twisting the control-steering handle to cut the speed so they wouldn't capsize in the violent sea.

Tommy forced his mind to concentrate on steering his skiff. That wave almost swamped them. The hurricane winds were from the direct South, blowing the Atlantic Ocean up into Narragansett Bay like a flood into a funnel.

"God, the wind must be seventy, eighty miles an hour," Tommy cried out loud. "And still increasing..."

Kathy had told him she had seen on her television early this morning that Hurricane Glenna had suddenly speeded up and turned toward Rhode Island. The change was so sudden that the Ocean State was caught unawares.

Glenna was an especially vicious hurricane, with wind speeds that could hit a hundred, even one-twenty or thirty miles per hour, and...

Tommy heard the roaring behind him. It grew louder, deafening. Risking being blown overboard by the violent winds, he quickly stood up and peered south into the slashing, horizontal rain. There was no mistaking it: a great wall of water was racing toward them.

"Oh, God!" he screamed. "It's coming!"

His frantic cries aroused Kathy, huddled in the bow of the skiff. She abruptly sat up in the sloshing water, blinking her eyes, dazed. Her clothes were plastered to her shivering, young body. Her pretty face was contorted in terror and weariness.

"W-What's coming?" she cried.

Tommy squinted his eyes to see further south, back toward the neck of Prudence Island, someplace behind them. In a momentary clearing he again saw that great wall of water.

There was no mistaking it now. It *was* a tidal wave! It looked exactly like what old Ben Brown had told them about—a monstrous wall of gray water bearing down upon them in their tiny skiff in the middle of Narragansett Bay. They would be drowned!

Within minutes the tidal wave would slam into them. There was no escape. It would kill them both!

"Forgive me, Kathy," Tommy yelled over the shrieking wind. "I didn't mean for it to happen this way."

"W-What do you mean?" White-faced, Kathy's dark green eyes were great in new fear.

Tommy struggled to keep the skiff's stern to the wind. He said nothing. After all the terror Kathy had already experienced, he couldn't add more. He couldn't tell her about the killing tidal wave bearing down upon them. He couldn't!

"A tidal wave," he thought bitterly. "Everything's ending with a wave..."

His frantic thoughts raced back to the beginning, back three months ago to his coming to Conimicut Village in Rhode Island, to crusty Granny Parker's home, to all the back-breaking work...and to lovely, tomboyish Kathy, to excitement, fishing and boating on beautiful Narragansett Bay.

It was ironic that everything was ending with a wave. It seemed only three short months ago his whole life had *begun* with a wave...

***

The heavy speedboat raced through the bright June day, trailing a huge wake. It streaked under Rhode Island's Jamestown-Verrazzano Bridge in Narragansett Bay's west passage. It passed the island of Conanicut, or Newport. It streaked past tiny Hope Island and continued north toward the gut between Prudence and Patience Islands.

Here it slowed briefly. Once free of shoal water, the boat's motor again screamed and the speedboat headed north toward Providence.

Eight minutes later it rounded the lighthouse dotting Conimicut Point and turned slightly northwest, following the channel.

Once past Gaspee Point, it knifed homeward to some unknown marina in Cranston or Providence.

Behind it, the boat's wake fanned out like an ever-widening inverted "V". The wave rolled toward both shores where it bobbed moored and anchored boats, startling seagulls and terns.

It jostled fishermen and quahaugers who automatically braced their sea-wary bodies and briefly glanced up and wondered why all the rush? Life was too short for such speed. A boat should be enjoyed.

Ten minutes after the speedboat had passed Conimicut Lighthouse, its wake rolled a small skiff anchored off the southwest shore of Conimicut Point near the mouth of Old Mill Cove. Its young occupant, new to the sea, lost his balance. He fell against the oarlock and cut his right arm near the elbow, forever to have a small scar, and never really knowing why.

"Ow!" Tommy Wayne cried and rubbed his elbow. The salt water on his fingers stung the wound, and he sucked in his breath in a hiss.

Curious about the origin of the sudden wave, Tommy stopped tonging for quahaugs and glanced to the east and open water. Nothing there. The mid-June day was calm and warm, the water smooth as polished glass. A superb day.

"Hum. Now, why would a wave suddenly appear out of nowhere to rock his borrowed skiff so he hurt himself?" he wondered. He sat down and stopped the bleeding with his handkerchief, wincing at the pain as he gently washed off the blood with salt water.

There was so much he didn't know about the sea—so very much. Would he ever learn?

A scrawny, towheaded boy of fourteen who looked two years younger, Tommy gazed thoughtfully at the school of bait fish winnowing around the skiff. They were silversides. He knew that much from his book study.

He had four books in his library, the most he had ever owned in his life. They were *his* books, not the orphanage's. He had personally bought them with his own hard-earned money.

Old Granny Parker, his temporary fostermother—(she was more like his grandmother, really!)—she promised she wouldn't touch them.

In the four fascinating weeks he had lived with her in the old house on the edge of the sea, she had kept her word. She had entered his tiny upstairs room only to clean and dust. And not very often, at that.

But Granny Parker was very old and crotchety. She was probably eighty, if she was a day. And she was stubborn, and she wouldn't admit that her eyes were old too. And she was independent and very set in her ways.

Well, so what was a little dust, anyway?

Tommy knew he was an intruder in her life. Granny Parker kept him only because she needed his working hands and his strength. He also knew she resented his presence in the weather-beaten old house on Bellman Avenue in Conimicut Village, Rhode Island.

Still, he wished she didn't resent him so. He wished she liked him, even a little. Oh, he didn't expect love, not at all. Just a little friendliness, a little warmth.

As for love, the crabby old lady seemed incapable of love.

Tommy sighed wearily as he sat thinking in his borrowed boat.

Maybe that's how a person becomes after living alone for thirty or more years. Still, it would be nice if she did like him— even a little bit.

He didn't enjoy being thought of simply as a strong back, or a doer of chores, or a noise and an appetite to be endured for services rendered. Who would like it?

"Brr-rr!" He shuddered at the thought that anyone would actually prefer to live alone, like Granny Parker did. To him, that was a horrible thing. It was terrible to be without friends or someone to talk to.

Tommy remembered back and was astonished that almost four whole weeks had passed since he had left the orphanage to spend the summer months with Granny Parker.

He had been terribly lonely that first week, but now, four weeks later, life wasn't so bad, really. Here on the edge of the sea there were many compensations. Here he had old Granny Parker to grumble at him, and a grumble was always better than nothing.

And if he was allowed to start school in the Fall things would improve. Oh, sure they would! And maybe Granny Parker wouldn't send him back. Maybe she'd—keep him, and even let him go to school. There was always a chance, he thought optimistically.

And if he could stay, and if he went to school, he'd meet other boys and girls his age, and—It would be wonderful having friends!...

Sitting in the gently rocking skiff, Tommy recalled his second week living with Granny Parker. He had been a bit lonely then, too, but he was beginning to feel more sure of himself.

The small seaside town of Conimicut Village pulsed with the eternal movement of the sea. Boating, waterskiing, fishing, quahauging, swimming—all were there for the taking.

On the beach he saw several boys his age. Girls too, like pesty Kathy Turner. They all seemed like they would be friendly. So maybe it was up to him to act. He just had to grit his teeth and plunge in and get wet.

But how? He was an outsider. He knew nothing about the sea that seemed so very important to these kids. Well, maybe he could learn. And that's why he was studying those books.

Of course, all his hard work helped salve his loneliness. Granny Parker—she really wasn't his grandmother, or any relation, but he couldn't call her Tillie, or Mrs. Parker or Ma. "Granny" seemed more appropriate, if only for respect for her great age and her cap of snowy hair. And "Granny" was okay with her.

Anyway, Granny Parker was a stubborn and fiercely independent old lady, and a demon for hard work.

"Work keeps me young," she had told him. "If I didn't work, I'd rust up like an old anchor weatherin' in the surf."

At first Tommy had resented all the work she thrust upon him. Since he didn't want to be sent back to the crowded orphanage where he was just another mouth to feed, a body to clothe, a mind to educate, he did as he was told. And work did help offset the loneliness.

He soon saw that the old lady did as much work as he did, if not more. She wasn't like some foster-parents who told you what to do, then sat around and watched you do it.

And once his work was done each day, his time was his own. That was the sweetest time of all, a free afternoon or evening in which he could explore the shoreline, skip rocks across the blue-green water, hunt fiddler crabs off Conimicut Point, Occupasstuxet Cove or Green's Island...enjoy countless seaside adventures.

He soon learned to do his work quickly and efficiently. Sometimes he even did more than he was told to do.

"Why not?" he reasoned. "If I do it now, I won't have to do it later."

Still, he wished he could learn to like the old lady. But how could he? No one enjoyed being thought of as a tool, a utensil, a strong back or a young pair of hands...and *that's all!*

Tommy sighed profoundly. "Well, maybe someday things will improve. Yes, things *will* improve." He would think positive.

The baitfish under his skiff suddenly ruffled the water and vanished. For several minutes he waited for them to return to feed on the debris he was stirring up from the bottom with his borrowed quahaug tongs. When they didn't return, he hauled the skiff two feet ahead and cinched up on the anchor line. If he was ever going to earn enough money to buy his own boat and outboard motor, he'd better get busy.

The ten-foot tongs—long wooden scissors with wire baskets with teeth at the end—were heavy. His hands were still sore and blistered from the previous day's tonging, but they were calloused in places too.

Tonging for quahaugs—hard-shelled clams—was hard work, but it was good, muscle-building work, and the money he got for the quahaugs would enable him to someday buy his own skiff and outboard motor. It seemed all the kids his age had their own boats and motors.

It had been Granny Parker who had first suggested he go tonging in his free time. She had the tongs stored in her barn. He had to make some minor repairs to the wire baskets and straighten the two-inch long teeth that scratched the bay bottom, but that wasn't very difficult. Kathy Turner's father helped him.

The tongs splashed and Tommy guided the open baskets to the bottom six feet below the skiff. Working his arms scissor-fashion, he opened and closed the toothed baskets, feeling for quahaugs one-to-two inches below the sandy bottom of the bay.

When the teeth scraped something solid, the noise could be heard and the obstruction felt though the wood stales.

Grinning, he worked the teeth deeper into the sand and mud, and around the quahaug, then pulled up the sea's treasures and put them in a bushel basket.

Collecting a bushel of quahaugs was slow, hard work. It took time and an agony of energy. His first bushel required over four hours hard digging, gave him blisters, aching shoulders, stomach cramps and an intense sense of personal satisfaction. When he later sold it for ten dollars, the satisfaction was still greater.

But a problem arose: He debated a long time about showing the money to Granny Parker, but finally decided he had to. After all, they were her tongs and it was she who had taken him from the orphanage—even if her reasons were purely selfish. She was his temporary guardian and she was feeding and clothing him. Best of all, she had given him his own room, the first he had ever had. Privacy was a strange and wonderful thing.

As he showed the money to Granny Parker, he hoped she would at least let him keep one dollar. He was in for a surprise.

The old lady snorted: "Huh? That's all you made in four hours digging?"

"All?" He was astonished. He drew himself up proudly. "I think I did pretty good my first day tonging."

"Well—" The old lady was hesitant. "—Mebbe you did."

He held out the money and she slapped his hand away. "It's your money. Go spend it," she cried. "Or bank it. Do what you want."

A great, joyous grin illuminated his young face. "Honest? I can *really* keep it? You're not fooling me?"

"I don't fool. Now, get your big feet out of my way so's I can make our supper..."

He had used that money to buy four used books on boating and the sea, the first books he had ever personally owned. They were a wonderful source of information and pleasure. The colored drawings of fish, shells and sea creatures continually fascinated him. That's how he had recognized the silversides beside his skiff.

Tommy grunted under the weight of the filled tongs. He rocked them against the side of the skiff, the way the professionals did to wash out mud and sand, then pulled them in and opened the baskets.

His take this time was four large quahaugs, two oyster drills, a pink starfish, a bent beer can and three barnacle-encrusted rocks. Not bad at all!

He added the quahaugs to his pile. Pausing, he placed them aside, along with four additional large quahaugs. He'd save them for Granny Parker. She loved sea food.

Besides, she made a delicious chowder and he sure did love chowder, Rhode Island style, with tomatoes.

The late afternoon sun was hot on his back. Perspiring now, he removed his shirt, doused his thin, tanned face with sea water, and had a drink from the water jug under the stern thwart, or seat. The bushel basket was only half-filled and he had a lot of tonging to do.

"Can't waste all my time thinkin'," he muttered, and the tongs splashed.

It was a half-hour later when he first noticed the small pram sailboat heading his way on a port tack. He admired it for several minutes.

"Sure is a pretty sight," he said aloud. Sighing wistfully, he returned to his tonging. Five minutes later he glanced around. The pram sailboat was almost on top of him.

"Hey, watch out where you're going, you nut!"

The boat's skipper expertly swung the tiller and released the mainsheet so the small boat nosed around and gently nudged his skiff.

"Hi, Tommy. I thought this was you. I came out to see you."

Tommy groaned audibly. He wanted friends, but not pesty Kathy Turner, a summer resident who lived three houses down from Granny Parker's.

Kathy was thirteen and "just starting to bud!", as Granny Parker put it. She was almost as tall as he, and a bit skinny, but she had a pretty face when it was clean, although that was rarely. She was always fooling around boats and motors, or scavenging like a seagull along the shore, or beachcombing. She acted like a boy and she wasn't, and sometime really soon even Kathy wouldn't be able to ignore that fact.

He watched sourly as Kathy scrambled into his skiff and tied her pram's bowline to the skiff's stern cleat. To her, the fact that she was uninvited made no difference.

"I was looking for you all over," she said agreeably. "It takes a long time to tack around Conimicut Point, you know." She pulled her pram closer and reached inside.

"I brought you an apple. Thought you'd be hungry. —Oh, you've cut your elbow!"

"It's nothing. Forget it." He was famished. He had been considering eating some littlenecks raw, but couldn't quite bring himself to do it. An apple was much better.

Maybe someday he'd learn to enjoy raw quahaugs like Granny Parker did.

"Thanks, Kathy." He bit hungrily into the sweet apple.

"You wash that cut real good. And put on iodine," Kathy warned.

"Okay. I will."

"—And you should take a lunch," Kathy chided. "I don't know why you don't. I always get hungry on the water. Always!"

"You're always hungry, period!" Tommy said, not unkindly. "I don't see how you can eat so much and still be so skinny."

Kathy flushed and turned away. "You—You're awful! And I sailed all this distance, over two miles, just to give you an apple." She looked at him, her green eyes shiny.

He hardened his heart. He liked Kathy, even if she was a tomboy and a pest. But if he wanted to be accepted by boys, he couldn't very well chum around with a girl. What would the guys think?

"Thanks. But no one *asked* you to bring me an apple." He munched at the core, finally tossing it into the water. Several silversides swam up and nibbled at it. More joined them.

Occasionally some tiny fish jumped over the core, playing leapfrog. He studied them thoughtfully.

"—I'm sorry, Kathy." He couldn't look into her eyes. "I—do appreciate the apple. Honest."

When Kathy turned, she was smiling and her young face was

almost beautiful. She had white, even teeth and a clear complexion. Her chestnut hair normally hung to her shoulders, curled up at the ends. Today, she wore it in pigtails. She looked like a ten-year old, all elbows and knees sticking out of her red-and-white striped pullover shirt and blue shorts. She was barefoot. A Band-Aid was wrapped around her small toe. Her feet were dirty from caked mud and sand.

She must have walked the boat a good part of the way, Tommy reasoned. He dropped the tongs into the water and started working them deeper, feeling for hidden quahaugs. He was very conscious of Kathy's presence. He wished she would leave. If any of the local boys saw her, they'd laugh and think he was a sissy. Or worse, they'd think Kathy was his girl.

At the thought, he felt his face heating up. He felt strangely awkward and confused.

"Don't have time for girls," he muttered to himself, and glanced at Kathy sitting on the rear thwart. She wasn't looking his way, but ashore, at Marshall's Mansion. He saw a faint shudder pass through her young body.

And for good reason too. Marshall's Mansion was the local haunted house. Facing due south on the edge of the sea and only four feet above mean high tide, it was vulnerable to abnormally high tides and hurricanes. So far, it had withstood three or four hurricanes and had not washed into the sea to break up as did so many other Conimicut, Long Meadow and Oakland Beach homes. But it had been vacant for many years, a wind-whipped derelict with empty window eyes and towering finger peaks.

And it was haunted with its own special ghost, a sea-breathing monster too horrible to describe.

Again he noticed Kathy's trembling. "What's the matter?" he asked. "Scared of ghosts?"

Kathy's face was white despite her tan. "Brr-r. It looks creepy even in the daylight. Have you gone there yet? I mean, at night?"

He shook his head, and Kathy said, "I wouldn't go there for a million dollars, especially at night." She swung her feet around to the deck, wiggling her bare toes in the half-inch deep water.

"How about you, Tommy?" Would you visit Marshall's Mansion at night?"

Tommy didn't believe in ghosts, but it didn't pay to take needless chances. He couldn't very well tell that to Kathy.

"Sure I would," he said boldly. "Someday I'll visit Marshall's Mansion at night, a windy, stormy night." He grinned at her. "It might be fun."

She stared at him in undisguised admiration. Her pretty lips parted in a wide smile. "I'll go with you!" she cried. "Oh, please say yes. I've been summering here for almost ten years and I've never gone to Marshall's Mansion at night. I've always wanted to go. Please say you'll take me, Tommy."

She seemed so earnest, so intent, he shrugged.

"Okay. If I ever go, I'll take you."

Kathy leaped up, excited, tipping the skiff.

"Hey, sit down!"

"You promise? Honest?"

"Yes, I promise. Now, sit down before you—*scuttle* us!" Yes, that was the right word. "Scuttle—to sink." A good nautical word from one of his boating books.

Pleased, Kathy sat on the stern seat, her legs dangling over the side in the water. She giggled happily at the baitfish nibbling at her bare toes. She had pretty legs.

For a long time Tommy tonged and said nothing. The bushel basket was almost filled with quahaugs. A late afternoon southerly wind rippled the water, rocking the skiff slightly. He was strangely conscious of Kathy sitting or lying on the stern thwart, her sailboat tied on back, its white sail luffing in the freshening breeze.

Occasionally he stole a look at her. She held her head high and proudly. Her eyes were closed and a faint smile played on her lips. She seemed completely alone, oblivious of everything, her pretty profile outlined against the blue sky. She didn't *look* like a tomboy.

He swallowed painfully, angry for even thinking Kathy was pretty. She was too skinny, and too young, and a pest and—yes, a *gabby tomboy!* He wished she would leave him alone.

He finally had a full bushel basket. "Wow! I'm bushed." He sat heavily. Kathy seemed to awaken from her daydreaming. She faced him and smiled.

"All done? Swell. Now, how are you getting home? I mean, to Granny Parker's?" Her cheeks reddened.

"But that's home to you, isn't it?"

Strangely annoyed, he said, "Yes, that's home to me. And I'm getting there the same way I came—rowing."

"Rowing?" Kathy was amazed. "That's over two miles."

"You got any better suggestions?"

For several moments Kathy was silent. "Yes, I have," she said. "We can sail back in my pram and tow your skiff."

"Huh! It wouldn't work, Smartie."

"Oh, yes it would." She was insistent. "The wind is stronger now, and from the south. Once we round Conimicut Point we can run with the wind. We won't even have to tack. So there!"

As much as he hated to admit it, he decided Kathy might be right. She was a good sailor and knew much more about boats than he did. Besides, his arms and shoulders felt like lead. Rowing that distance would take forever.

"Well, you want to try it?" Kathy asked.

"Sure." He hauled the anchor as Kathy moved her pram sail-boat around to the skiff's bow. She tied the anchor line to the pram's stern, making sure it cleared the tiller. They stepped into the pram and sat on the floorboards.

"Ready?" Kathy grinned joyously.

Tommy nodded, and she pushed down the centerboard and pulled in the mainsheet. The small sailboat nosed into the wind and around.

"Duck your head," Kathy warned, and the boom swung around to port. The single white sail filled, billowing out like a bed sheet in the wind, and Tommy heard the pleasing sound of water gur-gling past the hull.

"Well, I'll be darned," he cried, amazed. "We're moving."

"See, Smartie. Let the wind do the work instead of rowing!"

He was about to make a nasty reply, but stifled it. Kathy was a girl and a pest, but this time she was right. And very welcome.

They sailed past Marshall's Mansion, parallel to Conimicut Point, past the row of stilt houses built sixteen feet above the high water line to protect them from hurricane tides. When they were opposite the great brown house near the tip of the Point, Kathy turned the tiller to the right and the pram headed in shore.

"What are you stopping for?" Tommy asked.

"Shortcut. The sand bar goes out almost a quarter mile under-water, all the way to Conimicut Lighthouse. We can walk both boats across the sandbar and save all that sailing time. Okay?"

"You're the skipper," Tommy said, and Kathy beamed happily as she pulled up the mahogany centerboard. She stepped into the shallow water and he followed her, dragging the skiff up on the sandy beach. They had made much better time sailing than if he had rowed. Sitting on the skiff's bow, Tommy looked around. In the four weeks he had lived at Granny Parker's house he had seen Conimicut Point from a distance, and he had rowed around it several times to quahaug near Old Mill Cove, but he had never seen it close up.

It was a strange, torn place. At the end of the Point there were several abandoned cellar foundations, and three gaunt chimneys, but all the houses but one were gone.

"What happened to all these houses?" He pointed to one of the chimneys.

"Hurricane," Kathy said.

"Hurricanes? Here, in Rhode Island? I thought hurricanes were down Florida and Cuba?"

"So did everyone else." Kathy dug her toes into the warm sand. "But long before we were born, back in 1938, there was a very bad hurricane here, Daddy said. There was another one in 1944, I think, and two in 1954, Carol and Hazel. There was Diane and Edna, and others also." Her young face was thoughtful.

"I sure hope we don't ever have a hurricane Kathy." She shuddered. "What an awful thing, to have a hurricane with your name. Brrr-r-r!"

Agreeing, Tommy stood up. Fifty feet away was a great, three-story brown house with a long seawall in front. A thin, white-haired old man was kneeling at the base of the wall. He had buckets and a shovel beside him.

"What's he doing?" Tommy asked.

"That's Mr. Brown. He's cementin' his seawall." Kathy beckoned to him. "Come on, Tom. Let's go over and talk. He's very nice."

"No, I'd rather not. I-I don't know him."

Kathy was persistent. "Oh, come on." She pulled his hand. "You like the sea and boats, don't you? I don't know of anyone who knows more about them than Ben Brown."

She pulled him closer to the seawall. "Hi, Mr. Brown. Repairing your seawall again?"

Ben Brown's sunburned, leathery face broke into a wide smile.

"Afternoon, Kathy. Yep, all the time. Have to keep out the sea."

His glance included both of them. "Out sailin', hey? Nice wind for it right now." He sat back on his bony legs and studied them. "Got many quahaugs, Son?"

The direct question was surprising. "How did you know—?" The old man chuckled, a happy, good-natured rumble deep in his throat. "Saw you out there through my binoculars. Besides, I see the tongs in your skiff. Not much escapes me out here on the Point."

"Oh— I got a bushel." Tommy studied the strong, craggy face marked with the pleasure wrinkles of a long, happy, seaside life. The friendly blue eyes were like burning sapphires. Tommy didn't understand why, but he liked the old man immediately. He sensed Ben Brown's quiet strength, his dependability. Here was a man to lean on.

His attention went to the long seawall. It was an old wall, patched and re-patched, but still strong, still durable. Granny Parker's old seawall was patched like this one, but it needed a lot more work.

He again glanced at Ben Brown who was quietly talking to Kathy about sailing.

Mr. Brown seemed like his seawall, Tommy decided. He was old, but dependable, able to withstand trouble and turmoil. Like Granny Parker, Mr. Brown was stubborn and independent.

They both could sell their seaside homes and forget all about the endless cementing and repairs. They could ignore the everlasting nibbling of the wind and the salt and the sea. They could sell—and relax—but they wouldn't.

They loved their land, and if love meant hard work to keep out the sea, then they would willingly work. The price of real love was work.

"You're Tillie Parker's ward, ain't you, Son?" The question wasn't impertinent, just Mr. Brown's way of making conversation.

"Yes, sir. For now."

"Fine old lady." Ben Brown nodded in warm appreciation and winked. "Hope I'm as spry when I'm *her* age. 'Course, I ain't got too many years to go...but I don't *ever* expect to catch up!"

He threw back his head and laughed easily. His expression then grew serious, but the twinkle in his eyes said otherwise.

"Now, don't you ever tell Tillie I said that. She'll crown me, if you do."

Tommy saw Kathy was giggling and suddenly realized that old Ben was teasing him.

Yes, he *did* like this old man. Very much. He glanced curiously at the great seawall.

"—Mr. Brown?"

"Yes, Tommy."

Tommy felt awkward. He was unaccustomed to talking to strangers, especially adults. He didn't want to sound foolish, but he was very curious about something. He drew in a deep breath.

"I—uh—Kathy told me hurricanes sometime come up here." He paused, saw the old man nodding, and continued.

"—But surely the sea wouldn't go over your seawall and into your home. I mean, that wall's over six feet high!"

The old man regarded him thoughtfully.

"Hurricane seas are that high, Son, and even four and six feet higher." He stood up, pointed to a white board fastened to the south side of his home.

"See that marker. That's over thirteen feet up, the height of the water during the '38 blow. And six inches below it is where the floodtide of Hurricane Carol was." He nodded in fearful admiration.

"I love the sea, but not when she's hurricane-mad. Where we are standin' right now, during a hurricane, we'd have over eight to fifteen feet of churnin' white water over our heads. More with swells and giant ocean tidal waves. Much, much more..."

Tommy gasped. "Fifteen feet!" He saw Kathy nodding in agreement. "See. I told you so," she said.

"—Ah, but you needn't fret," Ben Brown assured them. "Fortunately, hurricanes this far north are few and far between. Chances are we'll never experience another one again... I hope."

Tommy wasn't sure, but he sensed a note of doubt in the old man's statement.

They talked for several more minutes, then said goodbye, promising to return.

Kathy walked her sailing pram along the shore until she was able to float it over the long, curving Conimicut Point sandbar.

Tommy followed her, dragging his skiff in the kneedeep water. Once they were on the north side of the sandbar they got into the pram and Kathy expertly sailed them homeward, towing the skiff.

All the way Tommy was troubled: Would a hurricane ever hit here again, like the one in '38? And if it did, what would Granny Parker do? Her busted old seawall was about six feet high and her old weathered house was only a foot or two higher. Was it high enough? Would it be safe? Or would the angry sea rush in and destroy it like it did to all those chimneyhouses remaining on Conimicut Point?

Chewing his lips, he tried to blot out the frightening thoughts...

"We're home," Kathy said, startling him. She pulled up the pram's centerboard as they neared the shore. Tommy stepped out into thigh-deep water and dragged both boats in closer.

"Thanks for the boatride, Kathy."

She grinned at him, then noticed his cut elbow. "Don't you forget to put iodine on that cut," she ordered.

"Okay, I won't forget."

As Kathy watched, he put his quahaugs and tongs on the beach, then returned the borrowed skiff to Mr. Cooley, a neighbor. He saw Kathy was still waiting.

"'Bye, Kathy. And thanks again."

He moved the tongs to the top of Granny Parker's seawall, then returned for the quahaugs. Kathy waved as she walked her pram sailboat along the shoreline to its mooring three houses down.

She was a good kid, all right, he decided, and he sure did appreciate that boat ride. He returned her wave and scrambled up on the seawall.

It had been a long day, but a good day. He was tired and hungry. He picked up the basket of quahaugs, groaning loudly at it's weight. Those eight big quahaugs on top were for Granny Parker. He didn't want to forget that.

Maybe Granny Parker wasn't the most friendly person in the world, and maybe her house was old and dilapidated, but right at that moment, it sure was *awfully good* to be home.

Chapter 2

The Cementer

"There is so much to learn!" Tommy thought dismally. "So much I don't know."

He was upstairs in his room overlooking Narragansett Bay. Opposite him on the east shore three miles away was Riverside and Barrington.

Providence was seven to ten miles to the north, and Conimicut Lighthouse was one mile to the south. Still further south, about 30 miles distance, was Newport and the Atlantic Ocean.

He gazed out the window. His new seaside world was big and strange and fascinating. Life on the edge of the sea was a continuous challenge, the most wonderful thing that had ever happened to him.

"If only I can stay with Granny Parker in this old house on Bellman Avenue in Conimicut Village," he said aloud, startling himself.

Yes, and if only he could win her love, and make friends, and be as carefree as the other young people on the shore.

All that was a mighty big order.

He thought of Kathy Turner. Kathy made friends with no trouble at all. Look how easily she had forced herself into his life.

"But she *belongs* here in Conimicut!" Tommy thought defiantly. With him, it was different.

He was an outsider, an orphan who couldn't even remember his parents, never mind recall his home. His first view of the sea and all her wondrous mysteries had been six weeks ago, the day he had been sent to Granny Parker's. That was the day his life really began.

But Tommy wasn't fooling himself. He knew Granny Parker

had only wanted a boy to work for her—any boy! In exchange, she would clothe and feed him. There never was talk of love. Or even of friendship. To her, he was a pair of working hands.

But she did need him, and that tiny thought filled him with an intense sense of pride. She needed him, and to be needed was a very good feeling.

"Oh, she's using me, all right," he thought as he gazed over the blue water at Kathy's small pram sailboat nodding at its mooring.

"But she's old and alone. She needs my strength to move things, to chop her wood, to help her repair her seawall. She needs my legs to run her errands, and my youth to climb on the roof of her old house and barn to make repairs. But so what? She needs me!"

And that was most important...to be needed.

His chin resting on his arms on the windowsill, Tommy watched the great, hot sun rising in the East. Funny how the July sun woke him up so very early. At the orphanage he had hated to get out of bed to meet the day. Now he was anxious to start the day, including doing his chores. The sooner he finished his work, the sooner the day was his to spend as he chose. And that was fantastic!

As much as he wished to go outside to greet the sun, Tommy had to wait until Granny Parker awoke, usually at seven o'clock, one hour from now. He never had to call her. She seemed to have a built-in alarm clock in her head. He never heard her rising, but once he heard the rattling of pans in the kitchen downstairs, he knew she was up and the day had begun.

Granny Parker was an amazing old lady. Even old Ben Brown who owned that big brown house on Conimicut Point admired her tenacity and her fierce independence.

Tommy glanced at the half-read book beside his chair. Ben Brown had given it to him a week ago, *Piloting, Seamanship* and *Small Boat Handling* by Charles F. Chapman. It was old and thumbed-through and had Ben Brown's marginal notes and underlining.

It was a storehouse of helpful information on boating and the sea, and on sailing, and navigation—all new and wondrous things.

If only he could remember all he read.

Ben Brown had given him several other books, all pertaining to the sea and her creatures. Now Tommy had nine books in his personal library, not counting the three borrowed books from Mr. Brown, or the two books Kathy's father had let him take.

He was glad Granny Parker didn't object to his reading. As long as he did his work she didn't mind. Several times he had noticed her watching him. She seemed pleased at his study, but as soon as she saw him look up, she'd pretend to be doing something else. Or else she would chide him.

"—If you're going to read, get better light!"

But she really didn't mind, he knew.

In fact, it was Granny Parker who had said, "Most all knowledge comes from books. Show me a person who doesn't read, and I'll show you a person who's mind has stopped growing."

A mighty profound statement, that.

"But *you* don't read," he had said once, and when he saw that painful expression on the old lady's face, he had immediately regretted his impulsive words.

"I-I'm sorry, Granny-"

The tired blue eyes behind rimless spectacles were deeply sad. "You're right, Tommy, I don't read much. But only because these old eyes of mine won't let me." She sighed wistfully.

"An' I do miss not bein' able to read... 'Specially the Holy Bible..."

Now, as he gazed out his east window, Tommy wondered if he should offer to read to her. Maybe she would like that. But maybe the suggestion would anger her by pointing up her shortcomings. Granny was a very proud woman.

No, he'd better not say anything. Not until he knew her better...

For the next hour, while waiting for the downstairs rattling of pans, he read and gazed dreamily out the window. Early morning seagulls shrieked, and argued, and mewed as the tide dropped. It seemed they were forever fighting for the same inch of ground.

From out of Occupasstuxet Cove sped several professional shellfishermen, their heavy gray skiffs skitting across the smooth water like buzzing waterbugs. Most of them tonged or bullraked south of the lighthouse in deeper waters.

Others bullraked in very deep water, their thirty-foot stales waving in the air like bent boat masts. Someday, when he was stronger—and if he wasn't sent back to the Home—he'd like to bullrake. It was harder work than tonging, but the quahaugs filled the baskets faster, and they were larger too.

Tommy reached for the cigarbox on his bureau and again counted the money he had saved from tonging. Thirty-nine dollars and seventy-two cents! He grinned in pleasure.

Maybe someday soon he could buy his own skiff, and still later, his own outboard motor. Second-hand, of course.

What a wonderful thought, his own boat!

At the sudden clatter of dishes, he ran downstairs and into the kitchen.

"Mornin', Granny. It's a beautiful day."

The old lady nodded. "Goin' to be a hot one—"

He waited. Granny Parker frequently began her thoughts with a preamble: "Going to be a hot day...so let's do this, or that, before the heat sets in..."

"—So what do we do before it gets too hot?" he anticipated her.

The old lady paused, then cracked two eggs on the side of the black, cast-iron skillet, dropping them into the hissing pan. Her own hot cereal was cooking on the other gas burner.

"Hum. Been with me only six weeks and already you think you know me like one of your books, heh?"

Tommy flushed. "I'm sorry. I just feel good. I didn't mean to be rude."

Granny Parker held up a thin, wrinkled hand. "Let it be. Let it be." A faint smile crossed her lips.

"—We'll do some cementin' on the seawall. Gettin' near hurricane season. We got a bag of cement left, haven't we?"

Tommy nodded, relieved. Living with Granny Parker was like walking on those eggs on the table. He had to tread softly or— squish! Back to the Home.

"Yes, Mam."

The old lady turned the eggs, frying them lightly on the other side, the way he liked best. She ladled them on to his plate beside four slices of buttered toast. She poured him a full glass of milk, then served herself a tiny portion of hot cereal and milk.

Tommy ate hungrily and thought about his temporary foster-mother. He really knew very little about Granny Parker. She was "Mrs." Parker on her mail, so she had been married. Her husband died thirty years ago, according to Ben Brown. Evidently, she had no children. She lived on social security and a small pension, but it was not enough, really. Yet, she survived. And those few dollars a month the Home was paying her to care for him probably didn't even cover expenses.

He thought about her as she poured her morning tea. At seventy-six years, or there-about, she was small and wiry, tough as catgut. Her hair was snow white, cut short; her wrinkled face, once beautiful, was still attractive and vibrantly alive. She had strong, calloused hands. The knuckles were big from heavy work. She knew how to pace herself so she didn't get over-tired.

Granny Parker thought nothing of repairing a porch, cutting her grass with a push-type lawnmower, mixing cement in a hand wheelbarrow and patching her seawall.

She also Lexonited her porch roof, and did a thousand necessary things. She and hard work were long-time friends.

But she and the house and barn were old now. Time had nibbled away at their vitality. Time could never defeat Granny Parker, but the buildings had really suffered.

Tommy's eyes drifted around the room. The house badly needed painting. The windows should be scraped and glazed and the doors weatherstripped. Maybe Kathy's father or Mr. Brown could tell him how to do it. And there was no central heat so the house was probably very cold and drafty in the winter. What heat there was was provided by a gas heater and a parlor potbelly stove in the fireplace.

The upstairs was unheated, and was probably closed off during the frigid winter months. Tommy shuddered at the thought of the cold. He wondered how the old lady could stand it.

His breakfast finished, he put his dishes and silverware on the sideboard next to the porcelain sink, a habit carry-over from the Home where help was always scarce. Besides, the less work he made for Granny Parker, the better it was for him.

"I'll go out and get things ready," he said, and reached for the barn keys behind the door. "Sure is a beautiful day today."

Whenever they repaired the base of the seawall, it was important that they catch the outgoing tide. That way, the sea was kept away from the hardening cement for almost ten hours, allowing it to set. Even then, Granny Parker preferred to put a barrier of rocks or upright boards between the fresh cement and the incoming tide. The barrier broke up the wave action.

"It's the waves that destroy the setting cement, not the sea water," Granny insisted.

Jumping down to the base of the seawall, Tommy moved rocks aside to expose the larger holes in the wall. He dug down to the wall's foundation, as the old lady had taught him. Granny had said, "A wall, like a building—or a person—is as good as its foundation! So you build the foundation well."

After washing sand and seaweed from the holes, Tommy filled them with rocks, stacking and dovetailing them neatly like a farmer's wall, but allowing room for a cement binder. Since he was stronger and more agile, he could do a better job. Granny Parker never exactly said so, but he could tell she was pleased with the work he had done on other days.

Small holes in the upper portion of the 150-foot-long seawall were easily filled with mortar cement mix, using a hand trowel. It was those larger holes at the base that needed constant attention or else you'd have to get an expensive skirt or capping. One winter's ice and frost could enlarge a tiny hole into a cavern, and the wall could collapse outward.

Then the next storm tide would enter inside the wall and bite off a six to eight foot strip of Granny's land.

Yes, protecting your land from the sea was an unending battle, according to both Granny Parker and Ben Brown.

"—But then, so's life," Ben had added. "But it's worth it, eh?"

"Yes, it is worth it," Tommy thought, and climbed back atop the wall. He gazed around happily. The shore front was slowly coming awake to greet the warming day.

He saw people sitting on their back porches overlooking the bay, their morning coffee cups to their lips. He smelled ham and eggs cooking. He heard laughter and the sharp bark of a neighborhood dog.

From her porch Kathy Turner yelled and waved. He saw she

was still in her pajamas. Mrs. Turner came out and shushed her inside, then called out in friendly greeting.

Further north someone was rowing out to a moored cruiser, the oar splashes audible over the still, smoky water. An outboard motor rumbled deep in its throat. Seagulls cawed and scrapped, as usual...and diving terns plunked into the shallow water for unsuspecting baitfish.

At Scallop Island, a tiny sand bar a quarter mile to the North, several small children were wading in the cool water, their delighted cries shrill and sweet in the bright, warm morning.

Tommy inhaled the sparkling, salt-tangy air.

"Ah! What a day!" But daydreaming didn't accomplish work, he reminded himself.

From the gravel pile he put ten shovelsfull of sand and gravel into the wheelbarrow, then added two shovelsfull of gray cement for a five-to-one mix. He mixed them thoroughly with the hoe.

Next, he added water from the garden hose, stirring it in carefully, as Granny Parker had taught him. Not too much water or the cement would be runny and hard to work. He hoed and chopped and mixed and splashed until the mixture was a smooth, uniform gray, then went up to the house.

"Cement's mixed. You ready?"

"Comin'." Granny Parker was dressed in dungarees and a light blue shirt. Atop her head was a floppy straw hat with a red ribbon. These were her "cementin' clothes", she called them.

They walked down to the seawall together. Granny inspected his work and nodded in approval. Tommy beamed happily.

Yes, indeed, today was a wonderful day!

Together they worked silently, smoothly and efficiently, with little lost motion. Granny half filled galvanized pails with wet cement and placed them atop the wall. Tommy, at the wall's base, worked the fresh cement between the stacked rocks, then coated the front with a thick layer of cement, troweling it flush with the original surface of the wall, as he had seen Ben Brown do. Granny seemed pleased with his handiwork.

But why didn't she ever tell him so?

The sun rose higher and grew hotter.

Perspiring, Tommy removed his shirt and undershirt, delighting in the warmth caressing his back. After that first sunburn a few weeks ago, he was tanning nicely so he looked like any other boy on the beach.

Noting Granny Parker's disapproval, he said, "I'll catch twenty minutes of sun, no more."

"Getting hot fast," the old lady remarked. "I'll go up and make us some lemonade."

Wiping his sweaty face with his T-shirt, Tommy watched her go.

He returned to his work at the base of the wall. As he completed each repair, he build a small rock-and-wood barrier in front of it. There was always plenty of driftwood and boards around. Besides, Granny Parker had a neat pile of weathered lumber near her wild roses behind the barn.

He turned at the sound of voices behind him. Several boys his age were walking along the shore, tossing stones in the water.

"Hi," Tommy greeted them.

"Hi, yourself. What'cha doin'? Oh, you're cementing?"

He nodded proudly. "Just about finished for now." He stood up, wiped his hands on his dungarees, and grinned.

"I'm Tommy Wayne." He held out his hand.

"Yeah?" The tall boy glanced at the gray, cement-stained hand. He moved his own hand away. He was a handsome boy with dark hair and a built-in smirk.

"I'm Pete Bender." He nodded at the others. "This here's Danny Booth, and the little one's Mike Higgins."

The two boys nodded, cautious. Pete Bender's black eyes raised briefly to the house.

"You livin' with the old witch?"

A sudden, sharp anger flushed Tommy's face. "You watch your tongue! Yes, I'm living with Granny Parker."

Pete shrugged. It was obvious he had no intention of fighting. It wasn't that important to him. He seemed completely disinterested.

Tommy's fists slowly unknotted.

"I thought maybe you were hired to work for her," Pete said. "Guess she's all right, but she keeps chasin' us off her old sea wall. You might think it was gold, or somethin'" He grinned.

"Man, you should see her when she's mad. Wow'ee!"

"You her grandson?" Danny Booth asked. He was also Tommy's age, but half a head taller and powerfully built, one of those fortunate boys who seemed almost a man at fourteen. His voice cracked when he talked and he had a faint, dark patch of hair on his cheeks. He seemed quite proud of it.

Tommy shook his head. "She's my guardian. My foster-mother."

Danny's freckled face registered surprise.

"Foster mother? What's that?"

"Yeah?" Mike Higgins moved closer, curious. "That like Pete's stepmother?"

Pete pushed Mike aside. There was no contest.

"No, stupid," he snapped. 'It's not like a stepmother." He faced Tommy. "Your folks divorced or dead?"

"Dead," Tommy said. "Killed in an auto accident when I was three."

"Oh—Then the old lady's taking care of you? You're an orphan?"

The too-familiar word hurt deep inside.

"—Yes."

"Sorry," Pete said. "I won't call her a witch again. My own mother died too, but now I have a stepmother. She's a little too bossy and nosy, but she's okay, I guess."

"You're living at old lady Park—at Mrs. Parker's—all the time?" Danny Booth asked.

Tommy shrugged. "I don't know. I—hope so."

"Well, what do you know?" Danny's voice cracked. "We thought you were just visiting." His grimy hand shot out, clasping Tommy's.

"Glad to know ya', Tom. I'm Booty."

Intensely pleased, Tommy grinned, despite the crushing pain of Booty's grip. He squeezed back, a silent duel of persistence.

Booty jerked his hand free, shaking it. "Hey! You got a pretty good grip for a skinny guy. You didn't look that strong." He slapped Tommy lightly on the shoulder and grinned crookedly.

"Come on. Let's go," Mike said.

Pete Bender picked up a pebble and tossed it into the wet cement. It made a faint plopping sound. He pushed it in with his finger and smoothed the surface.

"Well... See you around."

Tommy returned his nod. He hoped so. He watched as the three boys idly walked along the shore, talking and laughing as they headed toward Conimicut Point, a mile away.

His body remained at the seawall, but his heart went along with them.

A few minutes later he saw Granny Parker coming toward him, carrying a clear plastic pitcher and two glasses. That lemonade would sure taste good. He was parched.

Pausing atop the wall, the old lady stared after the boys. Without saying a word, she filled the glasses and gave him one.

Tommy drank it down without pausing. She filled it again. He sipped at it.

"Mmmm. That sure hit the spot. Thanks."

"Watch out for that Peter Bender, you hear me? He's a troublemaker."

"I suspected that." He grinned up at her. All the time she had been watching them from the house. She could have returned when the boys were at the wall and they would have left before he had a chance to meet them. He appreciated her thoughtfulness. At times Granny Parker seemed to have an amazing insight into the mind and thoughts of teenagers.

He saw the look of approval on her face. "You've done quite a bit today," she said. "Don't get too tired."

He worked his shoulders to ease out the stiffness. "Just about done. All the big holes are patched. See?"

Curious, the old lady cautiously climbed down the ladder to the beach. As she studied his work, a faint smile played on her lips.

"My, you did right fine. You accomplished so much this morning. It would have taken me two weeks or longer to fill in all those holes."

Tommy was delighted with her praise. It was something she rarely gave away, hoarding it like a miser hoards his wealth.

"Well, you helped too," he said. "I didn't do it all."

Granny Parker's blue eyes glistened behind her spectacles. "Well—maybe I did. A mite, anyway. You got any cement left?"

"Uh huh. A quarter bag."

"Hum. I'll have to order more from Lakewood Hay and Grain store, but a quarter-bag should be more than enough. Come on up to the barn."

He looked up curiously, but her wrinkled face was inscrutable.

He'd never be able to read her mind.

Puzzled, he followed her up the ladder and across the lawn. She motioned him to wait while she went into the barn. A few minutes later she brought out a large washtub, then some scrap metal, and a length of heavy chain.

"Here. Carry these down to the wall."

She again went into the barn, returning with a foot-long bolt with an eye at one end. When she saw he was still waiting, she scowled fiercely.

"Well, come on, boy! Get a move on!"

"Yes, Mam." He tossed the metal into the tub and carried it to the seawall. This *couldn't* be what he was thinking. Could it? He mentally shook his head. No, he didn't dare let himself think of that.

"—What's all this for?" he asked softly.

"Never you mind. Just do as you're told."

He placed the tub on the grass near the wall. "Okay. Now what?"

"Mix cement in the wheelbarrow, of course."

Mix cement? She was teasing him. She had to be. Or was she?

"Okay, and—then w-what?" he stammered.

Granny Parker looked hard at him. "Come on, Tommy. You're not that dense. I've seen your Chapman book. You left it lying around enough. From all your studying, I suspect you ought to be able to cast a mooring block."

"—A mooring block!"

His throat tightened. His eyes suddenly misted up.

"Of course. You can't moor a boat without a mooring block." There was a faint sparkle in her eyes. "—Or can you?"

Delightfully numb, Tommy mutely shook his head. Suddenly he laughed out loud. His heart hammered in his throat.

"You can't mean you have a boat hidden away in that crowded barn of yours?" he said incredulously.

"No, I don't!" Granny Parker snapped. "I mean *you* have a boat!"

"I—? But—I don't—"

"Oh, yes, you do! Granny cried. "I spoke to Mr. Cooley and he'll sell you his skiff for ten dollars. He likes the way you take care of it. Anyone else, he'd charge fifty dollars."

She smiled briefly. "Besides, he said you use it more than he does anyway."

Tommy's mouth fell open. He was dreaming all this. Any moment now he'd wake up and—

"Well. You interested or not?"

"Interested?" He suddenly dropped the shovel and caught the old lady around the waist and danced her merrily around the yard. She sputtered and fumed, but he knew she wasn't really angry.

Laughing, his eyes stinging with joyful tears, he suddenly kissed her on the cheek. Her wrinkled face reddened and she made weak noises of protest.

"Oh! Now, you cut that out! Get on with you, now. Go make your mooring." Her hand lightly touched her cheek.

"An' make it strong. And bury it deep!" she cried.

"I will, Granny. Oh, I will!" He frantically shoveled gravel into the wheelbarrow. Such fantastic good luck. He could hardly believe it. His own skiff! And it was in excellent condition, worth much more than ten dollars, or even fifty dollars!

"Thank you, Granny," he cried, remembering. "I'll pay Mr. Cooley when he comes home from work. Thank you."

The old lady snorted, once again in complete command of her composure. "Huh, don't thank me. Maybe I did it for selfish reasons. Maybe I did it because I like quahaugs, and you get them for me for free."

She picked up the tray and glasses.

Tommy studied her, wondering if she was teasing him. A second later he knew she was, for she faced him and added:

"And don't you pay Mr. Cooley anything for that skiff. You pay me. I bought that skiff three days ago!"

Chapter 3

Tommy's Outboard Motor Lesson

"Well, what are you going to do?" Kathy cried, greatly annoyed. "You going to sit in that silly old boat another whole day?"

Tommy grinned at her. No matter what she said, he couldn't get angry. After all his dreaming and wishing, he actually had his own boat, a major goal achieved.

And he still had twenty-nine dollars and seventy-two cents toward an outboard motor. He was the happiest he had ever been in his entire life!

But Kathy wasn't very happy about their hanging around, he realized. She was pouting and about ready to clobber him.

He slipped the bailer under the stern thwart, or seat. "I'll be done here in a minute, Kathy."

"But how many times do you have to bail a dry boat?" Kathy cried. "Or study every screw and bolt?" Her young, pretty face sobered.

"Aw, look, Tommy, I know you're very happy about owning your own skiff, and I'm happy for you. But let's use your boat. Let's go fishing or quahauging or *something!* You'll grow barnacles just sitting here."

Tommy laughed easily. "Okay, it's a deal." He rolled his denims past his knees and stepped into the cool water. His skiff was at its own mooring a hundred feet out, directly in front of Granny Parker's seawall. The tide was low. Mr. Cooley, the former owner, had also given him the oars, fifty feet of manila line and a grapnel anchor. And all for only ten dollars! It was a fabulous bargain.

"What and when?" Kathy persisted.

"We'll go fishing tomorrow morning. Early. Okay?"

That seemed to mollify Kathy. "Swell. Where?"

"Conimicut Lighthouse. I have to row, you know."

Kathy's eyes went wide as an idea formed. "Maybe—you won't have to. I'll ask Daddy if we can borrow his ten horse Johnson. It's an old motor, but dependable. You wait here."

She splashed to shore, running girl-fashion, knees close and bare feet apart. Her dark hair bounced off her shoulders. Her faded denims were getting a bit too tight for her hips and thighs.

Stepping back into his skiff, Tommy again sat in the stern. Kathy didn't understand the intense pride a man could take in his own craft. The half dozen times he had borrowed this skiff, he had cared for it as though it was his own. But now—now it really was his own! It was odd how that simple fact changed his entire viewpoint.

Before, she was a good, dependable 14-foot, lapstrake skiff of the Amesbury type. But now she was a personality, and he knew her thoroughly, even her faults.

For example, she leaked slightly, and had the tendency to turn to starboard. Maybe that was because the right oar was slightly heavier than the left one, or maybe his right arm was stronger, and he unconsciously rowed harder with that one.

Also, she had a brass plate screwed near the bow below the water-line where the bottom planking got splintered by a rock during a storm. Most of the leak came from around the plate. The repair was solid, but the deck boards gave slightly under wave stress and let in a little water. Mr. Cooley had it caulked with Kuhl's underwater compound. It stopped the leak during normal use, but not during a heavy sea. Then it leaked.

A plastic bleach bottle with the bottom cut out served as his hand bailer. Tommy kept it stored under the stern thwart.

But whatever her faults, the skiff was his, and he loved her. Granny Parker's only firm stipulations were that he continue to do his work and that he handle the boat with safety. She was insistent upon that. He had readily agreed.

He saw Kathy run from her porch, across the back yard, waving furiously at him. She stopped at the top of her father's seawall—a beautiful, solid, newly-capped wall that wouldn't require repairs for years.

Instead of climbing down as most girls do, Kathy leaped to the sandy beach. He winced when he saw her fall forward, rolling over headfirst. But she immediately scrambled to her feet, unhurt.

"Crazy kid!" he muttered, relieved she wasn't hurt. "When will she ever learn to act like a girl?"

Kathy splashed into the water, not caring about her clothes getting wet. As she ran closer, she was grinning like a pixie, and puffing like a steam engine.

"Whew!" She flopped into the boat. "Tommy, Daddy said yes! We can borrow his motor tomorrow."

"Wonderful!" Tommy was elated, but then he remembered something, and groaned out loud. Kathy scowled at him.

"Well, what's the matter now? Aren't you happy?"

"Yes, Very happy, but— Well, I—I read a lot about outboard motors and I know how they work, but—" A pink flush colored his cheeks and he pretended to study a horseshoe crab crawling on the bay bottom, a foot below the water's surface.

"—I've never run one."

Kathy exhaled in relief. "Heck, is that all? I'll show you. It's simple." She stepped out of the skiff, beckoning.

"Come on. I'll ask Daddy to show you. He's a man, and you and he can talk about details, and navigation, and things I don't know."

Mr. Turner not only explained the motor, but he demonstrated it, using Tommy's skiff. He showed Tommy how to start and stop, how to mix gas and oil in correct proportion, how to prime the motor by pushing the button on the remote gas tank, even how to remove and clean carbon from the two spark plugs.

With Kathy grinning in the bow and her father sitting on the center thwart, Tommy guided the skiff parallel to shore, following instructions. His boat handled beautifully.

Tommy learned fast, whether from books or verbal instructions.

Mr. Turner reached into his pocket and drew out a screwdriver and pliers, plus a small envelope. He waited until the boat stopped.

"Always keep these with you on the boat, Tom." He put the tools into Tommy's hand, then poured the envelope's contents into his other hand. There were five inch-long solid metal cylinders about a quarter-inch in diameter.

"These are shear pins for the propeller," Mr. Turner explained. "If the propeller hits something like a rock, the shear pin will break so the propeller won't get damaged. You'll need the tools to replace a broken pin."

At Mr. Turner's recommendations, Tommy guided the skiff into shallow water. Following instructions, he tilted the motor to expose the propeller. Replacing a shear pin was easy and he completed the job in less than five minutes. Mr. Turner nodded approval.

"You're pretty clever with your hands, Son."

Tommy grinned happily. "Thank you."

"Oh, I'm not flattering you. I've seen what you've been doing for Mrs. Parker. You do good work. I like that."

Tommy flushed. In the bow, Kathy was wrinkling her nose and grinning idiotically at him so he almost burst out laughing. At times she was such a nut!

"Every motor has its own peculiarities," Mr. Turner was saying. "Like a car, they're all slightly different. This old motor of mine has a bad habit of breaking shear pins." He patted Tommy's arm.

"Enough said, Son?"

Nodding, Tommy pocketed the tools and shear pins. He eased the motor down into the water. After pushing the skiff into deeper water, he pulled the starter cord and the motor barked into life. He let it idle and checked the exhaust port for cooling water—as instructed—then pulled the shift lever forward and the skiff moved slowly ahead. Its forward speed was controlled by rotating a hand grip at the end of a long steering handle.

Within a half hour, he was as familiar with the outboard motor and controls as with his own fingers. He steered for shore.

Mr. Turner stepped out into shallow water.

"Remember, Tom, keep the speed low and your gas will last much longer. Speed gobbles gas, and it makes your hull pound. Take it easy and enjoy your boat." His glance included both of them.

"Okay, kids?"

"Thank you, Daddy." Kathy waited until her father was beyond hearing.

"See, Tommy. I told you he'd teach you. He likes you. I can tell. He likes you a lot."

"He's very nice," Tommy said thoughtfully. He must be a wonderful father."

"Oh, he is! He is."

For several seconds Tommy said nothing.

Kathy gazed at him curiously. He noticed her and seemed to stir awake. Sighing, he slowly unfastened the motor from the boat's transom.

"How much gas do we have left, Kathy?"

"Over three-quarter tank. That's almost five gallons. Plenty for fishing tomorrow."

"Good. I'll dig worms in Granny's garden. You got any hooks and sinkers? I'll make up a hand line."

"You will not!" Kathy was indignant. "We have plenty of fishing poles at our house. You can borrow one until you can get your own."

"I'd like to buy one from you. I have some money."

Kathy resolutely shook her head. She lifted the gas tank, found it too heavy, placed it down again.

"I said *borrow!* Daddy won't mind. Later, you can buy your own new pole and reel."

Tommy sighed heavily. "Okay."

He hefted the heavy motor and half-carried, half-dragged it to shore, then returned for the gas tank. Girls sure were stubborn.

The motor was awkward and bulky. He finally got it to Kathy's house, grateful for Kathy's help. He then returned for the gas tank.

They put the motor and gas tank in the Turner's outside tool shed. Mrs. Turner called them inside for cake and milk.

"They sure are a wonderful family," Tommy thought as he ate. "Warm and courteous and thoughtful...just like a family should be. A family was really very important!"

Later that afternoon he dug worms. He found an old box which he made into a tool kit. When Kathy brought over a fishing pole and equipment, he patiently dismantled the reel and cleaned and oiled it. Once reassembled, it cast beautifully.

As he lay in bed that night, Tommy thought over the day's events. He wished he was going fishing with the guys instead of with Kathy. She was nice enough, but she was a girl, and it didn't seem quite right that he should go fishing with a girl.

He sighed deeply and rolled over on his stomach. Who was he

kidding? Kathy would probably catch more fish than he did. Besides, girl or not, it sure would be fun to go fishing in your very own boat.

Chapter 4

Riverside Crooks And The Terrifying Boat Ride!

*T*ommy was awake before Saturday's sun. His hands clasped behind his head, he remained in bed, thoughtful. Lately, things were going pretty smoothly for him and he was deeply grateful. He had his own boat now, and he and Kathy were going fishing.

And Granny Parker was—well, he couldn't exactly call her cordial, but he did detect a tiny ember of warmth in the old lady's eyes, didn't he?

And wasn't it she who got him the boat? She must like him, if only a little. But with Granny Parker it was hard to tell.

At first, she had obviously resented his presence in her house. Old and set in her ways, she disapproved of a stranger upsetting her routine, her habits of a lifetime. But lately she seemed to be tolerating him, and that was a giant step forward.

Tommy loved living on the edge of the sea. He was slowly making friends. He'd hate to be sent back to the Home now.

He glanced at the small alarm clock on his bureau just as the sun popped above the horizon. Quickly he dressed, crept down stairs so as to avoid awakening Granny Parker, made toast and ate breakfast.

Kathy was waiting for him at the beach. She was yawning violently, her green eyes puffy with sleep. She wore her usual denims and tennis sneakers, and a heavy, hooded gray boat sweater. She looked like a sleepy little elf.

He was pleased she had remembered her fishing equipment. When he jumped from the wall to the beach, her face suddenly came alive.

"Yuk! What an awful hour!" she groaned. "I bet the fish aren't even up yet."

Tommy grinned and waded out to the skiff. He paddled it ashore and quickly loaded their equipment aboard. Kathy had brought two sit-on type life cushions. That was something else he'd have to buy, he reminded himself. Safety is most important.

With Kathy's help, they got the motor and gas tank from the shed. By the time they were ready to shove off, it was past seven o'clock, according to Kathy's watch.

"Daddy gave me some money." Kathy flashed the five dollar bill. "He told me we should go across the bay to Riverside, to the marina, and buy some clam worms. Flatfish like clam worms better, and so do tautaug, and Daddy's hungry for good eatin' fish, he said."

"Fine. You direct me," Tommy said, as he helped her into the skiff. Kathy wasn't really helpless, but somehow, this early in the morning with the mist hovering a foot over the water, she seemed more like a little girl than a tomboy. He ignored her teasing grin.

The motor started on the first pull. Conscious of his gas supply, Tommy drove slowly, skirting the small waves to minimize pounding. The wind was a bit strong, with a heavy cross-chop driving up from the south.

While they were in the channel, some water splashed over the starboard side. Tommy was slightly concerned, but where they planned to fish in the lee of Conimicut Lighthouse the water would be calmer.

And with some clam worms, maybe they'd catch some tautaug. Granny loved baked blackfish—or tautaug, as they called them in Rhode Island.

Once across the bay, Tommy eased the skiff up to the marina dock and cut the motor. Kathy nodded approval. He nodded back.

"I'll go buy the clam worms," she said. "I know where to go."

"Okay." He watched her run up the long dock to shore and around a building, then he started bailing out the water that had splashed over the side.

Tommy was so intent on bailing, he didn't see the two men walking up the dock until they stood directly above him, staring down.

Their eyes bored into his neck. They watched him as if bailing out a boat was a fascinating thing. The bigger man tipped the scales at 250 pounds. He carried his dark suitcoat and was already sweating, even though it was early and the sun wasn't very hot yet.

He had a bulldog-mean face and huge hands, and was almost bald.

The other man was small and skinny. He had a gray complexion and hard, dark, deep-set eyes that looked bloodshot, as though he needed eyeglasses.

"Nice lookin' boat you got there, Kid," the big man said finally.

Tommy nodded and glanced ashore. What was keeping Kathy?

"Travel fast?" That was from the little, red-eyed man.

"Fast enough, Mister."

"Take you all the way across the bay? Say, to Conimicut?" the big man asked.

Cautious, Tommy nodded, and the two men withdrew and talked. Tommy wished they would leave him alone. Something about them wasn't right. And where was Kathy, anyway? What was she doing, digging the clam worms?

He wished she would hurry so they could catch the tide change. Ben Brown said that was the best time for tautaug fishing.

"Hey, kid. Give you five bucks to take us across."

Tommy saw they were actually serious. Five dollars would buy a lot of gas and oil. He was tempted, but something wasn't right about them.

He saw their lone car in the marina parking lot, in the no-parking area close to the dock. For no apparent reason they wanted a ride across the bay. They had probably picked him because he was the only one around. It was still pretty early. Besides, the seas were choppy enough to discourage a lot of boatsmen. He shook his head.

"No, thanks. I'm waiting for a friend. Why don't you drive around?"

The little man's face twisted into a snarl and he yanked at the bow line. "What are you, a wise guy? We don't wanna drive around. That adds over twenty miles. We just want a ride across!"

The big man kicked him in the leg, none too lightly. "Sam's impetuous," he said, his eyes hard. "Will ten dollars make you happier?"

"Ten dollars?"

"Tax free, like they say."

Tommy sensed a black threat behind the stiff smile. "N-No, thanks."

He continued bailing out the quarter-inch of water covering the deck, hoping all of it was from spray, and not from the bow leak with the brass plate. Mr. Cooley, the former owner of his skiff, had warned that pounding made the leak worse.

At the sound he looked up. Kathy was waving, the small, tan box of clam worms in her hand. She stood at the far end of the dock, cautiously hesitant about coming closer.

"Who's that?" the big man snapped.

"Kathy Turner. I've been waiting for her."

"A girl," Sam, the skinny man, said. "Mike, another kid. What are we going to do?"

"We're goin' for a boat ride, that's what." Mike yanked the skiff closer to the dock, almost toppling Tommy.

"Hey, what are you doing? Tommy cried. "Leave that line alone."

"Shut up, Punk!"

"You have no right in here, Mister. Give me that oar. Please."

The big man was angry. "I said, shut up!" He shoved Tommy back so he fell hard, his jaw slamming against the motor handle.

"Ow!" Dazed, Tommy's face smarted, tears filling his eyes. His jaw felt broken. He spat out blood.

"Come on, Sam. Get the lead out," Mike cried and Sam clambered to the edge of the dock carrying a large black suitcase. He jumped to the skiff's deck, tipping it violently.

"Siddown, stupid!" Mike yelled. Want to sink us?" He pushed the boat away from the dock with an oar. "Start that motor, kid. Fast."

His jaw numb, Tommy struggled to his feet. His tooth was loose. Some blood leaked from his mouth to the wet deck, mixing with the salt water.

He pulled the starter cord and the motor turned over, but didn't catch. As he tried again, he saw Kathy timidly watching at the far end of the dock. He motioned her to stay there.

"What's the matter?" Mike cried.

"No gas in the line." Tommy again motioned Kathy away.

Mike shook the gas tank in the bow. "You got a whole tankful, almost. What are you tryin' to pull, no gas?"

There was no sense explaining. Obviously, neither man knew anything about boats and motors.

"Pump that little button on the top of the tank," Tommy said. Mike did, and on the next try the motor started.

"All right, punk. Now, take us across to Conimicut—free!" Tommy couldn't feel a thing now. His whole lower jaw seemed to have vanished. He pulled the shift forward. The boat, lying deep in the water with the extra weight, responded slowly.

The big man, taking up the space of two normal people, was sitting on the center thwart. Sam was huddled in the bow, hugging the black suitcase as if it contained a fortune.

At the sound of the outboard, Kathy ran out on the dock, her young face concerned. "Tommy. Wait for me!" she pleaded.

"Tell her you'll come right back for her," Mike ordered.

"I'll—be right back," Tommy yelled. The words sounded funny because of his throbbing jaw. He hoped Kathy would realize he wasn't voluntarily taking these men for a boatride to Conimicut. He hoped she would realize he was being forced. He hoped she would call the police.

But Kathy was just staring at him, her mouth open, her feelings hurt. And there was nothing he could do about it.

As soon as the skiff cleared the protection of the cove, they hit the rougher water of the channel. A variable, southwesterly wind was blowing about fourteen knots, but it was gusting up to twenty, driving up waves which occasionally broke over the low gunwales.

The two men seemed very nervous.

"This tub rocks," Mike said. "Hold on tight to that suitcase, Sam."

Sam nodded violently, his mouth a firm, white line. He looked seasick already, Tommy noted. He was skirting the choppy seas to minimize pounding .

"Mike! Water's coming over the sides!" Sam screeched, and the big man glanced around, his face momentarily distorted with fear. He saw the metal bait bucket Tommy had stashed under the forward thwart. Moving carefully, he picked it up and casually tossed it overboard.

"No. Don't! That's our worms," Tommy cried.

"You won't need 'em. Sit down!"

Tommy sat, more angry than frightened. He sure had a score to settle. First the shove, and now the bait.

"What's all this junk?"

Mike picked up Kathy's fishing poles. They had been lying between the seats, close to the starboard gunwale, out of everybody's way.

"They're not bothering you," Tommy cried. "Please, Mister. Put them back."

Mike snorted. "Ha. Got to make the boat lighter."

Laughing, he flung them overboard.

Fury blocked reason. Tommy lunged at him, fighting and kicking, but the big man handled him liked a puppy.

Finally tiring, he slapped Tommy across the face several times and shoved him back to the stern thwart.

"Stay there and steer this tub, Punk. Don't get up again for any reason. I'm tired of playing with you. You understand?"

Tommy nodded mutely. He understood, all right. If Mike had been only playing, Tommy wondered what he would have done if he was really angry.

Dutifully, he steered the boat. He could hardly breathe, he was so furious.

What could he tell Kathy's father? One of those borrowed fishing poles was almost brand new. He'd have to replace them. Now he'd never be able to buy his own outboard motor.

He stared dully ahead, struggling to hold back tears. He watched Mike throw over the tackle box, the bailer and Kathy's fish net.

Now everything was gone. Why didn't he also toss over the oars and anchor? And the motor, too? Mike had no cause to toss over that gear. He knew the boat wasn't sinking. He did it out of plain, cussed meanness.

Tommy stole a glance ashore. Kathy was a tiny gray dot on the edge of the dock. He hoped she had seen what just went on, but she probably hadn't as they were too far away.

Besides, she wasn't running for help.

He was alone, and a growing terror gnawed at him. He pushed it away. Desperate, he tried to think of some way to let her know he needed help.

He suddenly turned the skiff south, directly into breaking waves. The bow leaped high and slammed down as a wall of water splashed against the hull and spilled inside.

In the bow Sam stared at the splashing water and whimpered in fright. The bow continued to leap and pound. The water wasn't really rough, just choppy. Not bad at all, if the boat was anchored. But Sam couldn't know that.

No... Sam and Mike couldn't know that, could they? Tommy thought.

And *he* couldn't know what they intended to do with him once they got across the bay. They certainly weren't going to reward him. Tommy didn't know what they were fleeing from, but they were running from something, all right.

The answer was probably in that suitcase, and Tommy was betting it was money or jewels they had stolen from one of the homes on Nayatt Point.

And he bet they had a car or friends waiting on the other side at Conimicut Point. The police would be looking for them in West Barrington and they'd be over on the other side of Narragansett Bay, laughing and racing toward East Greenwich, Arctic or Cranston. They thought they were pretty darn clever.

And maybe they were...

Tommy certainly didn't know what he could do about it.

"Hurry it up, Punk," Mike snapped. "Sailin' Sam's gettin' green around the gills."

Sam didn't look good at all. He was drenched from the heavy spray and pounding. His lined face was a tarnished-brass color, his mouth slack, lips wet and tight.

Tommy almost felt sorry for him.

Glancing around, he couldn't see Kathy at all. Too far away. Or maybe she had gone for help. She must have, he decided, because he needed to believe she had. But he had to give her time. Somehow, he had to delay their crossing. But how?

Mike yelled at him. "Come on, Punk. Hurry it up!"

"I—I'll try." Tommy turned the speed control, racing the motor, holding the bow into the on-coming waves. The skiff started pounding and slamming, shaking everyone and everything.

It was poor seamanship to do this, but it satisfied Mike. He had the sensation of going faster, so he decided they were going faster.

"Oh. Oooooh!" Sam groaned and suddenly leaned over the

side.

Tommy turned away because the power of suggestion is very strong.

But Mike didn't, and in another minute he didn't look very good either.

He started sweating. His ruddy face lightened to a pasty-white color. He kept wetting his thick lips with his tongue. He closed his eyes, but the sight and sound of Sam being very seasick had done its damage.

Now Mike was also violently ill...

Tommy kept the skiff's bow heading into the waves. With each approaching wave the bow leaped high, tossing skinny Sam into the air. As the waves passed, the bow slammed down in the trough, and so did Sam.

White water broke over the railings and streamed into the boat. Tommy's subtle varying the speed of the motor helped make it worse. Fortunately, the two men didn't know that.

Soon both men were so terribly sick Tommy felt sorry for them. He made himself remember the rough treatment and the lost fishing gear.

There was another thing too: Suppose Kathy didn't go for help? He'd still have to escape from them, and that might be easier if they were seasick.

The big man read his mind. "Get us over to that shore fast." He groaned, his hand to his mouth.

"Don't try anythin' funny. I'm warning you, Punk."

"Y-Yes, sir."

They had passed the black channel buoy and were heading for calmer water in the lee of the long sand bar of Conimicut Point. In another five minutes they'd hit the beach on the west shore of the bay. Tommy desperately tried to think of some way to delay their landing. He couldn't.

"Oh, God... Help me!" he prayed, as he had heard Kathy often do.

As though in answer, he had an idea.

He headed into the highest waves with the motor wide open, rocking the skiff slightly. The bow leaped up, then slammed down, bouncing San so he almost slid under the bow thwart.

Again Tommy did it, and heard a loud crack. Maybe it was enough. He saw water trickling toward the stern.

He slowed down, despising himself for what he had done. The deck planking near the brass plate at the bow had opened up from the violent pounding. The seam compound had worked out, and bay water was spurting in under the floorboards supporting the gas tank. The leak looked serious, but he knew they could make shore with time to spare.

He was counting on Mike and Sam *not* knowing.

But Sam noticed the water first. "Ooh! We're sinking!" he screamed in terror. "Look at the ocean comin' in. I can't swim, Mike!"

The big man saw the split seam and the spray of water. He muttered something profane.

"Stop the leak," he ordered Tommy.

"I can't," Tommy said. "I have to steer the boat. If I don't, we'll capsize... roll over."

"How can I stop it?"

Tommy said nothing, stalling for time. The beefy hand raised high and ominous.

"—Stuff a handkerchief in the crack!" Tommy cried, wincing.

After moving the gas tank and floorboards, Mike rammed a cloth into the crack using a prong of the grapnel anchor. The spurting stopped, but water in the boat was almost four inches deep, sloshing noisily.

The additional weight slowed them still more, Tommy noted happily.

"We're going too slow. Make this tub go faster," Mike yelled over the motor's labored roar.

"I can't. The water's slowing us. We have to bail it out."

"Well, bail then, Punk."

"But you threw the bailer overboard."

Mike stared at him. He slowly shook his head. He seemed about to cry.

"Of all the boats around Riverside and I had to pick yours! Why, oh, why?"

But they were still moving too fast, Tommy realized. He had to give Kathy sufficient time to get to the police—if she understood his signal. He knew he was putting a lot of faith in a girl, but Kathy wouldn't disappoint him. She couldn't!

They were about three-hundred yards off Conimicut Point,

close to the north side of the sandbar. Although still far off shore, the water was shallow. Fortunately, it was also murky and strewn with floating debris and straw from the high moon tide.

Counting on Mike and Sam's ignorance of the bay, Tommy eased the skiff closer, parallel to shore. He watched for ripples that indicated the underwater sand bar. Seeing them, he headed toward them at full throttle, the motor locked down.

"It's about time you headed toward shore," Mike grumbled.

Suddenly the motor shuddered as the churning propeller bit into the hidden sand. The boat stopped abruptly. The motor screamed as the shear pin snapped.

Tommy twisted the speed control handle to shut the motor off, then quickly released the tilt lock. He tilted the motor up to expose the propeller. Pretending surprise, he spun it around. He was secretly delighted:

He had a beautiful, broken shear pin!

The cooperative southeasterly wind was now moving them away from shallow water and back toward the channel.

Mike spun around, his sweaty face furious. "What's wrong now?" he bellowed. "What more could possibly go wrong?"

"T-The motor," Tommy stammered. "The shear pin is broken."

The big man was puffing as he hovered over the motor, his clothes drenched, body trembling, face slack and puffy white.

"What's that mean?"

"It's broken," Tommy repeated. "The propeller spins free. See?" He rotated it slowly. "It's like a broken transmission on a car. The motor runs, but the wheels won't turn."

Mike stared mutely at the motor. His mouth worked soundlessly. Finally, he said, "Can't you fix it?"

He seemed almost begging, Tommy thought.

"I—I—"

For the first time in almost five minutes, Sam spoke: "Mike. We're floating back to Riverside!"

"Damn it. I know it!" Mike snapped. To Tommy, he said, "Can you fix it?"

Tommy winced as though struck. "I—could, but—but you threw the extra shear pins overboard. They were with my fishing gear and the tools I need."

"Oh, hell!" Mike slumped to the center seat, heavily rocking the boat. He put his head in his hands and shook it.

"Everything went perfect, and then we had to meet *you!*"

The wind was steadily blowing them northeast, toward the channel. Mike suddenly glanced up. He picked up one of the oars and Tommy was panic-stricken, afraid Mike was going to test the depth of the water. It couldn't have been more than five feet deep.

He was relieved when Mike slipped the oarlock into place and motioned to him.

"You row us in, Punk."

Dutifully, Tommy obeyed. He didn't do very good alone. The wind was strong and against him, and the boat was heavy with all that water and the weight of the two men.

Mike swore and took the oars. He fumbled and puffed, and his beefy shoulders popped from the unaccustomed exercise. But slowly they made headway.

It took him over twenty minutes to reach the Conimicut shore. Both men immediately jumped out on to the beach.

Tommy dragged the skiff up on the beach and sunk the grapnel anchor in the sand. He was terrified now. Mike and Sam were still weak from seasickness, but they were again on land, and they'd soon feel better. Tommy saw no help had come. Kathy had misunderstood his signal. She was probably still waiting for him to return to her.

A very wet Sam still carried the suitcase, only he wasn't hugging it like before. He looked like he wanted to toss it away, or exchange it for a clean, dry bed.

"The car should be over there behind that tall grass," Mike said. "Close to that big, brown house."

He shoved Tommy ahead of him. "Come on, Punk. We're taking you with us."

Tommy's heart thundered in his chest as they walked over low sand dunes and through tall marsh grass toward the car on the dirt road several hundred feet ahead.

He thought of Kathy, and of Granny Parker, and of all the work that needed doing around the old house.

He thought of his own personal library of ten books, and of his own private room overlooking Narragansett bay.

He thought of Ben Brown who was nowhere near his big,

brown house today.

He thought of a lot of other important things, and none of them made any sense because they all needed a future, and he had no future, only a bleak and dismal present.

He was wondering if he should make a run for it. He was small and fast, and they were still queasy from their boat ride. He might make it.

But he didn't try...

Out of the corner of his eye he saw movement in the tall grass to his right. For a moment he thought it was a neighborhood dog. But it wasn't. Thank God. It wasn't!

At the signal, Tommy darted abruptly to the right, dropping over an embankment into an abandoned cellar foundation where there used to be a summer home before the hurricanes.

There was no noise. The action was swift and brief. Tommy looked up cautiously. There were a half dozen Warwick policemen with their guns pointed at Mike and Sam. One of the policemen held the suitcase.

Tommy choked in relief. Hot tears brimmed in his eyes and he was terribly afraid he was going to cry. And he did. A little.

Mike glared at him as the police handcuffed his hands.

"I should have thrown *you* overboard, Punk!"

Tommy watched them being led away toward several Warwick police cars with their friendly message on the doors: "Courtesy is our Motto!"

The lieutenant in charge told him that the two men had burgled one of the houses on Nayatt Point. He said there might be a reward for the things in the suitcase and, if so, it was theirs, his and Kathy's.

He explained that Mike and Sam had carefully planned to skip across the bay in a boat—any boat. They chose his because he was a kid, a pushover.

The lieutenant grinned warmly. "Ha! That's what they thought."

Tommy smiled gratefully.

"But how did you know? Did Kathy—?"

"Yep. The little Turner girl told us," the lieutenant said. "She called the Barrington police and they notified us. They're bringing her home now. She said she didn't know what was wrong, but two men forced you to leave her and you'd never do that to her.

"And she said she knew you were in bad trouble when she saw you make your boat go into the waves with the throttle wide open. She said you'd never do something dumb like that."

He grinned in admiration. "She's observant and smart. A pretty spunky little lady."

Tommy nodded in agreement. Kathy was that, all right.

The policeman's big hand rested on his shoulder. It was a friendly gesture, man-to-man.

"—And that was a very good job of stalling you did out there, Son. We thought you'd *never* get here."

The unexpected praise brought a hot flush of pleasure to Tommy's face. He felt he had done a pretty good job, but little Kathy had done even better. He was anxious to see her so he could tell her so.

"Poor Kathy," he thought, and grinned secretly to himself. "She never did get to go fishing. Now it's too rough to go."

The policeman shook his hand, and they walked to the patrol car. Tommy watched the car drive off. Sighing, he walked back to the beach and his skiff.

"—But we'll go fishing some day real soon," he promised himself.

"Kathy and me."

Chapter 5

To The Victor Go The Spoils!

*T*he tide was ebbing and for five weary minutes Tommy struggled to push his heavy skiff back into the water. Puffing, he sat down and slowly slipped the oars into position.

"Oh, I'm bushed," he moaned.

He was wet and tired, but with a broken shear pin the only way to get his boat home was to row it. Fortunately he was in the lee of Conimicut Point and the water was calm. The southerly wind should help too.

He rowed smoothly and steadily, anxious to talk to Kathy and to let Granny Parker know he was all right. Certainly she would be worried about him.

As he rowed closer to shore, he saw Kathy waving from Granny Parker's back porch. She raced across the lawn to the seawall, jumped down to the beach, and waded out to greet him.

He saw Granny Parker and a Warwick policeman talking on the porch. The policeman was writing in a little notebook. They both were facing toward the water.

He rowed past his mooring buoy into shallow water where Kathy caught the skiff's bow. She removed the grapnel anchor and pulled the skiff on to the beach, sinking the anchor into the sand. She hurried to Tommy's side and seized his arm.

"Oh, Tommy. I was so scared for you! I saw that big man slap you and—" Her eyes widened in concern.

"Oh, your cheek. It's swollen. They hurt you!" Her fingers touched the bruise.

Wincing from the pain, Tommy caught her hand. "It's—all right, Kathy. Just cut the inside of my lip." He grinned and squeezed her hand.

"Say, you were wonderful, Kathy. I'd hate to think what would have happened to me if you hadn't called the police. They were crooks and they were taking me with them...probably to their hideaway. Boy, I was relieved when the Warwick police caught them."

"M-Me too," Kathy whispered. She held tightly to his arm as they walked around Granny Parker's seawall to a low spot where piled rocks at the base served as a step.

Tommy helped Kathy up and suddenly realized how exhausted he really was. Now that the danger was over, he was trembling like a frightened puppy. And it wasn't from being wet either. He wasn't the least cold.

He felt foolish and embarrassed. This was a crazy time to get the shakes—after the event.

He remembered Kathy's fishing gear. "They—threw everything overboard!" he choked. "Your dad's fishing poles, the tackle box, the bait... I-I'm sorry, Kathy. I'll replace it all. I promise."

Kathy pulled him on. "Don't worry about that now. You're safe, and that's more important."

She glanced toward the house. "Come on. They're waiting for you."

They walked around the wild roses and through the tall eel grass to the mowed part of the lawn. Granny Parker looked angry, and Tommy was afraid to continue.

He eased away from Kathy's possessive grip. He saw Granny Parker was scowling.

"H-Hi, Granny," he choked out.

The old lady's face was dark and ominous.

"Tommy, you all right?" she asked. "You're all wet!" she scolded.

"Fine job you did out there," the young policeman said. "I need a few more facts for our records."

"You're sure you're not hurt?" Granny Parker said .

Tommy shook his head. "No. Just my cheek is cut inside." Tears rushed to his eyes. He ran to the old lady.

"Oh, Granny. They threw Mr. Turner's fishing gear overboard. All of it. I couldn't stop them. I tried. But I couldn't stop them..."

The policeman made a notation in his book. Kathy seemed about to cry in sympathy. The stern lines of the old lady's face relaxed a bit. She sat on a cane rocking chair she had recaned herself only two weeks ago.

"We'll worry about that later," she said, and leaned forward, scolding. "You shouldn't have taken Kathy over there in the first place. She's just a child, and you're not much more than a child yourself. Besides, if you had listened to the weather forecast you would have heard small craft warnings were posted. You shouldn't have gone fishing at all."

The policeman sighed wearily. "Please, Mrs. Parker. I have a few questions to ask."

"It wasn't Tommy's fault those men came," Kathy cried defensively.

Granny Parker sighed. "'Course it wasn't, child." She looked hard at Tommy and finally got up. "I'll make you some hot cocoa to warm you up. And change those wet clothes just as soon as that policeman is done talking to you." She went into the house.

The policeman waited until the screen door slapped shut. "And now those questions?" he said.

Kathy sat in the cane rocker, fascinated as Tommy gave his account of the incident. She listened, enthralled, like reading a novel.

The policeman asked several additional questions, marking replies in his book. He wrote down Kathy's and Tommy's names and addresses, and Kathy's telephone number. Granny Parker didn't have a telephone. It was a luxury she didn't really need, she had said.

"Thanks, Son. Guess that's about all. That was a brave thing you did." His glance included Kathy. "*Both* of you."

They walked him to the patrol car at the front of the house. Its two-way radio was squawking static and occasionally coded short messages. Several small children were hanging around the car. There were older boys too, including Tommy's new acquaintances. They weren't friends yet, Tommy reminded himself.

"Say, what happened?" Booty's voice cracked. "Tommy, we heard you captured some crooks. Is that true?"

Pete Bender snorted. "Huh! Tommy couldn't capture a fiddler crab with a net."

"Yeah? Then why is the cop here, huh? And there were four or five police cars on Conimicut Point an hour ago." Booty faced Kathy.

"And a policeman brought *you* home, didn't he? A Barrington cop."

Kathy nodded vigorously. "It's all true. Tommy *did* capture some crooks. He was just wonderful!"

All eyes converged on Tommy. He blushed furiously, but was secretly delighted with the attention.

"Is all that true?" Pete Bender asked the policeman.

"Yes. He and Kathy caught some real live crooks. They did a fine job, too." He winked at Tommy. "And I wouldn't be surprised if they got a nice reward too."

He got into the car and closed the door, motioning the small children back. As he turned the corner of Bellman and Troy Avenues, he honked the horn twice.

"Wow! A reward!" Booty nudged Pete in the ribs with his elbow. "What do you think of that, Grumpy?"

"Huh." Pete snorted, but it was apparent even he was impressed.

An hour later some reporters from the *Providence Journal-Bulletin* and the *Warwick Beacon* stopped at the house. Dry and rested, Tommy and Kathy again repeated their adventures. The reporters took notes, asked questions, took several photographs, and left.

Kathy danced up and down. "We're going to have our pictures in the papers," she told Granny Parker. "Oh, aren't you excited, Tommy?"

Tommy grinned and nodded. He was far more pleased than he let on. But he was concerned too. Granny Parker had been cool toward him since the incident, even more distant than usual.

Of course, she was glad he was unhurt, but she was obviously annoyed too. She didn't enjoy having the responsibility of a boy who got into trouble. She didn't like the police and strangers upsetting her routine, trampling her flowers, trespassing on her property. She enjoyed her solitude and preferred to keep things that way.

Another thing that bothered Tommy was the missing fishing gear. He had to explain to Mr. Turner that he intended to replace everything that was lost.

It was the least he could do. Kathy's father had been wonderful to him, letting him use the outboard motor, teaching him to run it, lending him books, encouraging his study of the sea. Somehow, he had to make things right again, even if it meant spending all his savings.

"Is your father home, Kathy?" he asked finally.

"Uh huh."

"Good. Let's go over and talk to him."

Kathy went inside her house and called. A minute later her father came out on the back porch. He vigorously shook Tommy's hand.

"Congratulations, Son. Heard all about it." He nodded at Kathy. "I'm very proud of you for keeping your head. Mrs. Parker must be proud too. Going to have your pictures in the paper and all. Yes, she must be *very* proud."

"Y-Yes, sir. She—is proud." He felt ashamed for the lie, but he didn't want to tell him Granny Parker seemed more annoyed over the incident than pleased at his safety. And not once did she say anything kind to him, other than ask if he was hurt. No, he didn't want to say that.

"You wanted to talk to me?" Mr. Turner said.

Tommy nodded. But how could he say it? He felt choked up, his heart thumping, face suddenly hot.

The best way to face trouble was head on, he recalled Granny saying. He sucked in a deep breath.

"Mr. Turner, I—" He swallowed painfully, his mouth full of cotton. "I—lost all your fishing gear."

Surprise distorted Mr. Turner's face. "*All* of it?" he gasped. "But how?"

"Tommy didn't lose it, Daddy," Kathy interrupted. "Those awful men threw it all overboard. It wasn't Tommy's fault!"

Her father's expression softened. "Oh—Is that true, Son?"

Nodding, Tommy felt himself filling up. "But I *borrowed* them from you." he said. "So they were my responsibility."

He reached into his pocket for his savings, twenty-nine dollars and seventy-two cents. He had put it there when he had changed into dry clothes.

"This is all I have for now." He pushed it into Mr. Turner's hand.

For several seconds Mr. Turner looked at the money, counting softly. Finally he shook his head. He put the money back into Tommy's hand.

He closed the fingers over it, patting the hand.

"No. I can't take your money. You keep it, Son."

"But—Your fishing poles. Your reels. Even the motor tools are gone."

Mr. Turner was insistent. "They can be replaced. Besides, they were old and I wanted to buy some new ones anyway. Now I can, and with a clean conscience."

"But—"

"No buts. I guess I can afford a couple of fishing poles. And as for the motor tools, I've got other pliers and screwdrivers. So don't worry about them." He ruffled Tommy's hair.

"Thanks for telling me. And I'm still mighty proud of both of you!"

"See," Kathy said when her father had gone into the house. "I told you Daddy wouldn't be angry. He couldn't. I'm going in for lunch now. See you later."

Exhaling in relief, Tommy pocketed the money and walked across the back lawn and along the seawalls toward Granny Parker's yard. Mr. Turner was wonderful for not insisting he replace the lost gear.

Nevertheless, Tommy decided he would replace Kathy's fishing pole and reel. He'd surprise her. Anyway, it was the least he could do.

And besides, he felt like buying her something. He didn't know why. Maybe it was because he was grateful for her saving his neck. There was no telling what those crooks would have done to him.

He kicked idly at a loose pebble. "Heck, does a guy have to have a reason for everything he does?"

That afternoon's *Providence Journal-Bulletin* carried the story about the robbery, the boat ride, and the rescue on page one. It had Tommy's and Kathy's pictures in the Warwick News section with a human interest story titled, YOUNG HEROES THWART THIEVES!

The article was vividly descriptive, glowing with praise, and, Tommy thought, a bit embarrassing to read.

Kathy loved the articles. She was thrilled with her picture in the newspaper.

"She should be," Tommy thought. "She takes a wonderful picture." Granny Parker said she would save the articles and photographs.

Later, Tommy went up to Joe's Drugs on West Shore Road and bought a second *Bulletin*. Joe congratulated him. On the street he was greeted warmly by strangers, slapped on the back, and asked hundreds of questions. He enjoyed every second of his new fame. Back in his room, he cut out the photograph, carefully clipped Kathy's picture, and put it in a secret place in his wallet. His own picture and the rest of the paper he burned in the evening's trash.

Fame was a sweet thing, a delicious thing, a sweetmeat to be enjoyed. For several days he and Kathy feasted on it. People who hardly knew he existed stopped to talk to him. The neighborhood boys were especially cordial. Even Pete Bender was friendly and offered to take Tommy on a boatride on his new boat, *Banshee*, a high-speed 18-foot runabout with a powerful 50-horsepower Johnson. He never did fulfill his promise, however.

But as the days passed, the friendly nods and handshakes and hellos diminished, and within a week things were back to normal.

"Fame," Tommy thought, "is like an ocean wave. It rises suddenly, lasts a short time, and smashes on the shore, and is gone." He was a hero one week and the next he was just another lonely boy.

He wasn't bitter about it, just sad and wistful. Still, it was fun while it lasted.

The next two day's free time he spent repairing the leak in his skiff. He was very pleased he was able to completely seal it so the boat was bone dry once again.

Several days later he was returning from digging soft-shell clams at Old Mill Cove when he saw the Connecticut car in the driveway. A sudden jolt of fear struck him. The Home was in Connecticut!

He walked slowly toward the house, his eyes stinging. Granny Parker heard him. She peered around the corner and beckoned him to hurry.

He saw Kathy was on the porch. And so was Mrs. Turner. They were sitting with a strange man in a dark suit. And they all were grinning. Grinning at him! Kathy looked like she was about to explode.

Finally, she did! "Tommy! Guess what? You have a reward

for catching those crooks!"

Tommy's mouth dropped open. The man *wasn't* from the Home!

"A—reward?" he said finally. "You're kidding." He placed the shovel and bucket of soft-shell clams down on the grass and wiped his sweaty face on his arm, glad the tears didn't show.

"You're kidding, aren't you?"

"No, I'm not," Kathy bubbled on excitedly.

The others let her do the talking.

"...And Mr. Dwyer from the insurance company has a check for five hundred dollars for you. Just think, five hundred dollars!" She clapped her hands in delight.

"Now you can buy a good second-hand motor. Think, Tommy, your own outboard motor. Oh, aren't you excited? I am. Oh, I can hardly sit still, I'm so excited..."

"Kathy. Kathy, honey..." Mrs. Turner laughed softly. They all were enjoying Kathy's enthusiasm.

Flushing, Kathy sat back in her chair. "There, I've said it all. —I think."

Grinning, the insurance man gave Tommy a check. "This is for you, Tommy."

For several seconds Tommy studied the green slip of paper. Oh, this was fantastic! Kathy was right: It was a check for five hundred dollars. And it was made out to Thomas Wayne, c/o Mrs. Tillie Parker.

A slow, delighted grin leaped to his young face. He beamed at Kathy.

"Half of it is yours, you know. You helped catch those crooks. You called the police."

Kathy shook her head. "We already talked that over, Mom and I. Granny Parker said half should be mine too, but Mom and I decided it was all yours."

She leaped up and seized his hand, squeezing it ecstatically. "Oh, isn't it wonderful!"

Mrs. Turner finally spoke. "Kathy called her father and Jim said it was wonderful news, and he would be very happy to go motor hunting with you after supper. He's very pleased for you, Tommy. And so am I."

As Tommy stared at the check, it seemed to shake in his hands. He couldn't read the printing anymore. He grinned widely. He had never had so much money in his entire life. This was fantastic. Colossal! Stupendous! He couldn't believe his wonderful luck.

This check meant he could buy his own motor: a second dream come true! First he got his own boat, and now he could get his motor. And he and Kathy had the whole, wide, wonderful Narragansett Bay to play around in!

The insurance man finally stood up. "Congratulations, Son," he said. "My client is deeply grateful. Those stolen items were of great personal value." He held out some papers and a pen.

"Will you sign here? It's just a receipt, saying you received your check."

When Granny Parker nodded approval, Tommy signed.

Thanking him again, the insurance man collected his papers, dealt them into a neat pile and placed them into his briefcase.

"Thank you, Tommy." He put on his hat. "—Oh, and the best of luck with your outboard motor." He nodded around agreeably and left.

"I really must be going too," Mrs. Turner said. "Jim will want an early supper if he's going outboard motor hunting. Congratulations, Tommy. Coming, Kathy?"

"In a minute, Mom."

Granny Parker went into the house to start supper. Kathy sat on the porch floor beside Tommy and studied the check, her pretty lips silently repeating the amount over and over.

"But half it *should* be yours," Tommy said. He wasn't saying it to be kind or generous. Half if it really *should* be hers.

"No, it shouldn't! And I wouldn't take it. You earned it and it's all yours. Besides—" she added eagerly, "—when you get your motor, I'll have lots an' lots of boatrides, won't I?"

"—Sure. I guess so. You usually invite yourself."

Kathy giggled happily. "That's what I mean. I'll have lots of boatrides."

After supper, Mr. Turner knocked on the door. For several minutes he talked with Granny Parker until Tommy returned from upstairs. Granny Parker endorsed the check with her shaky signature and presented it to Tommy.

"You're sure you don't need any of this money?" Tommy asked her.

Granny Parker shook her head. "Nonsense, child. Wouldn't

take it anyway. Go buy your outboard motor. You won't be happy 'till you do."

"Thanks, Granny. 'Bye." As he rounded the corner, Tommy groaned audibly. Kathy was sitting in the car.

"Oh— Is Kathy coming with us?"

Mr. Turner looked at him curiously. "Yes. She wants to. Why? Don't you want her to come?"

"No, I don't," Tommy blurted out. "I mean, I'd *like* her to come, but—" His voice choked. Kathy's coming would ruin everything.

Tommy's thoughts stabbed frantically for a suitable explanation, one that would not hurt or be misunderstood.

"Well, buying an outboard motor is a man's business," he said finally.

Mr. Turner seemed surprised and hurt. His voice was husky. "Okay... If that's the way you want it, Tommy."

"It's *not* the way I want it!" Tommy protested. He suddenly hated himself. "But—it's the way it's got to be."

Mr. Turner sighed. His voice came strangely cool. "Kathy will be very disappointed. All right. I'll tell her."

Holding back, Tommy watched him. He saw the surprise on Kathy's pretty face, then the sharp pain and the sparkle of tears.

Despising himself for his crazy idea, he gave it up and ran to the car.

"No! You can come, Kathy. I want you to come with us!"

Mr. Turner scowled at him. "But, you said—"

"I know. I was wrong. I'm sorry." Tommy opened the back door and sat beside the sobbing girl. Mr. Turner got in front and loudly slammed the car door, obviously annoyed.

Tommy looked at Kathy for a long time, and then he said, "I'm sorry, Kathy. I really wanted you to come with us. It's just— well, I was planning to buy you something and I wanted it to be a surprise. I'm very sorry..."

The words were miraculous: The tears stopped. A smile leaped to Kathy's lips.

"A surprise? Something for me? What? Oh, please tell me, Tommy. Please!"

Her intense delight made him feel even more awkward. Kathy was such a sparkling, vital enthusiastic young lady. In an eyeblink her emotions varied from deepest despair to joyous animation.

"Oh, come on," she begged. "You tell me now."

Grinning, Tommy assented. "Okay. A fishing pole and a reel and line. Now, you know."

Kathy jumped up so she was kneeling on the car seat. She flung her arms around Tommy's neck and loudly kissed him on the cheek.

"Oh, that's *wonderful!* There's nothing I'd like better."

Flushing, Tommy eased away from her. "But you took the surprise out," he said. He was acutely conscious of Mr. Turner's gentle, silent laughter.

Kathy again sat beside him. "No, I didn't, Tommy. When you give it to me, I promise I'll be *just* as surprised and happy as I am right now. Honest!"

And true to her word, she was. Kathy was so enthused with her gift that passers by in the store stopped to enjoy her pleasure.

"Oh, I'll cherish it forever and ever!" she promised and fondly caressed the fiberglass rod and new spinning reel.

She finally gave them to her father who was also carrying her other gifts: line and tackle for fishing.

Catching Tommy's hand, Kathy pulled him toward the parking lot at the rear of the store.

"Now, let's go buy your outboard motor."

Chapter 6

Tommy Gets His Outboard Motor

"Then this is the motor you want?" Mr. Turner repeated, and Tommy nodded in pleasure.

"Yes. This is it." His hand caressed the shiny fiberglass housing of the Johnson.

"Oh, it's a beauty!" Kathy whispered, awed.

Her father grinned warmly at her. "Yes, she's a good choice," he said to Tommy. "She's clean, in good condition, and she sounds fine."

To the marina dealer, he said, "And you'll put in new plugs and points, right?"

"That's right," the dealer replied. "She's greased and the lower unit's full of fresh hypoid oil. She's an excellent used ten horse Johnson, and guaranteed. Your son won't go wrong with her, Sir."

Tommy glanced up, surprised. He waited for the correction. None came. Kathy nudged him gently with her elbow and giggled. He wasn't Mr. Turner's son, Kathy's brother, but it sure was a nice thought.

He and Kathy admired the motor while the two men drew aside and dickered about final price, finally agreeing. While the papers were being signed and the money paid, Kathy thumbed through the instruction book the dealer had given Tommy.

Later, the dealer shook Tommy's hand and put the motor and six gallon gas tank into the car trunk. When the dealer left them, Mr. Turner gave Tommy the receipt and bill of sale.

"You now own an outboard motor, Tommy."

His heart thumping in his chest, Tommy was so excited he could hardly sit still in the car. Several times he thumbed through the instructions, reading snatches, delighting in the information. Tonight he'd study the booklet until he knew his outboard motor from cover to skeg.

He read a passage out loud to Kathy and when she didn't reply, he looked at her. Kathy hadn't even heard him. Sitting alone in the back seat, her new fishing rod on her lap and extending to the front of the car, she was oblivious to everything but her gifts. Her small hands repeatedly caressed the polished wood handle and she had a dreamy, far-away expression on her young face.

Watching her, Tommy was glad she did come with them, after all. He had brought her a six-foot fiberglass boat pole, a spinning reel, two hundred and fifty yards of 15 pound test Ashaway nylon line, some lead sinkers and two packages each of tautaug and flat-fish hooks.

It was just fishing gear, but the way Kathy was carrying on, you might think he had brought her a whole new wardrobe of clothes.

Mr. Turner had protested his spending so much of his money on Kathy, but Tommy had insisted, and now, seeing Kathy so wonderfully happy, he had no regrets whatsoever.

Besides, didn't he still have money left over in his pocket? He would bank it tomorrow. And with his boat and motor, he'd be able to go tonging for quahaugs practically every day. It wouldn't take very long for his savings to mount up.

The car slowed and turned into Ban-I-Mar's Gas Station on West Shore Road and Stokes Street. Kathy suddenly looked up.

"What are we stopping here for? I want to show Mommy my fishing pole."

"Gas," her father said. "For Tommy's motor. Right, Tom?"

"Right."

"And this will be my gift to you. A full tank of gas and a quart of outboard oil."

"But I have money," Tommy said.

Mr. Turner shook his head. "Keep it. Save it. You'll need it."

The tank full and Tommy's heart overflowing with happiness, they completed the short ride home. Mr. Turner helped carry the tank and motor to Granny Parker's seawall.

"There. It's all yours, Kids. I'll watch from the porch."

Tommy ran up to the house and called Granny Parker. She walked with him to the wall, admired the motor, said it looked like a right fine choice, and then went back to the porch and her favorite rocker—an interested spectator.

Once the motor was clamped to the skiff's transom, the gas tank hose connected, the motor primed, Tommy sat on the center thwart and nodded to Kathy.

"Go ahead. You start it. I want you to."

"But—Okay." Trembling in excitement and pleasure for the great honor, Kathy pulled the starter cord. The motor purred into life. Kathy moved toward the center thwart, but Tommy waved her back to the stern seat.

"No. You drive it, Kathy. I'll sit in the bow."

"Are you sure?"

"Of course, I'm sure."

Kathy's pretty face was flushed with pride as she sat on the stern thwart and pulled the motor's shift lever forward. She carefully steered the skiff into deeper water.

"Oh, Tommy! It's—wonderful! It's so quiet I don't even have to yell to be heard."

Tommy grinned at her. He felt a bubble of excitement rising, pushing up into his throat. Finally, he could no longer control it.

"E-yow!" he cried. "Wow-eee. Yeow!"

Kathy started, then she too yelled, and they both laughed joyously. Whooping and hollering, they headed north toward Mark Rock with its Indian markings, located at the end of Rock Avenue.

For two hours until dusk they rode around, cruising to Green's Island, along the marshes of Occupasstuxet Cove, over to the partially sunken wreck of a wooden coal barge near Gaspee Point, and back along the west shore to Conimicut Point where they frightened several hundred seagulls parading along the sandy spit of the Point.

As they drove around, Tommy familiarized himself with the controls. With Kathy's help, he adjusted the high and low speed jets for maximum economy. He repeatedly checked the exhaust port for cooling water.

He shifted into reverse, tried the tiltlock, everything he could think of. And yes, everything worked perfectly!

"Yep. Sure is a right fine motor," he said, and Kathy nodded. Later, he wiped the motor down with an oily rag and stored it in Granny Parker's garage-barn beside the gas tank. He locked the door and double-checked it.

"You do real good out there," Granny Parker greeted him as he entered the house. "I'm glad you're a safe boatsman, not like some people."

"Thank you, Granny. Oh, what a wonderful day!" He yawned loudly. "Boy, I'm bushed. Me for bed. Good night, Granny."

"'Night, Tommy..."

Once he had changed into his pajamas, he was too excited to sleep. For two hours he studied the motor instruction booklet, underlining passages, making notations in the borders like Mr. Brown did. He knew a great deal of the information already, thanks to Mr. Turner and Ben Brown, but the data on motor maintenance and winterizing was new and most welcome.

The next morning he purchased some inexpensive tools, shear pins and Cotter pins at Salk's store on West Shore Road. Chapman's book was insistent upon always having spares and tools aboard, plus the knowledge to use them correctly.

He was cruising around alone when someone yelled from the shore. "Hey, Tom!"

Recognizing Booty and Pete Bender, he headed in, stopping the motor and tilting it before the skeg hit bottom. The boat nosed easily to the shore.

"Hey, where'd you get the nifty outboard motor?" Booty cried.

"Yeah," Pete Bender said. "My Ma said she saw you and Kathy Turner riding around late last night."

Tommy stepped into the cool water and pulled the skiff's bow higher on shore. The three boys sat in the boat and he told them about the reward money.

"Wow! Five hundred bucks!" Booty cried. "You lucky dog, you!"

"Oh, five hundred bucks ain't so much," Pete said derisively. "Heck, my motor alone cost over one thousand dollars." As an afterthought, he added, "They should have given you a lot more reward."

"I'm satisfied," Tommy said. "And speaking of your boat, where do you keep it? I don't see it here."

"Here?" Pete was horrified. "Not me. I keep it at Plant's marina in Warwick Cove. My Pop doesn't trust moorings here in Conimicut. Too many violent storms. He lost his sleek 36-foot inboard cruiser in Hurricane Carol. Smashed her to bits against the seawall. Maybe I'll drive the *Banshee* up here one of these days. Okay?"

"Swell, but no racing."

Pete's handsome, dark face was scornful. "What's the matter? Chicken?"

Tommy shook his head. "No way! But a ten horse can't race a fifty horse and win. You think I'm nuts?"

Pete laughed. "Oh, I get what you mean." He glanced at the motor and nodded approval, a big concession for him.

"Well, wish you luck with it."

"Five hundred bucks reward..." Booty was still awed by the sum.

"Want to go for a short ride?" Tommy said.

The boys glanced at each other. "Sure do."

Tommy got out and pushed the skiff into deeper water. Booty sat in the bow, facing them. Pete sat on the center thwart.

After paddling into deeper water, Tommy lowered the motor and pulled the starter cord. He was delighted when the motor growled into life on the first pull.

"Boy, she sounds swell," Booty grinned. "I'm going to get me a boat someday."

"What do you need a boat for?" Pete cried. "You always manage to mooch a ride with someone."

Booty shrugged, unoffended. "I'd just like to have one." To Tommy he said, "Do you think this will pull a water skier?"

"Don't be silly," Pete snapped. "'Course it won't. Not enough power." He grinned and winked secretly at Booty. His voice was syrupy.

"Oh, maybe it'll pull Tommy's girlfriend, Kathy Turner. She's skinny and light."

Tommy flushed so his ears felt aflame. "Kathy isn't my girlfriend. She's just a kid."

"I don't think she's a kid," Booty said simply.

But Pete laughed loudly and slapped Booty on the knee. "Hey, look. Tom's blushing! Oh, I never would of believed it. Tommy's sweet on little Kathy Turner. Ha ha. She must be all of nine years old."

"—I think she's kind of cute," Booty said.

"Come on, knock it off!" Tommy cried. Pete's teasing annoyed him. "Besides, Kathy's not nine. She's almost—fifteen. And she's *not* my girl."

Hoping to change the subject, he rotated the motor handle too far and the skiff's bow suddenly leaped high with the increased speed. The sudden lurch startled Booty who cried out.

"Hey!" He clutched the gunwales and clung for dear life. "Come on, slow down. You're shaking out my teeth."

Kathy forgotten, Pete grinned in delight. "That's it, Tom. Open her up. Come on, Man. Go. Go. Go... Faster. Wow-ee!"

The skiff streaked along the choppy water, her bow pounding, plumes of white spray flying from her slapping bow. Pete was yelling and rocking the boat to heighten the effect of still greater speed. He was laughing at Booty who was bounding around and hanging on and yelling.

Tommy suddenly realized he was behaving stupidly. He was taking his anger out on the boat. He turned the motor handle counterclockwise and the motor quieted down. The bow dropped and the spray vanished. And so did Pete's smile.

"Aw, come on, Tom. Open her up again. Don't plod around like an old lady. Ke-rist, you're as poky as old lady Parker."

The name calling was like a knife-thrust. Sharp fury pumped hot blood through Tommy's veins.

"You shut up!" he cried. He suddenly hated Pete Bender. Pete was a smart-aleck, a selfish, spoiled, only child. Granny Parker had warned him about Pete. She had told him a dozen times that Pete was a troublemaker.

Pete noticed Tommy's anger and calmly waved his hand. "No offense meant about the old lady, Tom. It's just that I like speed and sharp turns. What good is a boat if you don't race it?"

Slowly relaxing, Tommy regretted his harsh words and bitter thoughts. This was no way to make friends.

"Okay, just watch what you say about Granny Parker and Kathy. I like speed too, but just as long as the water's calm and no one gets hurt.

"Besides, pounding a boat is stupid. It opens the seams, and I've already got a bow leak. And all those books I've studied warn about speed and dangerous boating," he added thoughtfully.

"Hell!" Pete's mouth hardened to a white slit. "Stop lecturing me. You sound like my old lady. And besides, *you're* the amateur around here. I've lived by the water all my life. You don't know beans...

"And I don't care how many dumb books you've studied. I'll *always* know more about boats than you do." He motioned toward shore.

"Take us back. I get enough preachin' at home. I don't need any of yours."

Tommy was astonished at Pete's reaction. He looked questioningly at Booty, but the taller boy merely shrugged and looked apologetic.

"Okay," Tommy said finally. "If that's the way you want it."

"Yeah. That's the way I want it."

Disappointed, the knuckles of his left hand white on the steering handle, Tommy guided the skiff to shore. Pete jumped out. Booty rolled his eyes and hunched his shoulders.

"Sorry, Tom. It's a nice motor. Thanks for the boatride." He stepped out and pushed the boat away from shore.

"Hey, Captain Bligh," Pete yelled derisively. "Hope you sink! And if I ever catch you out when I'm in my *Banshee*, I'll personally sink you." He laughed loudly, scornfully, humiliatingly.

"Wise guy," Tommy muttered to himself. He paddled the skiff into deeper water before dropping the motor down. Humiliated, angry at Pete and at himself, he watched the two boys run along the beach.

What happened? For a short while they were friendly. Everything was going fine. Beautiful. And then—whammo!

Now he was alone again, without friends.

But why? Had it been his fault? Had he been wrong to defend Kathy and Granny Parker? Is that what had angered Pete?

Or was all his studying and talk about boats, and his intense interest in the sea... were they the cause of Pete's antagonism?

He had studied all those books so he could be like the other boys, so he wouldn't be different. Was it his fault he had developed a genuine interest in boating and the sea?

Tommy chewed thoughtfully on his lower lip. But his study hadn't made him like Pete and Booty, or any of the local boys.

His new knowledge had somehow set him apart even more. He was enthusiastic and eager to learn, and to share. Maybe he even knew more about the sea than Pete did, and Pete resented that...

And him too.

After starting the motor, Tommy let it idle as he thought over Pete's warning. Would Pete really try to sink him with his powerful boat?

Oh, that was probably just an angry threat, he decided, and shifted into forward speed.

He headed out toward the channel, cruising slowly, thoughtful, a tiny, lone figure slicing up the great, reflected blue of the water.

He felt even more isolated now, even more alone...

Chapter 7

Attack Of The Screaming *Banshee*

*H*is young, tanned face flushed in raw anger, Tommy savagely twisted his motor to bring the port bow of his skiff into the huge wake that threatened to swamp him.

His skiff's bow leaped high, then slammed down sickeningly, and the wake passed. If he hadn't turned when he did, his small boat would have taken still more white water over the side and maybe even sunk.

But that was Pete's intention—to sink him.

Pete has promised he would, and he sure was trying. This was Pete's definition of fun.

The big 18-foot plywood lapstrake runabout that had almost run him down raced off. Tommy glared after it, humiliated by the raucous, whooping laughter from Pete Bender, skipper of the *Banshee*, "The Fastest Boat On The Bay!"

"And the most dangerous too, with Pete driving her," Tommy muttered bitterly. "Someday I'll give him a taste of his own medicine. I'll fix him good."

Slim and bronzed, his hair sun-bleached from the countless hours on the bay, Tommy headed toward the north shore of Conimicut Point. He was glad Kathy wasn't with him. She would have been badly frightened.

—Or maybe she would have clobbered Pete with an oar. There was no telling with Kathy.

Tommy was suddenly conscious of the wetness around his bare feet. Despite his fast action, a considerable amount of salt water was sloshing around the deck.

He stopped his boat a dozen feet off shore, swung the motor up and let the skiff nose in, sweetly kissing the beach. When landing, he avoided letting his bow plow hard into the gravely shore as some boatsmen did, and as he had done occasionally, up until a week ago.

From his books and Ben Brown's teachings he knew it was a bad practice. It ruined the bottom's anti-fouling paint. And neither did he drag his skiff up on the beach to hold her there. Instead, he anchored her off shore, the proper way. He wouldn't always have a planked-bottom skiff, so it was best to learn to do the right things now.

Noting the wind direction, Tommy sunk the grapnel anchor so the boat floated parallel to shore, then got his plastic bleach bottle bailer from under the stern thwart. He had over three inches of water to bail out, thanks to Pete's horsing around.

"Crazy fool character!" he muttered.

Pete's *Banshee*, a sleek plywood racer, was now south of Conimicut Lighthouse. She was a beautiful white boat, powered by a factory fresh fifty-horse Evinrude, and capable of pulling two water-skiers at thirty miles an hour.

His own fourteen-foot skiff was tiny in comparison. It was powered by ten second-hand horses, but he was intensely proud of her.

He continued bailing, thoughtful. This was the third time this past week Pete had almost sunk him. Playing his new and dangerous game—sink Tommy's skiff—Pete had zoomed close, the throttle wide open. A few yards away, he would suddenly whip the steering wheel around, his beamy boat skidding and throwing up a huge white wake.

The *Banshee's* propeller would scream in cavitation, then growl throatily as she bit into solid water and streak off.

Pete laughed hilariously at Tommy's frantic struggles to keep afloat. Oh, this was such great and wonderful fun!

And today Pete was working hard to impress his new girlfriend Marilyn. But from what Tommy could see, Marilyn had seemed more terrified than impressed.

"Pete knows better than to pull this stuff," Tommy grumbled as he bailed out the water. "If he doesn't, he should. It's against the boating laws, subject to fines. A person is responsible for his boat's wake, and that's a fact..."

Pete was sixteen and a half-head taller than Tommy. His father had given him the sleek _Banshee_ several months ago, a birthday gift. She was docked at a Warwick Cove Marina, but shortly after Tommy got his skiff and motor, Pete had started bringing the _Banshee_ to Conimicut.

Granny Parker disapproved of Pete. He was wild and irresponsible, a menace on the water, according to Granny. He handled the _Banshee_ the way he'd eventually drive his car—carelessly, recklessly, for thrills.

As often as he tried, Tommy couldn't understand Pete. Pete had everything he ever wanted, but he wasn't happy. He seemed angry at the whole world...

"He almost got you out there, boy."

The deep voice startled Tommy. He recognized the old eel fisherman he had seen bottom fishing out on the Point. The man's smiling face was windburned a deep red, the skin weathered like parchment. He was an old sailor and clam-digger who obviously spent more time in the wind and sun than in a house. Somewhat like old Ben Brown.

"Yes," Tommy said. "He almost did."

"That crazy kid coulda swamped you with that dang fool trick! Did you get his boat number? You ought to report him. It's kids like him that ruin boatin' for the rest of us."

It had never occurred to Tommy to report Pete. Besides, this was a personal battle.

"I don't need his number. I know him. I don't want to turn him in."

The weathered face twisted in surprise. "You don't? Why, if you hadn't moved quick and knowed what you was doin', your skiff would of been swamped for sure."

Tommy smiled nervously. "But I wasn't sunk," he said. "I was lucky."

The old fisherman snorted. "Call it luck if you want to, but I calls it good boatin'. Does my heart good to see someone like you. Almost makes up for all the dang fool Sunday Id-jits on the water now-a-days."

His gray eyes burned into Tommy's. "I'd _still_ turn him in before he hurts someone, Boy."

The old man's praise was intensely pleasing to Tommy. Maybe all his studying was finally paying off.

"But Pete's just horsing around," Tommy said, feeling mildly defensive.

"Horsin' around like that can kill you."

The old man shook his head. "Well, I'm glad you're okay, anyway." He hefted his fishing pole and continued walking in a wide, rolling gait, heading out to the long sand bar on the Point.

Tommy called after him. "Thank you. And good fishing!" He returned to his bailing. Using a rag, he sopped up the dregs, sand and seaweed, then rinsed his equipment and stored it.

Straightening up, he shaded his eyes against the sun reflecting on the water. The *Banshee* was far south of Conimicut Light, heading toward Prudence and Patience Islands.

"Maybe I should turn Pete in," he thought, but immediately changed his mind. "No. That would only make him angry and resentful. He'd never be friendly. And it wouldn't teach him anything!"

He sighed heavily. Pete would have to learn safe boating the hard way.

Once again Tommy looked south. Judging from the *Banshee's* flying spray, Pete was running her wide open, as usual. And she was probably gobbling gas like a glutton. Well, Pete had the money for it. His father was most generous, giving him everything he wanted. Except, maybe, personal attention and love, according to Granny Parker.

The *Banshee* had two six-gallon tanks, enough gas for plenty of high-speed running around. Tommy's boat had only one six-gallon tank and he was lucky when he was able to say, "Fill her up!" It took an awful lot of lawn-cutting and tonging for quahaugs to pay for six gallons of gas and a quart of outboard oil.

But he had no complaints. He had as much fun running at a quarter-throttle and used much less gas. His ten horses got him to the fishing holes and back. He and little Kathy enjoyed exploring the coves, visiting the many marinas on Narragansett Bay, or just plain boating around and eating picnic lunches on the water. Besides, running a 50 Evinrude at full throttle as Pete did took all the pleasure out of boating. It turned it into work. High speed required intense concentration. You had to keep your eyes peeled for waves, cross-chop, wind shifts, floating debris...

And at high speed the water was as bumpy as an old potholed

Providence street after an icy winter. You had to continuously wrestle with the steering wheel.

No, speed wasn't fun. Not Pete's brand of speed...

Tommy noticed the wind was picking up, from the southeast. It was stirring up a sea, capped with "white hubcaps", according to little Emma Parenteau, a local great grandmother.

Out where Pete was racing around was rough water. In contrast, Tommy was in the lee of the Point in relatively calm water.

"Well, this isn't catching any fish," Tommy said, and hauled anchor. He pushed the skiff into deeper water and noted his gas gauge. He had a half tank, enough gas to last him all afternoon, if he didn't rev her up.

His motor started on the first pull, bubbling and gurgling, spitting a steady stream of steam and cooling water from the exhaust port. Out of habit he touched the two spare shear pins taped inside the steering handle, a recommendation from Kathy's father. His tools were stored in a cigar box fastened under the stern thwart, another recommendation. They were oiled and wrapped in a waterproof plastic bag.

Pete was lucky in one respect, Tommy decided. He didn't have to worry about a broken shear pin. He had a slip clutch on the propeller shaft to take any prop jams.

Easing into forward speed, Tommy headed toward the channel. He had gone a hundred yards when he noticed his motor sounded strangely loud. He saw no water was coming from the exhaust.

He immediately stopped the motor and tilted it up. Sure enough, a ball of seaweed was stuck in the water intake screen. Ten minutes driving like that and his motor would have heated up and seized, ruining it.

The motor running smoothly again, he continued east toward Conimicut Lighthouse. The north side, near the granite foundation rocks, was a choice tautaug hangout.

Tommy wished Booty could have come with him, but Booty had to help his father repair a car. Maybe tomorrow the two of them could go fishing for flats, or maybe even striped bass.

This Fall he, Booty and Kathy were planning to take the Coast Guard Auxiliary course on safe boating. Tommy had suggested that Pete come with them, but Pete had snorted in contempt.

"What? Me go to school to learn about boats? Are you kidding? I was born on the shore, remember? Besides, I have enough troubles with day school, never mind goin' nights."

...Anyway, he had tried.

As he rounded Conimicut Point, Tommy saw the water was choppy. And dirty too, with patches of floating seaweed and debris from the earlier full moon tide. To minimize pounding, he guided his skiff at a 45-degree angle to the waves so her bow sliced smoothly through them. Chapman's book recommended that.

The water was now too rough to fish at the lighthouse so he headed southwest toward the stakes over at Lambrecht's old place off Long Meadow, a quarter mile away. There the water would be calmer.

Riding parallel to the rocky south shore of Conimicut Point, he delighted in the salt air smell, the prickling chill of spray on his face and bare arms. Several hundred yards to his right the waves were breaking hard and loud on the rocks, shooting up plumes of white spray like great walls of smoke.

More waves were smashing against Ben Brown's patched seawall, trying to get at the great brown house near the end of the Point. Where one wave failed, another tried, again and again...

Tommy suddenly heard a new sound, like a giant buzzing bee. He glanced to his left.

"Oh, no! Not again."

It was the *Banshee*. She was bearing down upon him, less than two hundred yards away. He knew Pete wouldn't deliberately ram him and destroy his own boat in the process, but worse accidents have happened from careless horseplay on the water.

Tommy knew he was in for a rough time. He held his course, bracing for action. He expected Pete to zoom in close, suddenly turn and speed off again. But would Pete cut across the skiff's bow or stern? Either way meant trouble. A sharp turn at high speed would slide the big runabout smack into him. It could even flip the *Banshee* over in a broach.

Tommy stood up and desperately tried to wave Pete off, pointing to the rough water, but Pete still bore down upon him.

Tommy could see more of the big boat's starboard, or right, side and decided Pete intended to cut across his bow on a left turn. Gambling on this, he shifted into reverse.

Pete saw him and altered his course slightly to the right. The big boat streaked closer. Her motor whined shrilly. Her bow porpoised in the choppy sea: _thump! thump! thump!_

Suddenly the _Banshee_ turned a sharp left. She skidded dangerously close...closer. _Wham!_ Her stern slammed hard into the skiff's bow, throwing Tommy hard against his motor, and momentarily knocking the breath out of him.

Tears of anger and rage sprung to Tommy's eyes. "You crazy nut!" he screamed, shaking his fist.

The _Banshee_ sped away. Tommy checked his boat. No real damage. Another inch or two and he would have been sunk for sure, his skiff's hull stove in.

But Pete still wasn't satisfied. Tommy saw he was making a tight turn, pounding and slamming the hull mercilessly. The runabout now headed back toward him. Within seconds, the big craft ringed the skiff, the circles drawing tighter, her great wake drawing the skiff around and around like a stick caught helpless in a whirlpool.

White with fury, Tommy shifted into neutral. "Get away! Scram!"

Pete laughed at him. Little Marilyn had her hands to her mouth, stifling a scream. Her eyes were saucer wide. Her face was white in terror.

The _Banshee's_ propeller suddenly spun air in the tightness of the turn. The motor screamed, an unusually loud and hollow sound.

It was then Tommy noticed the steam. He remembered the dry sound his own motor had made when the water intake port had been blocked. He recalled the great amount of floating debris and seaweed on the water. Should he warn Pete? Should he?

He saw Pete was oblivious to the ominous sound and the steam cloud pursuing him.

He had to warn him. He shouted.

Laughing, Pete waved back. The _Banshee's_ wake was now dragging the skiff—stern first —in a tight circle. Pete was having a real ball.

"Pete!" Tommy yelled again. "Cut your motor. You're overheating!" But shouting was useless. The sound of Tommy's voice was killed by the runabout's shrill whine.

Suddenly the whine stopped. It was replaced by a loud metallic clanging, like a muffled fire alarm. That sound stopped. The _Banshee_ shuddered, then abruptly plowed to a stop, her bow pushing up a great wall of water. She settled level, her motor dead, enveloped in a cloud of smoke and steam. The sound of wind and surf took over.

Still trembling in anger, Tommy restarted his motor and pulled alongside the crippled *Banshee*. Marilyn was sobbing. She insisted she would never again go boating with Pete who was frantically fiddling with the useless remote controls.

Tommy dropped his anchor, then shut off his motor. He caught the bowline tossed by Marilyn. He made the line fast to his stern chock and scrambled aboard the *Banshee* to survey the damage.

"Whew!" The wide cockpit smelled of gasoline and oil and something else—the stink of burned paint and metal. Fearful of an explosion, Tommy forgot his anger and disconnected the two gas tanks. He moved them toward the bow, and then faced Pete.

"You crazy nut! Now you're in trouble, bad trouble." He tilted the big motor to check the lower unit. Sure enough, the intake screen was plugged solid with junk. He unhooked the fiberglass hood and removed it. The stench of scorched metal was overpowering. When the acrid smoke and steam finally cleared, he examined the motor.

"Oh oh!"

The motor was a mess. Deprived of cooling water, the powerhead had overheated, the metal pistons expanding, but instead of jamming from the binding friction, one of the connecting rods had let go and the piston had smashed through the motor's side.

Pieces of aluminum and magnesium were strewn about. The speed control linkage was shattered. Through the five-inch jagged hole Tommy could see the bearing end of the burned connecting rod.

Pete was breathing heavily beside him.

"Gee, Tom. Is it bad?"

Tommy held up several pieces of broken metal. "Bad? Look at it. Here's what your horsing around did, Pete. Ruined your motor. The power-head's shot. The block too, I think. Satisfied now?"

For a long time Pete stared at the smashed motor. Behind him, Marilyn was coughing softly from the fumes.

Pete stammered: "B-But how? I mean, it's almost *brand new!*"

Tommy explained as best he could, drawing from the instructions he had received from Kathy's father, and from what he could recall from the booklet describing his own outboard motor.

Pete nodded, chewing nervously on his lower lip .

"Oh, boy," he groaned finally. "My Pop will crown me. He'll clobber me for this. Probably take away my boat."

He stared vacantly at the ruined motor for several seconds, then faced Tommy.

"I-I didn't know it was overheating, Tom. Sure, I noticed it sounded louder, but I thought that was okay. Tom, I didn't know it was heating up..."

Tommy faced away, suddenly embarrassed. He wasn't getting the satisfaction he had expected from Pete's downfall. Instead, he felt sorry for Pete, and the unexpected emotion angered him. He hardened his heart, refusing to feel sorry for Pete.

Didn't Pete bring this on himself? Wasn't he the big man, too big to learn? Besides, what about that deep crease in his skiff's bow caused by the *Banshee's* fins? Fixing that was going to take a lot of time and woodfiller and sanding and paint. No, Pete got what he deserved.

"She's all yours," Tommy said. He helped Marilyn into his skiff, then started his motor, leaving it in neutral. His mouth firm and determined, he hauled his anchor and cast off the bowline from the *Banshee*. "Wait," Pete cried. "You're not going to leave me out here!"

"Why not? Throw out your anchor and wave for help. Maybe the Coast Guard will rescue you. Swim to shore. It's not far."

"But I don't have an anchor! I lost it." Pete glanced around apprehensively, a whiteness bracketing his lips.

"And I'm drifting toward the rocks. The *Banshee* will smash up. Please, Tom, help me!"

Ignoring his pleas, Tommy put his hand on the shift lever. He was suddenly acutely conscious of the brisk southeasterly wind steadily blowing both boats closer to the rocks.

"Why should I help you?" he cried. "Ever since I got my motor you've hounded me. Twice you almost swamped me. Go ahead, let the *Banshee* break up. I don't care. Your father will probably buy you a new one anyway."

He shifted into forward speed and slowly headed his skiff toward the lighthouse.

"Tommy. No!" Marilyn gasped. "You can't leave him!" He ignored her.

He had travelled less than twenty feet when he slowed his

motor and shifted into neutral. For several seconds he sat motionless, choking up, tears welling in his eyes.

He felt ashamed. He couldn't look at little Marilyn staring at him from the bow. He glanced at the crippled *Banshee*. He hated himself.

Darn it! There was no joy, no satisfaction in revenge. It was a bitter, empty feeling. He couldn't live this way. He wouldn't!

He abruptly jammed the shift into forward speed and turned the skiff around. Regardless of what Pete did, he couldn't leave him adrift. He'd never be able to look at himself in the mirror. And what would Ben Brown, or Mr. Turner—or Kathy—think of him?

Besides, he rationalized, wasn't it the duty of all boatsmen to help a craft in distress? And all those past two months, wasn't he studying and working to be a good boatsman—*and* a better person?

Tommy glanced ahead at the *Banshee*. But maybe he was already too late. Pete's big boat was very close to the rocky shore. He raced his motor, streaking closer.

Swiftly guiding his skiff alongside the *Banshee*, he tossed a line. "Fasten it to your bow chock, Pete," he yelled.

"Thanks, Tommy." Pete cried. He held the line in his hands, apparently bewildered.

"Hurry," Tommy yelled, but Pete still seemed confused. He kept staring at the rocks a few yards away.

"Come on, Pete!" Tommy cried. "Tie that rope on the metal bar on the front of your boat." He watched nervously. "That's it. Now move the gas tanks to the back and stay in back. Get your bow up as high as possible."

Nodding in understanding, Pete scrambled back over the windshield into the cockpit. He moved the gas tanks from forward to aft. "Okay."

"Swell." Tommy shifted into forward speed and the *Banshee* slowly turned. Heavy waves splashed against her starboard bow, holding her tight, pushing her still closer to the rocks. The crippled big boat was dragging Tommy's skiff with her. Marilyn gasped behind him.

Acutely concerned, Tommy twisted the throttle wide open. His motor screamed, but nothing else happened. The driving force of the waves was equal to the small motor's pull, and now *both* boats drifted closer to the jagged rocks.

"Oh, no! Were not going to make it," Marilyn cried .

"Yes, we will!" Tommy continued running wide-open. The tow line stretch taut, snapping spray. The little motor screamed and strained. Tommy silently prayed.

"Please. Please!" Marilyn begged.

Slowly...ever so slowly...the big boat nosed around and her bow headed into the waves, a giant hauled by a flea.

"Oh, thank God," Marilyn cried.

Tommy agreed. He headed directly into the on-coming waves, getting soaked. He finally turned his skiff slightly toward the east and saw the deadly shoreline, and the rocks behind him, slowly receding.

It was not until they were well clear of the rocks that he allowed himself to relax.

"Wow! That was _too close_," he breathed.

Marilyn exhaled in relief. "It sure was." She smiled warmly at him. "Thanks for helping Pete, Tommy." A wide smile brightened her pretty face. She glanced back at Pete sitting in the _Banshee's_ stern, and then at Tommy.

"I think maybe now Pete's learned his lesson. He'll attend that Coast Guard course. We'll both go."

She moved to the center thwart and rested a small hand on Tommy's knee.

"Pete was very wrong about you, Tommy. I think you're very nice."

The unexpected praise brought a hot flush of intense pleasure to Tommy's face. "T-Thank you," he stammered. "I-I'm just sorry Pete had to learn the hard way.

"So am I. But my daddy says most of us do. And many of us _never_ learn."

A concerned look creased Marilyn's brow. "But will you be able to tow the _Banshee_ all the way home, Tommy? She's a big boat and your skiff's small. And you don't have much gas left either."

Tommy eased the speed control down a bit. "I think so. I hope so. My skiff isn't sleek and fancy like Pete's boat... She's slow and small, like a turtle." He grinned.

"But she's dependable and good on gas. She'll get us home, all right."

Compensating for the wind at his stern, Tommy expertly guided his skiff with its larger tow across the submerged sandbar and slowly headed in toward calmer water in the lee of the land. He saw the old eel fisherman on the north shore waving triumphantly at him. Grinning widely, he waved back.

He didn't quite make it back home before his motor coughed and stopped, out of gas. But they were in shallow water. Pete jumped overboard in the waist-deep water and walked both boats to shore. He borrowed Tommy's anchor and line, and walked his own boat home.

Later, the *Banshee* anchored, Pete came up to Granny Parker's house. He stomped up on the back porch.

Seeing him, Tommy slowly rose to his feet, tensing for the fight to come. Granny Parker just watched, saying nothing.

Tommy was surprised when he saw Pete was carrying his grapnel anchor and line. Pete gave them to him, smiling slowly. He held out his right hand for a handshake.

"Friends, Tom? —If it's okay with you?"

Tommy seized the offered hand and violently shook it. The sudden elation was almost overpowering, threatening to suffocate him. At long last, Pete Bender wanted to be a friend!

Tommy grinned up at the taller boy. "It's okay with me, Pete," he said happily.

"—Friends!"

Chapter 8

Of Time And Changes

Summertime on the seashore was a sweet and continuous joy. Tommy was never happier!

A hot July melted softly into a still-hotter August. The weeks raced by and the lawns browned from lack of rain. Cicadas buzzed shrilly, in sun-baked contentment, and fat June Bugs bumped into everything and everyone.

Sunny, hot day followed sunny hot day, and the people of Conimicut Village and Warwick, and all of Rhode Island, and New England too, mildly complained about the heat and lack of rain, but all agreed, it was, indeed, an incredibly beautiful summer. One of the best in years!

Far south, the first hurricane of the season dallied west of Cuba. Alice fussed and fumed, then went away. Then came tropical storms Barbie and Cleo and Dora, Elsie and Francie, but all proved to be strictly southern belles and shy to set foot on land.

Then came Glenna. She hung around Bermuda, indecisive.

On Tommy's fifteenth birthday on August 10th., Kathy shared his cake and ice cream and happiness. Her gifts to him were two boatcushion life preservers, and a size-fifteen collar sport shirt. Tommy was growing rapidly, and many of his clothes were tight across the chest, choking around the neck, and too short. But who needed dress-up clothes in lovely August, anyway?

These days Tommy practically lived in swimming trunks. He swam every day. After cutting Granny Parker's lawn, or cementing her seawall, or working on the barn roof, he'd race down to the shore where he plunged in and cooled off and relaxed.

Often he'd anchor his skiff in front of the house in deeper

water and dive from her stern. He'd swim down and hastily dig for quahaugs with his fingers. He usually managed to locate one or two, sometimes three, in one breath.

These he used for bait for fishing, never for eating. The quahaugs in front of the house in Conimicut Village were considered polluted. Granny would never eat them. Neither would he.

Tommy wasn't exactly sure what pollution was, but thought it meant the quahaugs were poisoned by something men had put into the water.

He loved this area and decided he'd learn as much about pollution as he could, and he'd do everything possible to stop it from destroying beautiful Narragansett Bay. And that was a promise!

His young body was now bronzed and strong. Hard work, deep, contented sleep, and a good, sensible diet were filling him out, hiding the embarrassing ribs, and padding his shoulders, arms and thighs with hard, firm muscles.

He no longer got blisters on his hands from tonging. And filling a basket with quahaugs usually took him less than an hour.

He was content: life was sweet and most delicious, like ice-cold watermelon.

Around the house he frequently did more than asked. He repaired and painted the back porch floor. With Mr. Turner's guidance, he reputtied and painted all the windows in Granny Parker's house. Now they were Winter-tight.

With the newly-glazed and painted wood storm windows—another project completed—the old house should be warm and comfortable, despite not having central heat.

He had never wallpapered a room in his life, but then he had never done most of the things he was now doing. With Kathy's commandeered help, and Mr. Turner's wallpapering board and tools, the job was completed in three days.

The change was amazing and most gratifying. His room was lighter and seemed much brighter. It was decidedly more relaxing.

He spent considerable time in his room reading, and now as he read the cheerful room filled him with intense pride. At long last he had a sense of belonging...

Soon after, he made a bookcase from driftwood lumber that had floated in from the shipyard at Providence. When he had sanded it and painted it white, he put it beside his chair and reading lamp. His prize collection of books filled the top two shelves, leaving the bottom shelf for expansion.

His library on boating and the sea had expanded to over seventy volumes and numerous magazines, plus borrowed books from the Warwick Public Library on Sandy Lane, a wondrous place filled with friendly, helpful people!

He had studied and thoroughly enjoyed all of Rachael Carlson's seaside books. Superb! He had purchased many second hand books at Spencer's Store in Oakland Beach, including five colored and illustrated *Golden Science Guides: Fishing, Seashores, Weather, Stars* and *Birds*. These he particularly enjoyed, frequently re-reading them and using them for reference.

He was unable to estimate how many fish, shells and birds he had identified with the aid of his books.

And it *was* true, as Granny said: "Books were a lasting companion and a constant source of pleasure and knowledge!"

They were fun, too, especially the novels of Jack London and Nordoff and Hall.

At Kathy's suggestion, Tommy started attending the Turner's church every Sunday. He especially liked the people there. They reached out to him in love and friendship.

He grew to understand more of the Turner's quiet sharing and giving of themselves to others. They were a very close and warm family. He liked that very much.

Occasionally, in quiet times, he and Kathy talked about God. Kathy seemed to know God personally, and talked to Him like He was a close friend.

Tommy also liked that, and began to copy her.

He and Kathy spent countless hours visiting old Ben Brown on the Point, delighting in his wondrous tales of the sea. Often they helped the old seaman repair his massive seawall. Ben Brown's wall was extremely vulnerable to the southern wind and sea. It required constant patching.

Granny Parker's seawall was located on the west shore of Narragansett Bay, in the lee of the great beckoning finger of Conimicut Point. In comparison, it was in a protected location.

Several times Tommy and Kathy had anchored Tommy's skiff to talk privately, and ended up visiting with the old man who showed them how to dismantle an outboard motor, or to make repairs or replacements.

He even showed Tommy how to remove the starter mechanism and replace and re-gap the points, how to check the coil, and to adjust the tappets for maximum gas mileage.

Mr. Turner was wonderful too, the closest thing to a real father Tommy had ever had. He had located an old split-bamboo fishing pole he had forgotten he had, and had given it to Tommy. The next day he gave him an old fishing reel.

Tommy immediately began working on them. After two afternoons of sanding, nylon whipping and varnishing, the fishing pole looked like new. The reel was old, but once cleaned and oiled, it cast superbly.

With the sultry weather of August, the tautaug had migrated to the cooler waters of the Atlantic Ocean, but the flatfish were still biting. Striped bass, those beautiful, silvered Kings of the Sea, were hitting on trolled clam worms and rigged eels. Most of the bass caught were "schoolies"—two and three pounders you released to grow some more. Some were "keepers" and they made delicious eating.

But the real big stripers were out there, somewhere, Tommy knew. Approximately once a week the *Providence Journal*'s sport section had a photograph of a monster bass and a delighted fisherman. So the big fish were being caught, but most of them came from the lower bay, twenty miles south, and much too far, Granny insisted, for a small skiff and two youngsters to travel.

"Well, maybe someday a bull bass will roam north," Tommy hoped.

"And when he does, I'll be waiting for him!"

Chapter 9

Kathy's Birthday Party

*T*ime had a way of changing things. Almost overnight, it seemed, Tommy was growing taller and stronger, his voice lowering slightly. To him, these were important and welcome changes.

"But Granny Parker doesn't seem to change. And neither does little Kathy Turner," Tommy thought.

But there really were changes in Kathy, dramatic changes, and they were brought to Tommy's attention in a startling way.

He had seen Kathy practically every day. True, she wasn't as pesty or tomboyish as when he first met her—he had noticed that much—but to Tommy she was a little neighborhood girl who wrinkled her nose when she laughed, and who was as frisky as a baby eel.

When you see a person daily you don't notice subtle changes, that sweet miracle of maturing, those changes from pretty to beautiful. It isn't like when you go away for a month or two, and then come back and see your friend. Then you would notice the changes. You couldn't avoid it.

For Tommy, Kathy's maturing came suddenly and startlingly, the day of her fourteenth birthday. And that strange day after...

Tommy had spent hours selecting her gifts, finally deciding upon a 2½ pound Danforth anchor, fifty feet of quarter-inch nylon anchor line, both for Kathy's small sailing pram, and a white sailor hat for Kathy. He thought they were good, thoughtful gifts. He hoped she would like them.

The Turners were having a family dinner and party, but Kathy had insisted Tommy come.

"After all," she had explained to him, "you're practically one of the family. You've got to come!''

Tommy agreed happily, and that evening he dressed with meticulous care, selecting his best clothes: tan trousers, a brown suitcoat, and that white shirt Kathy had given him a few weeks earlier.

It seemed strange to wear long trousers and a shirt after living in shorts and swim trunks practically all summer.

Tommy stood up tall, noticing how his trouser cuffs were inches above his ankles.

They had fit perfectly only a month or so ago.

As he walked about his room, he winced and rubbed his right heel. His shoes pinched, the result of going barefoot and wearing loose tennis sneakers most of the summer.

"You hurry it up, Tommy!" Granny Parker called up the stairwell. "Kathy said be over there at six."

"Coming." Excited about his first dinner party, he thundered down stairs, but suddenly remembered Granny Parker's aversion to loud noises .

The last three steps he took on tiptoe.

"My! Don't you look nice." Granny Parker looked up at him. She looked up at him, Tommy realized.

"Goodness, how you've grown. Your clothes don't fit you."

He grinned in pleasure. "It's about time, isn't it? I thought I was going to be a midget all my life."

"Have no fear of that." The old lady pushed a small white package into his hand.

"You give this to Kathy for me, Tommy," she said. "'Tain't much, but she's a girl an' I think she'll like it. Have a nice time."

"Thanks, Granny. Oh, and thanks for wrapping my gifts."

They were on the chair by the door. The anchor line and sailor hat were neatly wrapped so Kathy would never be able to guess what was inside. But the anchor—who could wrap an anchor?

Granny Parker had compromised: She had tied a gaily-colored, red-and-green ribbon on each of the flukes, and a third ribbon with a huge red bow on the shank.

She shrugged apologetically. "It's the best I could do."

Tommy grinned warmly at her. "It looks just fine." He slipped the small white package into his pocket and left with the gifts. Excited, he ran the distance, three houses down.

Mrs. Turner let him in. "Don't you look nice, Tom." She studied him intently, from head to toe.

"You're getting tall. I never noticed before."

"It's these clothes," Tommy said. He felt awkward and embarrassed to be stared at so. Why didn't clothes grow with you? Except briefly for Sunday church, he hadn't worn these dress-up clothes since leaving the orphanage, almost four months ago. And then they had fit perfectly. He'd have to use some of his savings to buy some trousers. And shoes too.

He glanced around the room. "Where's Kathy?"

Mrs. Turner laughed softly. "Still dressing. Her father brought her a new dress for her birthday and everything has to be perfect. Come in to the parlor, Tom. She'll be right down."

As Tommy entered, Mr. Turner folded the evening paper and got up from his chair. He shook Tommy's hand.

"Evenin', Tom. Bring your appetite with you?"

"Yes, sir. Thanks for inviting me."

"Thank Kathy. She insisted, and we're very glad she did." He reached for a book on the mantle.

"Here's a Hemingway novel I think you will enjoy. I know I did. You may keep it."

"Thank you very much." Tommy grinned in appreciation. The book was *The Old Man And The Sea.* He had heard of it and was very anxious to read It.

"It's about this old fisherman, see?" Mr. Turner explained. "He hasn't caught a fish for weeks and then he hooks on to this monster swordfish, and is dragged out to sea. He fights the fish for two days and finally ties it to the side of his boat. Then along come some sharks and—" He grinned apologetically.

"Sorry. You read it, Tom. Beautifully written." He glanced up at the noise overhead.

"I think maybe Kathy is about to make her grand appearance."

They walked toward the hallway. Mrs. Turner hurried from the kitchen, wiping her hands on her apron. Wonderful, festive odors filled the house.

"Are all of you ready?" Kathy called down.

"We're ready and waiting," Mr. Turner replied.

To Tommy, he said, "She's very excited. Fourteen is an important age, you know. She'll be wearing her new dress and her first pair of nylons and—other things." He chuckled goodnaturedly.

"Jim, you cut that out!" Mrs. Turner warned. "She'll hear

you."

"Come on, honey," Mr. Turner yelled. "We're hungry."

Tommy realized he was very anxious to see Kathy. Except briefly on Sunday mornings, he had rarely seen her in a dress. And by the time she came over to Granny Parker's, she was wearing denims again and an old shirt, and her chestnut hair was windblown or else tied back with a ribbon.

He heard the creak of the top stair and looked up.

"Here I come," Kathy cried.

"Ta daa! Ta daa!" her father bugled and waved his hands, the signal to sing.

"Happy birthday to you. Happy birthday to you-u..." They chorused. "Hap—"

Tommy suddenly stopped, speechless. That wasn't Kathy. It couldn't be! Before him stood a stranger, a very, very attractive young lady with soft, wavy hair, a touch of lipstick, wide soft eyes and a captivating smile.

She wore a vivid red dress and somehow she wasn't skinny anymore. And she wasn't a little girl either. She was a lovely young woman.

"—py birthday to you-u-u!"

"Oh, you do look lovely, dear," Mrs. Turner said, and Mr. Turner nodded and caught Kathy's hand.

He proudly led his birthday girl through the parlor and into the dining room.

"Come on, Tom, boy," he yelled after him.

As though suddenly awakening, Tommy followed them. The table was filled with delicious food. In the center was a huge birthday cake with fourteen pink candles. The gifts were on a chair against the wall.

His anchor, he realized now, looked stupid and out-of-place. The little girl Kathy he knew would have loved it, but this slim and very adult young lady Kathy would only laugh at its childishness. He wished he hadn't come.

Mr. Turner helped Kathy into her chair. She sat like a queen, regal and confident.

"You sit here, Tom, next to Kathy," Mrs. Turner said, pointing.

Tommy felt awkward and clumsy. He tripped over the rug as he sat into his chair. He realized he was staring at Kathy and glanced down at his plate, his cheeks hot.

Somehow in the short time of Kathy's walking downstairs, his and Kathy's relationship had changed. Kathy was no longer his little friend. He realized he was in awe of her, almost afraid of her.

Mr. Turner stood up for attention. "Shall we eat dinner or open the presents first?"

It was then that the little Kathy abruptly returned. Her voice, anyway:

"Oh, no!" she cried, excited. "Let's open my presents first!" To Tommy, she said, "Hey, you look swell, Tommy. How do you like my new dress? Isn't it lovely? I've always loved red, and this is my first dress-up teenage dress even though I'm fourteen, not thirteen. But I was too skinny last year. I didn't want nylons, and so—"

"Kathy. Honey!" Mrs. Turner laughed in delight. "Take it easy. Slower. Don't bubble on so."

Kathy squealed on in pleasure. "Ooooh! I'm so *happy!*"

Chuckling, Mr. Turner piled some of the gifts on the table.

Giggling, Kathy tore off the wrappers. One of the gifts was a brilliant red one-piece bathing suit.

"Oh, it's beautiful!" Kathy stood up and held it in front of her, modeling it.

"Wow-ee!" her father said, and they all laughed, but Tommy blushed. He suddenly remembered Granny Parker's little gift and pulled it from his pocket.

"This is from Granny Parker. She said, 'Happy birthday'."

"Oh... Isn't she sweet," Kathy whispered. She unwrapped the gift slowly, a small bottle of toilet water.

"Perfume!" She beamed at Tommy. "You tell her—No, I'll tell her myself. After our party I'll bring her over some cake and ice cream and I'll tell her thank you."

Unscrewing the cap, she sniffed, then touched a drop to her throat, and one behind each small ear. "Mmmm."

"Very dainty," Mrs. Turner said, sniffing the perfume. "Mrs. Parker has excellent taste."

Kathy sidled up to Tommy. "Smell me. Don't I smell pretty? Huh?"

Tommy blushed furiously and backed away. Kathy smelled of soap and liveliness and vitality and—

"Open your other gifts," Mrs. Turner said, grinning at

Tommy's intense discomfort.

When Kathy got to Tommy's anchor, she held it to her breast, her eyes bright and moist.

"Ooooh— Tommy! Thank you. I really need an anchor for my sailboat." Holding it out in front of her, she admired the ribbons.

"And I'm not going to unwrap it. It looks too lovely!"

Tommy was both embarrassed and delighted. She *did* like it, after all.

At the unwrapping of the nylon anchor line, Kathy's eyes filled, and she did a most unlady-like thing: She wiped them with the back of her hands. Her voice choked. "T-Thank you. Oh, gee, this is swell!"

"—And one more gift from Master Thomas Wayne."

Mr. Turner was obviously having a wonderful time at his daughter's birthday party. They all were.

Kathy tore at the wrappings. "A sailor hat!" she exclaimed and plunked the white hat atop her beautifully coiffured head. The unexpected action brought startled expressions to everyone, and they burst into laughter.

Tommy also. For the first time since Kathy had come downstairs, he felt himself relaxing.

Kathy flung her arms around her father's neck and kissed him. She hugged her mother and kissed her. She came up to Tommy, the sailor hat still jauntily on her head. For several seconds she looked up at him. He was half a head taller now. He looked down at her, saw a hesitant smile pulling at the corners of her lips .

As though suddenly deciding, Kathy took a step forward, pulled his head down, and loudly and firmly kissed him on the lips!

Beaming, she turned. "Thank you, all of you. It's a wonderful party!"

Dinner with the Turners was a warm, relaxed, family affair. Kathy wanted to eat with the sailor hat still atop her head, but her mother insisted she remove it.

Dinner over, .Mr. Turner lighted the candles on the cake and Kathy furiously blew at them.

"With that mighty blow, I'm sure you're going to get your wish," Mrs. Turner said.

"I've already *got* it!"

Kathy did not elaborate. She smiled and sliced the cake. The first piece she gave to Tommy, then served her father and mother. She cut a fifth piece, carefully wrapped it in a napkin and placed it in a clear plastic Baggie.

"That's for Granny Parker," she explained.

They had cake, ice cream and soda, then sat around the table talking and laughing, reliving the evening's events.

Later, as he walked to Granny Parker's house, his new book, *The Old Man And The Sea*, clutched tightly in his hand, Tommy knew things had changed. But not too greatly, happily.

Kathy was a young lady in many ways, but she was still a little girl, and still his gabby little friend. He was glad of that.

But he thought a lot about that kiss she had given him...an awful lot.

The next day when Kathy joined Tommy for their morning swim, she was wearing her new red, one-piece bathing suit. Suddenly, again that painful shock of change jolted him.

Kathy was no longer skinny. She was—well, rounder, and fuller and...

From now on Tommy knew things would always be slightly different between them.

Oh, sure, he and Kathy would continue to have fun. They'd still fish and sail and laugh, and even continue to insult each other goodnaturedly.

But there was that certain sweet and warm and easy friendship of a young boy and a girl that would never, ever again...be quite the same.

Chapter 10

The Young Man And The Sea

(The Big Fish)

*T*he expression on Kathy's pretty face would squeeze tears from a hardshell clam, but Tommy was determined to resist her pleading.

"But you promised to go sailing with me," Kathy cried, her young face acutely pained and intent. "You did!"

"I know, but not today," Tommy answered. "I want to go fishing." He made a distasteful face. Lately, Kathy Turner was becoming so—so girlish. Not at all cooperative and agreeable as she used to be.

Before, she was anxious to go *anyplace* with him, and never a complaint or an alternate suggestion. In fact, she had usually insisted upon going, and invited herself.

It had to be that adult red dress and red bathing suit she got for her birthday that was bringing about the changes in Kathy, Tommy decided grudgingly. They had gone to her head.

"Please, Tommy—" There were tears in Kathy's eyes.

Annoyed, Tommy shoved the plastic handbailer under the stern seat of his skiff. He sat down heavily and glared at Kathy.

And that was another thing new about her that annoyed him: She cried. Before, she *never* cried. Not even that time she had cut her hand on the barnacle-clad rocks off Rocky Hollow in East Greenwich when they went crab hunting with Mr. Cooley. And that was a deep cut with salt water in it, and it probably stung like murder too.

But then she didn't cry. Her little mouth had tightened, and her eyes went wide, and her face had scrinched up something awful and she *almost* cried, but she *didn't!*

But lately—Tears in mid-sentence.

What was wrong with her? He sighed heavily and shrugged.

Sure, he had promised to go sailing in her eight-foot pram, but Danny Booth said he had heard the big striped bass were cavorting around Providence Point at the north end of Prudence Island. Summer was rapidly drawing to its end and he desperately wanted to catch a big fish before school began—providing Granny Parker let him stay and go to school.

Not for a second had he forgotten that Granny had "borrowed" him from the orphanage for the Summer. And Summer was over in two short weeks. Every night he prayed to God that Granny wouldn't send him back.

And maybe catching a big bass wasn't important to Kathy, but it was very important to him. It was another one of his life's goals.

Again he glanced at Kathy. She was standing in the bay water next to his skiff, her denims rolled past her knees, and her sailing pram beside her. She already had the sail up and luffing, and the rudder was in place. She was wearing the sailor hat he had given her, but not the way sailors wore it, square atop their heads.

Instead, she had it plunked on her chestnut head like an old pan, the stiff brim shading her eyes and almost hiding her tanned face.

And worse, she had written his and her names all over the brim. It was disgusting and it looked silly, but she wouldn't part with that hat for anything. She'd told him that often enough.

As for those other two birthday presents, she had put them to use the day after her birthday. Both the anchor and fifty-feet of line were neatly stored in her pram, one end of the line newly spliced around a thimble on the anchor, the handiwork of her father.

"Please, Tommy," Kathy said. "I'll go fishing with you tomorrow. I promise. Cross my heart and hope to die. Honest."

She was so intent and serious, Tommy stifled a grin. What's a fellow going to do? He sighed heavily.

"Okay. You win, Kathy." He knew she'd win anyway. She always did win—lately.

Kathy beamed in pleasure. "Oh, thank you, Tommy. We'll have a wonderful time. I made us a picnic lunch and we can sail all the way to Prudence Island and back."

"Prudence Island?" That's where the stripers were, Tommy remembered.

He grinned widely as the idea formed. He put the skiff's oars into the pram sailboat.

"What are they for?" Kathy asked quickly, suspicious.

"A deal," Tommy said. "We'll go sailing, but I'll take my fishing gear and the oars. I'll troll for bass on the way down, and when we get to the island, we'll spend one hour rowing about Providence Point while I fish. Is it a deal?"

Kathy was hesitant, then nodded slowly. "Okay, it's a deal. But I think you're awful."

They loaded their gear into the eight-foot sailboat, waved good-bye to Granny Parker on shore, and dropped the centerboard, locking it down. Kathy pulled in the mainsheet and the small boat quickly heeled on a starboard tack.

"Whee-e, we're off," she cried.

At Conimicut Point the southerly wind hit them head on. Kathy set her boat on a port tack, then a starboard, another port, and another starboard.

All the way to the island Tommy trolled for striped bass. He exchanged the clamworm and spinner for a plug, then a spoon, but still no strikes.

"Maybe there's bass in the upper bay, but where?" he cried.

He lay back on the pram's floorboards, eyes closed, listening to the gentle gurgling of the water against the hull, delighting in the sweet comfort of the late August day.

Sitting beside him, her right knee holding the tiller amidships, Kathy held on to the mainsheet. The sail billowed out sweetly.

"Man! Sure is a swell day," Tommy breathed.

"Uh huh. Now, aren't you glad you came?"

"Yep. But where are all the fish? We're sailing at a beautiful trolling speed. Not one hit. Boy, I've got to catch a striper!"

Tommy sat up, leaning on his elbow, and grinned at Kathy.

"Say, wouldn't it be swell if I caught a huge bass and he fought like a demon, and the sharks came and bit at him, and—"

Kathy giggled, her eyes slitted against the sun's glare on the water. "You've been reading that book Daddy gave you, *The Old Man And The Sea*."

"It's a good book," Tommy cried defensively. "I read it twice."

"I liked it too," Kathy replied. "I like lots of books you like, but I don't imagine myself in the stories like you do. Who do you think you are, the young man and the sea?"

Her gentle teasing brought a great, gay grin to Tommy's face.

"Think you're pretty clever, don't you?"

"Don't think. I know I am."

"Ha ha."

"Ha ha, yourself." He sat up. "Well, we're almost there. Remember your promise. You'd row me around Providence Point.

Kathy groaned. "I was hoping you'd forget. But let's eat lunch first."

They sailed past the point and through the gut between Prudence and Patience Islands in Narragansett Bay. Kathy headed the boat toward Coggeshell Cove on their port quarter. After several tacks they beached the pram. Tommy sunk the anchor in the hot sand and straightened up.

"Hey, this is nice, a beautiful place for camping." They were on the extreme northern end of Prudence Island, in a small sheltered cove surrounded by trees, shrubs and marshes. Not a house in sight.

The shore abounded with fiddler crabs. Six inches below the moist tide line sand were delicious soft-shell clams for the digging. The shallow water of the cove held plenty of quahaugs, most of them small cherrystones, the kind seafood enthusiasts enjoyed raw, or with prepared sauces, catsup or vinegar.

In the past months Tommy had even learned to enjoy raw quahaugs.

Granny Parker had kidded him, saying, his loving quahaugs would greatly please cartoonist Don Bousquet who made his living drawing about quahaugs, clam-diggers, tongers and bullrakers.

"Wow! I never knew this place existed," Tommy declared. "A fellow could live here all summer." He spread the blanket and helped with the sandwiches, pickles, hard-boiled eggs and tomatoes.

"What would you eat?" practical Kathy asked him. "I mean, if you lived here."

"Well, I wouldn't starve. There's plenty of food. Clams, quahaugs, fish, crabs. There's wild duck too, and I saw some pheasant over there in the marshes. I don't think I'd starve."

Kathy flopped on the blanket. "You go eat your raw clams and things. I want liverwurst sandwiches on rye bread." She bit hungrily into her sandwich. "Mmm. Num num!"

They ate and talked and finally Tommy got up. "Let's go fishing, Miss Robinson Crusoe. And remember your promise."

Kathy groaned. "Okay, slave driver."

With the warm south wind at their stern, sailing north to Providence Point was fast and easy. Tommy hooked two fat clam worms on his spinner and trolled them behind the boat.

"Come on, fish," he cried. "Look at those luscious worms!"

Kathy giggled and moved the tiller to avoid bumping Louie Rock, humorously named after a young, Conimicut Village, enthusiastic bass fisherman who was acutely conscious of the submerged rock.

The story goes that whenever Louie fished Providence Point, he consciously strove to avoid the hidden rock at high tide, but almost always had the bow of his outboard boat, or the skeg of his motor, nudge the rock.

Fortunately he was usually trolling too slow to do any real damage, but he was continually amazed, and annoyed, at always doing the very thing he strove *not* to do.

So one wild day at low moon tide, when most of the rock was out of water, Louie had painted his name on the rock: "Louie Rock."

The name stuck. And some of the letters were still visible, Kathy noted.

"You're cheating," Tommy said. "You're sailing, not rowing. But that's all right. You're doing fine."

"Thank you, *kind* slave driver."

After one pass Kathy turned the pram into the wind and ran down the sail, tying it to the boom, then fastening the boom securely to the mast. She slipped the rudder inside the pram and pulled up the centerboard, then put the oars into position in the oarlocks.

"So now I row," she groaned.

Tommy checked his bait. Not a nibble. Not even a choggie bite.

"Maybe too hot," he decided, "or too late in the afternoon."

He cast out astern of the pram and let out fifty feet of line, occasionally jerking his pole to entice the fish.

"Now, if my one girl-power outboard motor will kindly start," he said, and Kathy grimaced. She rowed close to shore where Tommy said bull bass liked to feed, past rocks and ripple-topped sandbars and low spots.

Twenty minutes later they completed the pass around Providence Point.

Tommy sighed in disappointment. There were no fish. Nothing.

Depressed, he picked up his pole and started to wind in. Maybe Kathy had the right idea after all. It really was a superb day, ideal for sailing. Maybe they should enjoy it.

Suddenly the tip of his pole jerked downward. The reel screamed as the line was pulled out. Tommy jerked back hard, sinking the hooks.

"I got one! I got one!" He tightened up a bit on the reel's drag. "Wow, I think it's a monster."

Kathy unshipped the oars and put them into the boat. She watched, fascinated, as the fish knifed the strong line around and around, trying to cut it against rocks.

Gripping the pole with all his strength, Tommy moved toward the pram's bow. The fish was pulling out still more line, despite the reel's drag...

"He's making a run for it," Tommy yelled. "Look! He's pulling us with him. He's pulling the boat!"

"Whee!—" Wide-eyed in excitement, Kathy hovered amidships. "Don't let him get away."

"I won't." Gritting his teeth, Tommy clung tighter to the pole, praying the line wouldn't break, or the bamboo rod split. This was a dream come true, his monster bass. It had to be!

The enraged fish towed the light eight-foot pram around the west side of Providence Point, then headed southwest toward the channel between Prudence and Patience islands.

The small boat moved faster. Soon it seemed to be flying, throwing up a surprisingly large bow wake.

Tommy stared ahead, giddy with delight. He had never hooked on to a fish so powerful. He was also terrified the line or the bamboo rod would snap, or the fish would throw the hook.

As they passed little Patience Island on their right, Kathy stared at it.

"I don't believe any of this, you know," she cried. "It's all too crazy, being towed by a fish. I'm dreaming. Any minute I'll wake up and I'll be lying on my blanket in Coggeshell Cove."

Tommy chuckled. "It's not a dream, Kathy." He gasped painfully. "Wow. I'm getting tired. My hands are killing me..."

But the big fish wasn't the least bit tired. As it swam south toward the Atlantic Ocean, it towed the pram like a stick of wood.

They passed the belly of Prudence Island and continued south toward Hope Island. Kathy watched as the tiny island with its seagull-clustered rocks passed by. For some unknown reason, she waved.

To Tommy, it seemed like hours had passed, and still the great fish wasn't tiring.

The fish was now heading toward Narragansett Bay's West Passage and Jamestown Island, effortlessly towing the pram on a fantastic Nantucket Sleighride.

"Whee... It's Moby Dick," Kathy cried.

They passed several anchored boats. Startled fishermen glanced up, curious. They did a double-take. They stared, scratching their heads. They blinked their eyes as if blaming a mirage, or something they ate, or drank.

A boat moving by itself? This couldn't be true!

Several boats upped anchor and followed at a safe distance, their occupants whooping and cheering.

As the pram passed under the great Jamestown Bridge, more anchored boats tooted their horns. And still more boats followed them.

Apprehensive, Tommy watched them, afraid some over-enthusiastic skipper would come too close and cut the fish line with his propeller. But, happily, all boat skippers wisely kept a safe distance.

Delighted men and women excitedly shouted encouragement: "Hold him, Son. Fight him!"

"Son-of-a-gun!..."

"Don't let him get away!"

"Jumpin' Jehoshaphat. He's hooked on to a whale!"

"Naw, it's a submarine from Quonset Point."

For a few anxious minutes Tommy was afraid maybe he had hooked on to a whale. Or a shark. But the fish made a sudden spurt to the surface, and in that instant he saw it was silvered and had a dark stripe down its side. It was a striped bass! And what a bass!

Still more boats joined in the nautical parade, hooting and honking, a gay, festive, maritime follow-the-leader.

Tommy held on to the pole, his face grim and determined. It was a fight to the end, he or the fish. But the fish seemed fresh and strong.

In contrast, Tommy's arms and shoulders were one massive ache. His body felt numb. His fingers were stiff and white on the pole.

The great fish towed them past Dutch Island. It continued due South, toward Beavertail Lighthouse at the extreme southern tip of Conanicut Island, also called Jamestown.

Beyond was the great blue ocean...

Tommy did not mention it to Kathy, but he was afraid now. Suppose the fish towed them right into the ocean? What would they do? As it was, it would take them many hours to sail the twenty miles back home. Kathy's folks would be worried. Granny Parker would be furious with him. Neither he nor Kathy was allowed this far south.

"Tommy!" Kathy's shrill voice was edged in panic. She pointed ahead. "Look. The ocean. He's pulling us into the ocean!"

"I-I know..." Tommy groaned in pain. He was tiring fast. He considered throwing the anchor overboard, but the sudden stopping of the pram would probably snap the fishing line, and the great fish would be free. He also realized the anchor probably wouldn't even touch bottom because Kathy had only fifty feet of anchor line. They were in very deep water.

They were also less than a half mile from the ocean and the water was getting rougher. Great, rolling seas bobbed the small boat. Fine sheets of spray drenched them. Occasionally, the white water splashed into the boat, frightening them.

Although deeply concerned, Tommy welcomed the coolness. Kathy didn't. She was annoyed at having to bail out her pram.

"This fight can't go on much longer," Tommy gasped. "It—can't!"

He glanced fearfully ahead. The ocean swells were far too high for their small craft.

After several more minutes, several of the smaller boats and runabouts following them turned back to calmer waters. The larger cruisers were still with them, fortunately.

"I've got to turn him," Tommy cried. "Somehow, I've *got* to!"

Clutching the pram's sides for support, Kathy moved closer to the bow.

"But how, Tommy? He's still pulling us without any trouble at all. How?"

"I-I don't know. But I have to try...even if I lose him."

Desperate, Tommy forced himself to think. Using the anchor was definitely out. Somehow, he had to *gradually* slow the big fish, to add more drag to tire him. But how? It seemed impossible.

Kathy moved back to the stern thwart. Her knee hit one of the oars, knocking it loudly to the deck.

Tommy suddenly had an idea. He yelled over his shoulder.

"Kathy, put the oars in the oarlocks. Sit in the stern and row—*backwards!*"

Trembling, her face shiny and wet, Kathy slowly lowered the oars into the green water as Tommy instructed. The wide blades created additional drag, plowing up white walls of water. The increased drag seemed to slow the fish.

"Atta girl. It's working!" Tommy shouted, delighted. All around them the spectator fleet honked congratulations.

But now the small pram was past Beavertail, the last part of land. Ahead was the wide blue ocean. Seven miles out on the left was the Brenton Reef Light Tower, and eleven miles out was tiny Block Island.

After that—Europe!

And the great fish was steadily towing them toward England.

"Row!" Tommy cried.

"I—am..." Kathy plunged the oars deeper into the water, holding tightly to them, creating still more resistance. The pram's forward speed diminished still more.

"Not enough," Tommy gasped, his young body now a mass of cramps and pain. He couldn't keep this up much longer. Somehow, he had to get even greater resistance, some kind of additional drag stern-wise.

"That's it!" he cried aloud. "A drag stern-wise."

He tightened the reel's star drag as hard as possible, then carefully wedged the pole and reel against the forward thwart and the pram's mast, tying them securely with one end of Kathy's nylon boom line. Should the great fish suddenly jerk, the reel's drag would slip so the line wouldn't break.

He hoped!...

"W-What are you going to do now?" Kathy asked nervously.

"It's all right," he assured her. "You keep rowing and don't worry. I know what I'm doing—I think."

He ignored her startled expression.

Cautiously, he moved to the pram's center. He stripped to his swimming trunks and tied the free end of the nylon anchor line around his waist, making a bowline knot.

"If this doesn't stop him, nothing will, he said." Grinning determinedly, he cautiously eased over the stern into the water, holding tight to the transom.

He loudly sucked in his breath. The icy water shocked him. He seriously considered climbing back into the boat and cutting the line, letting the fish go free.

But he didn't. He couldn't! Ever since coming to the seashore at Conimicut Village and getting interested in boating and fishing, he had dreamed of catching a monster bass. To cut the line would almost be a sin. He had to boat this grandfather fish!

Gritting his teeth, he yelled to Kathy. "Now. Row backwards!"

At the same time she dipped her oars he bent his body around into a large U-shape, creating great currents behind the pram.

The icy water bubbled and foamed into his mouth. It tugged at his young body, threatening to break his grip on the transom. He clung tighter still, and somehow kept his body bent for maximum drag.

Would the great fish never tire?

Gasping and choking, he forced himself to hold the torturous position. Spectator craft tooted encouragement. People yelled approval.

Sobbing in fear for Tommy, terribly concerned, Kathy continued to row backwards.

"—Ow!" Tommy couldn't do it any longer. Gasping in pain, he let his legs trail behind him. Every muscle in his body seemed afire.

But, despite all his efforts, he hadn't stopped, or even turned, the great fish. In fact, the pram seemed to be moving faster still. He had failed!...

Panting, choking on the salt water, Tommy clung to the stern, weary and defeated. He had failed...

"Tommy," Kathy begged. "Let him go. Please. I don't want you hurt."

"No!" he cried. "I—Just one more time."

He summoned every ounce of strength and again bent his body. The frigid seawater slammed against him. It jerked at his sore fingers. It bubbled and boiled into his face, mouth and eyes.

"Row, Kathy!" he yelled.

Kathy pulled hard on the oars...

Suddenly, the pram stopped so abruptly Tommy bumped head-first into the transom.

"W-What happened?" he gasped, as soon as he was able to speak.

"I—don't know. It just stopped." Kathy helped him climb back into the boat. In the bow, Tommy saw the fishline was slack.

"Oh, no!" He slumped to the deck. "He's gone. He got away. I lost him..."

Acutely depressed, his body an agony of weariness, Tommy untied the rod and reel and slowly wound in the line. It was half in when he felt an odd, dead weight. It seemed as if he had hooked onto a heavy boot filled with mud, or a massive string of rubbery kelp.

—Or maybe... Just maybe...

Cautiously, his breath panting through dry lips, Tommy wound in more line. Easy, gently...

Suddenly, twenty feet away, something bobbed to the surface. It was silvery.

It had a long black stripe down its side.

It looked a mile long!

"The fish!" Tommy cried. He laughed shrilly, wonderfully joyous and triumphant. "I got him, Kathy. I got him. He *didn't* get away!"

Quickly he wound in the remaining fishline. The great fish came in peacefully, exhausted, not moving a fin.

When it's snout touched the pram's side, Tommy quickly

looped the anchor line around its tail several times, then he and Kathy tilted the pram so its edge was close to the water.

Together, they strained and struggled, and finally pulled the great fish inside.

The monster was boated! The great and majestic King-of-the-Sea was caught!

All around him, boats tooted and people waved and cheered.

Tommy slumped back on the center thwart and stared at it. The striped bass was over four feet long. It probably weighed over seventy pounds, more than Kathy, a true tackle-buster.

His fingers hesitantly touched the cool, silvery scales. He glanced at Kathy hovering close.

"It's—dead," he whispered. The beautiful fish had worked so hard to escape it had burst its heart.

Tommy felt a sharp stab of sadness. Now that the long fight had ended, he felt sorry for the fish. It was such a beautiful, streamlined, noble creature, so full of life and fight. And now it was dead...

But his sadness was short lived.

Laughing, Kathy flung her arms around his neck, hugging him tight.

"Oh, Tommy. He's beautiful! I've never seen a fish so big in my entire life. I'm so proud of you!"

The two dozen spectator craft came closer, honking and tooting, their crews shouting and cheering. It had been a spectacular fight, and the fish was now boated, and they were happy and anxious to share in the victory.

Tommy grinned at them, proud and pleased. He was too exhausted to do more than wave his hand.

The cruiser *Free-Lancer* out of Conimicut came alongside and tossed them a line.

"We'll tow you back home, kids," the smiling skipper said. "Seeing you boat that monster bass was worth the price of admission. That's the best dang fish fight I've ever seen. Congratulations!"

"Thank you," Tommy said.

He made the line fast to the pram's bow ring, then grabbed his clothes. He and Kathy climbed into the big boat.

Tommy dropped, exhausted, to the padded seats as the *Free-Lancer* headed north, towing the sailing pram with its great striped bass cargo.

On all sides they were surrounded by neighboring craft, all honking and tooting and blasting their horns and sirens like at the Newport Cup Races, or the Tall Ships visits.

Smiling happily, Kathy elbowed Tommy in the ribs. "Gee, this is fun, Tommy. I didn't know bass fishing could be so exciting. Let's go again next week, huh?"

Tommy grinned feebly at her. "You're kidding—Aren't you?"

"Uh uh!" Kathy replied. "I love fishing—now."

Nodding slowly, Tommy slumped lower into the padded seat. He closed his eyes. It looked like he had a fishing companion from now on, and there was nothing—absolutely nothing—he could do about it.

Tommy was dressed and sleeping, wrapped in a warm blanket when the *Free-Lancer* stopped at Nick's Dock in Oakland Beach.

Skipper Don, a writer himself, telephoned the story to the *Providence Journal-Bulletin*. With Tommy and Kathy in tow, he had the fish weighed and photographed—just like in the sports section of the papers: Tommy and Kathy were standing with the fantastic striped bass hanging from a line in the center. They were holding fish poles and grinning triumphantly.

The bass' total weight of seventy-two pounds, four ounces, was dangerously close to the world's record for the largest striped bass ever caught on hook and line. It was a true tackle-buster!

Later, once home and the great fishing adventure over, Tommy fell into bed. Sleep was instantaneous.

But activity on the Narragansett Bay waterfront was just coming awake. All over the east and west shores, at marinas, coves and inlets, the spectator fleet pulled into port.

Their skippers hailed other boatsmen, in person, and on their ship-to-shore radios, and, like all true fishermen, they delighted in the telling and re-telling of a fantastic boatride and a wondrous fish story. Only this time it was true.

Skipper Don, the writer-owner of the *Free-Lancer* out of Conimicut, was the most vociferous. He had to tell everyone he met. His mouth split in a grin as he talked:

"...I tell you, it was the most fantastic thing I ever saw! There were these two kids, a boy and his girl. I was fishing under the Jamestown Bridge when I first saw their sailing dingy zip right past me.

"But it had no sail up. No motor. Nothing! I thought I was seeing things. Then I saw they were being towed by a fish. Yeah, *by a fish!* And what a fish!...

"A whole bunch of boats were following them, all tooting and cheering. I decided I had to see the end of this chapter, so I upped anchor and joined the parade. That monster fish had towed those kids in that little boat over twenty miles, all the way from Prudence Island, down the west passage, and right out into the Atlantic Ocean before those two wonderful kids finally stopped him cold.

"And the *way* they did it. Beautiful! Fantastic! I'll tell you later how they did it... Oh, he was a monster bass!...

"I picked up the kids and their little boat and towed them back home in my cruiser. I hefted that giant bull bass, and helped weigh him at Nick's Dock...

"He was huge, that fish. Over seventy-two pounds of fighting mad striper bull bass..."

Skipper Don of the *Free-Lancer* out of Conimicut shook his head in great admiration and enthusiasm.

"I still don't believe it. I saw it all with my own eyes, but I still don't believe it! Oh, I've got to write a story about these two wonderful kids and their giant fish.

"And I will! And that's a promise..."

Each fisherman who heard this fish story saw another fisherman or friend, and the story was told and re-told again and again, and would forever be legend, forever remembered and told among sportsmen and women along the Rhode Island waterfront.

It was a fabulous fish story! And it was *true!*

And what's more, there were photographs and official weight records to prove it!

Chapter 11

The Mounted Fish And New Fame!

Slightly under one hour later Tommy awoke, refreshed and eager to go outside and view his wonderful fish.

He was amazed that it was only six o'clock in the evening of the same day he had caught his great fish. It seemed as if it should be tomorrow.

From his upstairs window, he saw all the activity on the beach. Over two dozen people were admiring the fish. Some people were taking pictures. Others were talking together, or hefting the striped bass.

He saw Kathy, her father and mother, Granny Parker, Pete and Booty, and many folks he didn't know. They all were at the seashore, talking and laughing, and occasionally glancing up at the house as though looking for him.

Kathy saw him in the window and waved, beckoning. He waved back, indicating he'd join them in a few minutes.

His body stiff, he took a hasty hot shower, towelled down, and quickly dressed. He felt much better. And he was hungry too.

Granny Parker's thin voice called from down stairs.

"Tommy. Hurry up. They're all waiting for you."

"Be right down, Granny."

He hastily tied his sneakers. They? he wondered. Who were "they?"

"They" turned out to be well-wishers, local residents, reporters and photographers from the *Providence Journal* and *Warwick Beacon*, and several members of the Rhode Island Stripers Club, and the West Shore Sports Fishermen. They brought with them congratulations and offers of honorary memberships.

Word of Tommy's catch had spread rapidly, thanks to Skipper

Don of the *Free-Lancer* out of Conimicut, and many, nameless boatsmen and women and fishing yarn-spinners.

It seemed his giant bull bass was a record size and many honors were due.

More cars stopped in front of Granny Parker's house and people rushed down to the beach. And then the television crews came, Channel 10 with newspeople Doug White and Mary Maguire, Channel 12's reporter and cameraman, and the Channel 6 crew.

Several men brought the bass higher on the beach where they hung it on an improvised, hastily-constructed tripod. The photographers and video people posed Kathy and Tommy beside the displayed giant bass, fishpoles in hand, the tiny pram nodding at anchor, and much of lovely Narragansett Bay in the background. They took many pictures and video shots.

This made "good copy", according to cordial Doug White of channel 10, and would be shown on the eleven o'clock news.

When the TV people left, the news reporters moved in for greater detail and local color. They bombarded Tommy and Kathy with questions, writing occasional notes, and snapping many pictures.

Finally the questions stopped and the photographers ran out of film. Members of the press thanked them and left to make their deadlines.

Now the sportsfishermen attacked with enthusiastic words and congratulatory praise. They extended invitations to meetings and dinners. They promised a trophy for both Tommy and Kathy at their annual banquets, and they insisted they attend. They also hinted at special prizes—new saltwater fishing poles and reels, lines and lures. There was even a request from a famous fishing reel company for a testimonial from Tommy.

Tommy and Kathy were delighted, and agreed to it all. That old Penn reel Tommy had used was the same reel Mr. Turner had given him a month ago. It was a good, dependable reel, and he'd be glad to praise its superb qualities.

"What are you going to do with him?" one man asked.

"With who? Whom?" Tommy corrected himself.

"That beautiful bass." Tommy glanced at Granny Parker.

"Eat it, I guess. Give some of it to Kathy's folks, of course."

"Eat him!" Several horrified voices cried simultaneously.

Tommy flushed. He had said a *bad* word.

"Well, what else do you do with a striped bass? God made them for eating, didn't He?"

One more-sensitive member of the West Shore Sports Fishermen shouldered his way into the foreground. After introducing himself, he gripped Tommy's hand proudly.

"Of course God makes fish for eating, Son. But what we all mean is—He's a record catch, a beautiful, noble creature. Wouldn't it be better to have many people able to admire and enjoy him for years and years? And your and Kathy's names would be on the metal plaque with him."

He glanced around at the others, as though seeking their approval. Again he faced Tommy and Kathy.

"We mean, we'd like to mount him for you." He grinned warmly. "And you'll still be able to eat him. That's a promise."

"But taxi- taxider- *stuffing* a big fish costs lots of money, Kathy cried.

The man nodded. "My club will pay the expenses. A beautiful fish like this one should be mounted. It would almost be a sin to cut him in little pieces for dinner. What do you say, kids?"

Kathy glanced at Tommy, awaiting his decision. "It's your fish, Tom. It's okay with me if it's okay with you."

Tommy looked to Granny Parker for approval, saw it, and agreed.

"Okay."

"Wonderful!" the man cried. "And you'll get the meat, all nicely packaged and frozen. That's my promise, Son."

"—But when it's mounted it will *still be* Tommy's fish, won't it?" Kathy asked.

"It will, indeed. All we ask is the privilege of displaying it. We'll lend it out for special sports events, let the Providence and Warwick Chambers of Commerce and the Rhode Island Development Council borrow it once in a while for special events. We'll also lend it to other state promotional groups for publicity purposes. And they all will mention Tommy and you as the award fishermen. But when Tommy wants it, it's his."

"Good!" Kathy declared defensively, and everyone laughed.

The agreement made and signed, the men carefully wrapped the fish in a wet gunny sack and took it with them for immediate refrigeration. Granny Parker slipped the receipt into the pocket of her apron.

Now the Turners, Pete and Booty, and many local residents moved in, shaking hands, marvelling, saying wonderful words of praise that filled Tommy and Kathy with elation. All this activity and excitement over his fish made Tommy almost giddy with excitement. The praise made him feel important, and that was a wonderful feeling—to feel important.

Maybe now Granny Parker would think of him as more than just a strong back or a pair of working hands. Maybe now she'd even begin to love him. He didn't ask for a lot of love, just a little—enough so she'd decide to keep him with her. He could do an awful lot of work for her, and be a lot of help to her...

That wasn't too much to ask for, was it?

Tommy considered how wonderful it would be if Granny did let him stay. Maybe he'd be able to go to Gorton Junior High School, or to Pilgrim Senior High with Kathy. Man, that sure would be swell, going to the same school!

But then he realized he couldn't do that because Kathy didn't live in Conimicut Village year round.

Gradually, the crowd diminished and the slight wind stopped so the water stilled, and the sky slowly pinked and darkened into dusk. Mr. Turner joyfully shook Tommy's hand for the fourth or fifth time. He joked about Hemingway's book and Kathy's nickname for Tommy: *"The Young Man And The Sea."*

"We're all *very* proud of you, Tom," he said. "But the next time you go fishing, take your skiff and motor." He shuddered.

"Brr-rr. I get the chills when I think of you and Kathy adrift in the Atlantic Ocean in an eight-foot sailing pram!"

"I will, sir," Tommy said. "I sure will!"

Mrs. Turner hugged him and kissed him warmly on the cheek. "I'm very proud and pleased for you, Tom. You may come over and watch the 11 o'clock news on our television, if you'd like. I know Mrs. Parker doesn't have a TV."

Flushing, but intensely pleased at the warm show of affection, and the invitation, Tommy nodded and gently eased free. He glanced at Granny Parker, but the old lady was gazing out over the water, her wrinkled face inscrutable. Not once in the almost four months he had been living with her has she ever displayed any indication of affection. Maybe she was incapable of love...

When the Turners and Granny Parker left the shore, only

Kathy, Booty and Pete Bender remained. The three boys and Kathy sat on the seawall and talked, reliving the adventure once again as the Barrington horizon slowly turned purple and melted into night.

Booty was enthusiastic and curious, but Pete Bender was indifferent, as though slightly annoyed that it had been Tommy who had caught the great fish. He wasn't hostile though, and Tommy was glad of that.

Since Pete's motor blew up, his boat had been hauled out of the water. His father had agreed to get him a new engine block and repairs for next Spring, but Pete's punishment was his loss of the *Banshee* for the remainder of the season. It didn't seem to bother him greatly, Tommy noticed.

He and Pete were no longer enemies, but they were not friends either. Granny was right about Pete, Tommy had decided. Pete was careless and irresponsible, and as badly as Tommy wanted friends, he realized that not all people were truly capable of friendship. But not having an *enemy* in Pete was sufficient.

With Booty it was different. He was warm and friendly and sincerely enthusiastic in his praise. He seemed to want to be a friend, but at the same time he was faithful to Pete.

"What was wrong with people, anyway?" Tommy wondered. "Why couldn't the four of them be friends?"

"Well, gotta go!" Pete jumped down from the wall. He idly scaled a few stones across the water. "You comin', Booty?"

Booty shrugged and jumped to the beach. Turning, he said, "I'll cut out the picture and article for you two when it's published in the *Warwick Beacon* on Thursday. Man, that sure was a beautiful bass!"

"Thanks to *you*," Tommy said to him.

"Me?" Booty's eyes saucered. "W-What did I do?" his voice cracked.

"Plenty! It was you who told me about the bass hanging around Providence Point. Don't you remember?"

Booty grinned widely in pleasure, feeling deliciously important, now that he was even remotely involved in the catch of the great fish.

"Well—So I did. Ha ha! Well, what do you know? I forgot all about that." He strode off with Pete, somehow seeming several inches taller. He turned and waved at them.

"See you..."

Kathy's hand briefly touched Tommy's, then moved away. "That was a nice thing you did. You made him feel like a million dollars. I like that, and I like Booty."

"I like him too," Tommy said. He thought of the smooth warmth of her hand. He took a loud, deep breath of the warm evening air.

"Booty wants to go clamming down Old Mill Cove with me tomorrow."

"I'd like to go too," Kathy said.

Tommy sighed. "Yeah. I expected you would."

With a sudden, unexplained surge of affection, he cupped Kathy's chin and gazed warmly into her green eyes.

"You know, I never did get to thank you. You were wonderful out there. I never could have caught that fish without you."

Kathy blushed and moved away slowly. "Oh, sure you could have." She grinned widely, obviously pleased.

"But thanks. It's nice to hear you say that, Tommy."

For several minutes neither of them spoke. Kathy was swinging her feet against the wall. Tommy stared at the Indian Class sailboat returning to her mooring after an evening's sail. He studied John Howell's sleek fiberglass sailboat, *Good News*, sleeping at its mooring. Neither he nor Kathy was conscious of the silence, or felt the least bit awkward about it.

As he thought about his future, Tommy became acutely conscious of the slim girl sitting beside him. He was going to miss Kathy. In two weeks she'd be gone. Her folks would move from their summer home in Conimicut Village to their winter house deeper inland, and she'd be gone all winter.

Perhaps forever, if he was sent back to the orphanage...

Neither of them had spoken of this, but both were acutely conscious of the swiftly passing time. The words, "two weeks" frequently escaped their lips, and there was a sudden, awkward silence before the sentence continued.

"Two weeks... Fourteen short days... The end of the Summer..."

The end of everything!...

Tommy felt the warmth of Kathy's body beside him, heard her gentle breathing, felt the brush of her hair on his cheek...

Kathy suddenly poked him with her elbow. "Old Mill Cove!"

she cried loudly.

"Hey, that hurts!" He rubbed his side. "What about Old Mill Cove?"

"Marshall's Mansion," Kathy said. "The haunted house. School starts in two weeks and we haven't gone there. You promised to take me to Marshall's Mansion at night, Tommy. You promised. Please?"

There it was again, that horrible phrase, "Two weeks... Pretending elation, Tommy lightly poked her back.

"And a promise is a promise, I suppose?"

"Uh huh. What about it? Tonight? Or are you too tired?"

Tommy was tired, but not that tired. "Okay," he agreed. "We'll get Booty to go with us. All right?"

"Sure. He'll be fun."

"Okay, it's a date. As soon as it's real dark, in about an hour from now, the three of us will go to the haunted house. You're sure you want to go now?" Tommy grinned secretly and whispered: "There's a monster there, you know, and he *eats* little girls."

"Oh, go on," Kathy cried, flushing. "Besides, I'm not exactly little any more, you know."

"That was true," Tommy had to agree. He got up and helped Kathy to her feet. "That was *indeed* very true."

Chapter 12

Visit To A Haunted House!

*T*he old house stood alone on a small hill, bleak and desolate in the black August night, its vacant windows, like empty eyes, staring forlornly at wind-whipped whitecaps dancing madly on Narragansett Bay.

It was a dead house, long ago killed by a hurricane sea. Conimicut Village residents called it Marshall's Mansion.

Tommy, Kathy and Danny Booth slowly walked along the long, dark, dirt road leading to Old Mill Cove on the south shore at Conimicut Point. They passed the five stilt houses on their left, regular homes set atop sixteen feet high steel poles to protect them from hurricane tides.

Tommy was surprised at the southerly wind and choppy sea. There had been little wind at Granny Parker's. But Granny's house was on the west shore of the bay, protected from a southerly wind, he remembered.

He grinned secretly at Booty teasing Kathy.

"Come on, you know there's *no* such things as g-ghosts," Kathy stammered. Her voice was tiny and nervous in the dark, eerie night.

"You're sure of that?" Booty said, and stifled a laugh.

Tommy bit his lip to keep from laughing. Booty was sure giving Kathy a good warm-up. But Kathy had wanted to visit a haunted house. She had insisted, and he and Booty had privately planned to make it a special spooky occasion for her.

"You sure you want to go through with this, Kathy?" Tommy asked her again. "You can still back out. Marshall's Mansion is a terrifying place. And as I told you, that monster especially likes little girls."

"You cut that out, Tommy!" Kathy cried, her slim, summer-tanned face white in the rising orange moon.

Black clouds scudded across the sky, seeming to cooperate in creating a haunting scene. Tommy thought Kathy seemed to be wishing she could back out of their agreement. But she wouldn't, he knew. Not Kathy. She was too stubborn and determined to do that.

"There's absolutely nothing to be afraid of at Marshall's Mansion, Tommy Wayne," Kathy cried defiantly. "It's just an old, deserted Conimicut house on the edge of the bay, and there never was a Marshall's monster. That's silly talk to scare little kids. So there!"

"We'll see," Tommy said. He remembered what Granny Parker had told him, how the raging waters of the 1938 hurricane had smashed into and through the old house. Again in 1954 Hurricanes Carol and Hazel had slammed frothy green seas against the strong timbers, doing still more damage, but not destroying the house.

The City of Warwick prohibited the owners from rebuilding, as the house was in an area of extreme hurricane danger. As a result, the house was abandoned.

Today, years later, and even in bright daylight, the Marshall house looked ominous and evil. But if it was haunted at all, it was by seagulls and terns, by crabs and dipper-ducks, and giant horse-shoe crabs.

Several times violent seas had entered the windows and doors, so now the sea creatures were taking over what they felt was rightfully theirs.

"Brr-r. Looks real creepy in the moonlight," Booty said, pausing under the last streetlight on Old Mill Cove.

"I wonder if the monster's there," Tommy said, his voice terribly serious.

"I heard he comes through underground tunnels from the sea," Booty added, "Maybe he is there tonight."

"Now, you two cut that out!" Kathy cried, her voice edged with annoyance. "You've already got me scared enough."

"Well, you wanted to visit a haunted—"

"Tommy! You stop that now!"

"You're too imaginative," Tommy said. He motioned them on. The moon was higher now, in the southeast, like a huge, orange

Jack-O-Lantern leering down at them. Long, crawling black clouds, like clutching fingers, reached for the moon.

Overhead, a twenty-knot southerly wind vibrated taut electric wires in a thousand moaning voices. Tommy thought the Walt Disney people would love this place.

Kathy's dark eyes were wide with apprehension, and Tommy felt sorry for her. But he wanted her to have a good time, and a pump-priming of juicy "ghost stories" and her own vivid imagination, all helped.

Besides, he wasn't exactly free from all apprehension himself. Of course, there were no such things as ghosts and monsters, but— well, you never could tell. Someday, you might meet a monster...

Where there's smoke, there's fire.

Ever since Tommy had come to Conimicut Village he had heard scary stories about Marshall's Mansion. But how much of them were really true?

Dr. Marshall was supposed to have been a mad doctor who had made a monster from dead bodies, like Dr. Frankenstein. Only Marshall's monster was supposed to be a sea and air-breathing creature that came back to its creator's place occasionally, usually in late summer. It was supposed to be huge, and horrible to see, something like a giant man and like a dinosaur, gigantic and silvery in phosphorescence from the sea, dripping fresh blood and seaweed from its massive jaws.

Tommy bit his lower lip. "Crazy nut!" he thought. "You're scaring yourself."

He knew he was letting his own vivid imagination run away with him. Besides, every neighborhood had its own "ghost" and "haunted house" story, didn't it?

"Well— There's Marshall's Mansion in the moonlight!" Booty said, his voice cracking. "Spooky old dump, huh?"

"You ready?" Tommy asked, and saw Kathy nodding slowly.

"Okay. Here goes." They left the protective light of the last street-lamp and walked through the scratchy eel grass and brambles. Mosquitoes and sand fleas bit them.

All around them crickets sang in shrill, scrapy voices. A seagull shrieked like a hurt child in the lonely night. Tiny tree frogs peeped warning:

"*Go back. Go back...*" they all seemed to say.

Kathy giggled nervously.

Tommy caught her small hand. It was icy cold. "Shh—We don't want to wake up the monster."

"That's right," Booty whispered. He gripped Kathy's other hand.

"Ow! Don't hold me so tight!" Kathy cried, and Booty's face reddened.

"Shh. I'm sorry."

The southerly orange moon shone brighter now, creating weird moving shadows that hovered close. A nightbird cried in final, desolate warning.

"Run...Run...Run!..."

Gingerly they stepped around debris, on crushed clamshells, over bits of driftwood, long deposited on the jungle-like lawn and forgotten, around rocks that had smashed windows long before they were born.

They stepped into the open doorway...

"Ooh, It's awfully dark in there," Kathy whispered, and held back.

"Come on, Silly," Booty said. "Darkness never hurt anyone."

Now they were inside the great, echoing house...and at night.

Tommy was more nervous than he let on. They had started this as a gag, a fun-thing to frighten and please Kathy. But now he wasn't so sure. And he strongly suspected Booty was just as nervous as he.

As his eyes accustomed themselves to the dim light, Tommy saw they were in a huge, cluttered room with a gigantic fireplace at the south end. Bits of broken window-glass were strewn about the floor, clinking and snapping as they walked over them. Near the fireplace the floor had a large rectangular hole where someone had removed and taken the hearthstone. Below the hole was a dank and dismal cavern that was the cellar. It smelled foul, of rotting seaweed.

They heard water gurgling beneath their feet, splashing and ebbing with the eternal movement of the sea.

"L-Listen to that!" Booty's falsetto voice was startling.

"—Yeah." Tommy gripped Kathy's small hand tighter.

"That must be the monster's underground tunnel."

"Tommy!" Kathy wailed. "You *promised!*"

"Okay. No more mention of monsters. Come on. Let's explore."

"But it's so dark," Kathy cried. "I can barely see."

Tommy moved slowly, feeling his way. The old house smelled of salt and the sea, of ancient dust and Time and Eternity...

"Yeow!" Kathy cried shrilly. "Oh, no. No! Oh, it's got me. The monster's got me!" Screaming and sobbing, she clutched tight to Tommy, her young body trembling violently.

"W-What is it?" Tommy choked. Kathy was almost crushing his hand.

"I—don't know. I touched it with my foot. It—moved! Then it grabbed my foot and—I-I pulled away and it just let go..."

"I think maybe it's blocking our way out," Booty whispered nervously. "See? It's over near that patch of moonlight on the floor. Now, we can't leave! What will we do, Tom?"

Huddling together, the three friends stared at the spot. The noise was muffled, like a grave robber cautiously moving a body.

Suddenly Tommy laughed, a greatly relieved sound.

"Oh, no!" Booty cried. "Kathy, you nut. Look at your monster."

Kathy stared incredulously as the dark figure inched into the moonlight, moving like a miniature tank.

"A horseshoe crab!" she groaned. "But I thought—"

"A small King Crab," Booty said scornfully. He shook his head and made clucking noises. "Kathy Turner..."

Tommy felt sorry for Kathy. Despite the darkness, he could tell she was blushing. He touched her shoulder.

"If I stepped on a ten-inch horseshoe crab in the dark and he snapped his spiked tail on my foot, I'd have yelled out too," he said.

A fleeting smile spread Kathy's lips. "Thanks, Tommy."

"Well, let's get on with our exploring." Booty beckoned and the others slowly followed.

The sea's perpetual roar filled the house with eerie echoes. The strong wind shrieked and moaned. There was a bitter taste of decaying seaweed and of iodine in the moist air.

Hearts thumping, the three friends crept from room to dismal room, up the creaking stairs to the second floor.

Cobwebs brushed Tommy's face, startling him. A spider

crawled up his cheek and he wiped frantically at it. "Ugh! A spider."

"Shhh," Booty warned, his eyes wide, face pasty white in the swath of moonlight from the hole that had once been a window. They were on the second floor now.

The great house creaked and groaned and shuddered in the blasts of wind.

They walked to the doorway leading to the widow's walk overlooking Narragansett Bay. This was the place, Tommy recalled, where the ghost of a woman in white was seen on severe stormy nights. He peered out. There was nothing there but a white curtain tied to the side railing. He felt disappointed.

"Let's go out and look at the water," Kathy said. Walking past him, she stepped out on the steel walk. She tripped on the rusted metal and screamed as she fell.

Tommy seized her arm and pulled her back inside. The entire front railing was gone. The widow's walk could easily *make* a widow. It was very dangerous now.

"Wow. That was too close," Booty said. "I'm glad you were quicker than I was, Tom. Kathy, take it easy, will you?"

Greatly shaken up, Kathy nodded in agreement. "I'm glad too," she cried. "Thank you, Tommy. Boy, that's a thirty foot drop to the rocks below. This whole place is falling apart. Let's get out of here."

"Yes, let's!" Tommy agreed. "We can get hurt in here. —But not by ghosts or monsters," he added. He led the way down the winding stairs, through the hallway toward the parlor.

He stopped abruptly as everything got black, inky, pitch black. A huge cloud had swallowed the moon.

Kathy gasped. "Oh!"

"I can't see a thing!" Tommy said.

"Oh, brother," Booty cried, his voice edged in fright.

"Give me your hand, Kathy." Fumbling in the dark, Tommy located Kathy's small hand. It was cold and clammy. The poor kid was terrified, he realized, and deeply regretted bringing her to Marshall's Mansion.

"We'll wait. The moon should come out soon," he said.

"But suppose it doesn't come out," Booty said, his voice faltering.

"It will. It has to."

"—Tommy. I'm scared and cold. Let's go home..."

"In a minute, Kathy. Soon as it's lighter.

Trembling, huddled close like three frightened puppies, they waited silently.

Two...three...four minutes passed. The blackness made the old house even more eerie. The noises and creaks and groans were all around them, moving in closer...

"Listen!" Kathy whispered. "Chains. I hear rattling chains." Clutching to each other, their imaginations racing free, painting vivid pictures on their receptive minds, the three friends listened to the terrors of night.

The sound was faint, Tommy noted, but it *was* the rattling of chains.

"G-Ghosts rattle chains," Kathy stammered. "Don't they?"

An icy chill raced up Tommy's spine. Goosebumps popped out, chasing each other all over his body. His hair seemed to ripple, stand on end.

"Is—it—the monster?" Kathy choked.

"No. Of course not. It's—" Tommy didn't know what it was.

Silence... The chains rattled again, soft and distant.

"Tommy!" Kathy clutched him tighter.

Suddenly Booty laughed, a painfully thin sound in the darkness.

"What's so darn funny," Tommy whispered.

"Us." Booty snorted. "Huh. We're scared of chains rattling. I remember seeing short pieces of chain on a bench near the fireplace. The wind must be shaking them.

"You're not fooling?" Kathy asked. "Honest?"

"Honest. Come on. I'll show you." Feeling their way, they cautiously inched up the dark hallway to the huge parlor, then along the east and south walls toward the fireplace. A chain rattled loudly, startling Tommy.

"See?"

It was Booty clinking and shaking the chain. He pushed it into Tommy's hand. "Here. Feel it. There's lots of pieces all around here. Probably old anchor chain."

Tommy exhaled in relief. "Whew! Don't mind telling you now, but I was real scared." He gave the chain to Kathy who let it drop to the floor.

"Me too," Booty confessed out of the blackness. "Well, we're this far and we haven't seen any ghosts or monsters. Let's feel our way out of this tomb. What do you say?"

"Oh, yes!" Kathy cried eagerly. "I'm with you."

"Me too." Tommy reached into the blackness. "Give me your hand, Kathy. Kathy? Where are you?" Silence...

Then out of the murky blackness came Kathy's tremulous voice. "Here I am. I—Oh. OOOH!" Kathy screamed.

"Kathy!" Tommy cried. He fumbled about frantically, blindly, in the darkness. "Please answer me, Kathy..."

No reply... Kathy Turner had vanished!

The boys called. They shouted. They yelled her name. Silence. Kathy was gone, disappeared, as though from the face of the earth.

"M-Maybe the monster got her." Booty's voice was husky, frightened. "I never really believed in Marshall's Monster before, but *now* I do. He has Kathy. He'll get us too. Come on, Tom. Let's get out of here!"

"We can't! Not without Kathy!" Tommy cried, deeply concerned. It had started as a great, joyous adventure, but now it was a nightmare. Kathy was gone. And Booty's fear of the monster and wanting to flee was making things even worse.

"No! We have to find Kathy," Tommy said.

"We can't!" Booty's voice was now a shrill falsetto, his words edged in icy panic.

"She's gone, I tell you. Come on, Tom."

Tortured by concern and indecision, Tommy said nothing. He also wanted to run from the old house, but Kathy was still in here someplace. She had to be! People just didn't disappear.

Maybe she was hurt and needed help. Maybe she was—dying!

"Are you coming?" Booty was edging toward the door. "We can go after help, get some flashlights. Come on, Tom."

The room was slightly lighter now. A cold sweat chilling him, Tommy shook his head. No, he couldn't abandon Kathy.

"No. I've got to find her," he insisted, and prayed for more light.

As if in answer to his prayers, the moon appeared, once again brightening the great room, but also filling it with even more frightening shadows.

Tommy saw Booty by the door, ready to leave. Alone and

terribly concerned, he picked up an old board for a weapon.

"Kathy? Where are you?" His voice sounded piteously thin in the huge, echoing house. "Please answer me. Kathy?"

Again and again he called, praying silently, afraid to think even one second ahead.

"Kathy. *Please* answer me..."

He heard a faint noise. His body suddenly stiffened, and his legs seemed bolted to the floor. Again he heard it: a soft moaning. It seemed beneath his feet.

"—Kathy?" The word choked in his throat.

"—Oooh. Help—me, Tommy—"

A wide, triumphant smile leaped to Tommy's face. In that one instant his fears vanished.

"It's Kathy!" he shouted. "Booty, she's in the cellar. I think she's hurt."

Booty returned, his face flushed. "I—was looking outside."

"Careful!" Tommy pulled Booty back. He pointed to the large hearthstone hole in front of the fireplace. "Kathy must have fallen through that."

They hurriedly searched the room for the cellar entrance, found it behind some boards leaning against the wall. They quickly cleared a passageway.

"Watch it," Tommy cautioned. "These old stairs are rotted and awfully steep."

Kathy had a lump as big as a cherrystone quahaug on her forehead. Her face was dirty and wet, her hair tangled with dried seaweed and sand. But she wasn't hurt, only stunned, thanks to the mound of beach sand beneath the hole.

Sobbing in relief, she clung tightly to Tommy. "Oh, thank you for coming to find me. Thank you, Tommy. Thank you!"...

The intense display of gratitude and tears both embarrassed and pleased Tommy. For several moments he allowed himself the sweet luxury of holding her close, her cheek against his chest. Finally, he gently eased away.

"Kathy, I'm so glad you're safe."

"Me too," Booty said. "I feel awful for running off like I did."

The boys helped Kathy up the steep stairs to the parlor where they stopped to rest.

Tommy gazed around the room, as though seeing it with new eyes, the eyes of fact, instead of the eyes of imagination and fantasy.

Everything seemed different now. The room was dark and dank and smelled badly, but he knew there weren't any ghosts or monsters in Marshall's Mansion, or anyplace else.

Tommy felt a bit sad and slightly disappointed. Tonight he had lost something precious, a priceless part of his youth, and he deeply missed the loss.

But he had gained something else too...something very valuable—a deep and warm affection for a pretty little tomboy.

He helped Kathy to her feet. They were about to leave when from behind the shadowed, jagged walls came a clanking and rattling of chains .

"Oh, you cut that out, Booty," Tommy cried, annoyed.

"Yes. One session of chain-rattling is more than enough," Kathy said. She sounded much better now.

"But it *ain't* me!" Booty insisted, his face as white as beach sand. "I'm here with you two and—that noise is from *over there!*"

An icy chill suddenly raced up Tommy's spine. The noise grew louder, closer. The moon again slipped behind a cloud. In the darkened room, a new and more horrifying sound was added.

"S-Sounds like a b-body being dragged," Booty whispered. "Let's get out of here!"

The two boys picked up Kathy by the arms and bolted for the door, carrying her. They fled across the clamshell yard and through the eelgrass to the dirt street.

In the safety of the street-light, they paused to catch their breath.

"Whew! Boy, that was too close," Tommy gasped, puffing loudly.

"Marshall's Mansion really *is haunted*," Booty cried. "Wait 'till I tell Pete."

"I'll never scoff at ghosts again," Kathy added. "Never!"

"Me neither." Tommy drew in a deep breath. "But in a way, I'm kind of glad it is haunted," he said thoughtfully. "That's the way I want to remember it. I think every kid should have a haunted house in his or her life."

To this, the others enthusiastically agreed.

Tommy continued: "A while back when we finally found Kathy in the cellar, and we realized she wasn't kidnapped by the monster, I thought I had lost my sense of fantasy and imagination. But now I realize I haven't lost it. I hope I never do. Imagination, wishing and dreaming are a superb part of growing up and—and of all your life!''

"I'll drink to that," Booty said, and Kathy agreed.

Tired and happy, their frightening adventure over, the three friends headed homeward, down the long dirt road toward Conimicut Point, and then north, down Shawomet Avenue to Bellman Avenue, and reality...

As Tommy walked beside Kathy, he felt her hand occasionally brush his. He smiled warmly at her. He knew he would never forget this very special night...or this very special day!

He also knew that if he went back to Marshall's Mansion and really looked around with a flashlight, he'd find a logical explanation for the rattling chains and the eerie shuffling noises.

But he had no intention of ever doing so.

As far as he was concerned, Marshall's Mansion really did have a monster!

—And that's the way it should be, he decided...

Back at the old house a weary, drying-out Horseshoe Crab, dragging a length of old chain caught on one of its many points, slowly, patiently, crept its shuffling, clanking, noisy way back toward the welcoming sea.

Chapter 13

Hurricane Glenna And The Mysterious Phone Calls

When something is anticipated, Time seems to creep at a periwinkle's pace, but when something is dreaded, Time is like the roaring wind of a cold front—swift and sudden.

Those two weeks Kathy and Tommy had avoided talking about suddenly shrunk down to only one week.

Only one short week...

Far south, tropical storm Glenna, after two weeks dallying around, suddenly matured into Hurricane Glenna. Like all women, Glenna wanted to visit the big cities of America's east coast, but she was undecided as to which city she preferred. It was a difficult choice, all so tempting, and she hesitated off shore, debating...

Far north of Hurricane Glenna, the hot, late August sun continued to scorch the land. It sent panting dogs to shade and freshly-dug holes in their masters' lawns. It sent happy families to Rhode Island's many lovely beaches.

Each day the *Providence Journal-Bulletin* displayed little temperature charts on the front page, comparing yesterday's heat record with today's newer and higher records.

The Scituate Reservoir was low, the water level steadily dropping. To conserve water, the sprinkling of lawns was prohibited until dusk, and then only on alternate evenings.

Despite the watering, lawns continued to brown and char, and leaves wilted and waved good-bye to trees. Old timers like Granny Parker, and old Ben Brown on Conimicut Point, were predicting a colorless, fire-endangered Fall season unless some rain fell, and soon. And that's a fact!

These hot days of late August, Tommy, Kathy and Booty practically lived in the water, on the water, or under the cool water of Narragansett Bay.

They swam, boated and skindived, seemingly doing everything with an added fury, as though the increased activity, and the gathering of sweet experiences, would store up a happy memory reservoir for Winter's long use.

Only one short week, then Labor Day, and school began...

"Only one short week. —And then what?" Tommy wondered.

Things were very different with Kathy. She knew her future. In a week she and her family would move to their winter home and she would attend school. Next summer they would return to the seashore. It was that simple, uncomplicated and secure.

But Tommy's future was locked tight in that steel-trap-mind in Granny Parker's head.

He tried not to think about the weeks ahead, but that was impossible, for the harder he strove to forget, the more he thought, and the more he wondered and worried. The unknown and uncertainty of his future was a special agony for him.

Many times he had considered asking Granny Parker about her decision. Will she keep him, or not? Several times he had actually decided he would ask her. But when face-to-face with the stern old lady, his heart sank and his tongue thickened in his dry throat.

The truth is, he was afraid to ask, afraid of her answer.

Suppose the answer wasn't what he wanted?

Suppose she said, "Yes, I'm sending you back to the Home. Your work is done here"?

The awful part of it was his work really *was done!* In the past few months he had worked extra hard to please the old lady, but in doing so, he had probably jeopardized his chances of staying on with her. His work was completed. She didn't need him any more.

It was a terrible, agonizing thing to be not needed or wanted.

And as for pleasing the old lady, he never knew whether he did or not. Neither by action, nor by motion, nor by emotion or word.

Oh, he knew she was pleased about his catching the big bass, and being on the television news, and all the publicity, but at the same time all that attention had intruded on her privacy. She didn't like that.

Yet, he knew she kept the newspaper clippings from the *Journal* and the *Warwick Beacon*. He had seen them tucked in her Holy Bible.

He wondered if there was something else that still needed doing—a long and heavy project that would require a young boy's strong back and agile hands. Oh, there must be lots of things he could do!

He could paint the old house. He could wallpaper all the rooms, like he did to his own room. He could insulate the north and east walls against Winter's icy fingers.

Yes, and the barn needed shoring up. And painting too, and maybe a new roof. Oh, there were lots of jobs he could do to earn his keep.

...But none of them *really* needed doing now.

The seawall was patched and strong, able to withstand Winter's tides and eight-inch layers of salt-water sheet ice.

With the newly-glazed and painted windows and the repainted wood storm windows the house would be warm and draft-free. The east porch floor had been painted. Twice! It's roof now proudly displayed a new, red roofing.

The holes in the barn roof had been patched and Lexonited, the hedge trimmed neat and even as the horizon. The large yard had been leveled and re-seeded...

Hundreds of smaller projects were completed. There was nothing really important left to do!

One week... One short, seven-day week remaining.

Oh, he couldn't bear to think of it! He wouldn't. That was only one-hundred and sixty eight hours. Ten thousand and eighty short minutes...

No . He *wouldn't* think of it! Instead, he would make himself indispensable so Granny Parker would have to keep him on.

For the next two days Tommy threw himself into a fury of activity, collecting rocks along the shore and stacking them neatly at the base of the seawall to act as wave breaks.

He shoveled sand from the beach to the top of the seawall, then moved it inside, behind the wall until the land was level with the wall's cap.

He raked the lawn and neatly stacked driftwood timber. He nailed new boards around the base of the barn, replacing dryrotted timbers.

Occasionally Kathy helped him. Booty too. But it was too hot to work, Booty complained. Too awfully, stinky, sweaty hot...

Anxiously Tommy searched the old lady's face for a sign, a tiny indication of approval or pleasure. There was nothing. He wasn't sure, but he sensed she was deliberately withholding praise or compliments, as though they were a commodity too precious to give away freely.

Or maybe she had other things on her mind. He could never tell. She certainly never discussed her business with him, or her plans, or anything, for that matter!

He was continually amazed at how little he actually knew about her. When it came to talking about herself, Granny Parker's lips were sealed tighter than a freshly-dug quahaug.

On the Wednesday before Labor Day Tommy was replacing some boards on the north porch when Granny Parker called him inside. She was dressed up to go down-town.

"Tommy, I have a few errands to do and I want to make a telephone call up the corner. If you're not planning to stay here I'll lock up the house."

Tommy was curious. Granny Parker didn't have a telephone because she said she didn't really need one, but this was the second telephone call she had made this week. That was a record for her.

"I'll stay here. I have a lot of work to do on the porch," he told her.

"Fine. I won't be long. An hour maybe." She put on her hat. No matter how hot it was, when Granny Parker dressed for shopping or visiting, she always wore a hat.

Tommy walked outside the house with her. The day was still young, but already the sun was hot, the air dry and still. Even the birds seemed too wilted to fly. By the dozens they sat motionless on the electric wires, looking like so many decoys. They weren't interested in anything, not even the bits of bread Granny always scattered about the yard for them.

"Why don't you use the telephone at the Turners?" Tommy suggested. "They never mind."

The old lady nodded. "Can't. Mrs. Turner took Kathy down-town Providence to buy school clothes. No one is home."

"Oh—"

He had forgotten that. Kathy had told him yesterday she was going "down-town," as Granny said it. Kathy said she would be back by midafternoon.

"You look after things," Granny cautioned.

"I will. I'll work here."

He returned to his work on the north porch. Quite a few boards were edged with dryrot and mildew. Kathy's father had told him the best way to avoid dryrot was to prevent the boards from resting directly on the wood joist where moisture could collect. The solution was simple: place some tarpaper on the wood joist, then nail down the flooring.

As he worked, Tommy again thought about Granny Parker. He got nowhere. Sighing, he spent the remainder of the sultry morning working on the porch.

That afternoon, despite the oppressive heat, he went tonging for quahaugs. He spent the greater part of the time in water up to his waist, treading for them. Filling a bushel basket this way was much slower, but it was too hot to tong.

He straightened to rest his back. Will the heat ever let up? They hadn't had any rain in over three sweltering weeks.

He gazed around solemnly. Not a cloud in the sky. The air tasted burned. It was hard to breathe.

The next day, Thursday, August 29, he was cutting brush when Kathy ran into the yard.

"Hi, Tom. Where's Granny Parker? Telephone call for her."

"In the house." He dropped the hatchet and joined Kathy. "What's going on?"

"I don't know." Kathy knocked and entered the house. A minute later she came out. Granny Parker followed her up the street.

"Be right back, Tommy," she called back.

For several minutes Tommy stared after them, then returned to his brush-cutting. Granny sure was getting popular all of a sudden. But it probably was about her social security, or her insurance company calling. They did that every so often.

Twenty minutes later he saw Kathy running up the street as though pursued by Marshall's Monster. She raced across the yard and slammed into him, almost knocking him down.

"Hey. Take it easy, little one," he said, laughing.

Kathy's eyes were wide and frightened, her mouth trembly and uncertain. She caught his hand and pulled him toward the seashore. "Come on, Tom. I've got to talk to you privately." She glanced around. "Let's get away from here."

He had never seen Kathy so upset. "What's wrong?"

"Not here," she cried. "Come on. Hurry!"

She sat on the seawall and eased down to the beach—the first time he had ever seen her do that. Usually she jumped down. But then Kathy was growing up fast, he reminded himself. He jumped down beside her.

"Now, what's so terribly secretive?"

For several seconds Kathy stared at him. Her face suddenly broke up.

"Oh, Tommy. Tommy..." she choked. "I—didn't mean to, but I heard part of Granny's telephone call. She was talking to someone at that—that place you came from. The orphanage. I didn't hear everything, but—" Her dark eyes filled and tears rolled down her cheeks. She slumped against him, sobbing.

"—But, what?" Tommy gasped.

Kathy held tightly to him. "Two men are coming tomorrow. I—think they're going to take you back!"

Kathy's words were a sledgehammer blow in his stomach. They savagely knocked out his breath, bringing stinging tears to his eyes. He felt icy cold.

Then it *was* true: Granny Parker was sending him back!

For a long time Tommy held tight to Kathy, afraid to let go, afraid if he did she would vanish, and he would plunge down into a deep, black pit of nothingness.

Granny Parker didn't want him. His work was done and he was being returned like—like a rented cement mixer. He wasn't...wanted...

An agony of confused thoughts raced through his tortured mind. He felt empty, as though a huge being had crushed everything, leaving only a hollow shell that looked like Tommy Wayne, but was nothing but paper-mache.

Slowly his pain turned to bitterness, but only briefly, and then to purpose.

Direction.

No! They wouldn't take him back! Not now, he resolved. He wouldn't let them. He loved the sea and boats and Kathy...

Yes, he loved Kathy—and her whole family, and Ben Brown, and the chattering seagulls, and the waves and the wind, and wondrous freedom.

He loved the wonderful people of Conimicut Village, Warwick, and Rhode Island. He couldn't leave all this simply because Granny Parker was through with him, because she didn't need him anymore...

—Because she didn't *want* him!

No! He wouldn't let them take him away from his first real home!

Easing back, he studied Kathy's face for a long time. She was rapidly changing into a beautiful young woman. He'd miss her greatly. He'd miss her vivaciousness, her frequent laughter, her magnificent zest for life, her delightful, happy, adventurous ways. Yes, he'd miss her very much.

He suddenly pulled her close, startling her. He kissed her on the forehead. His lips brushed her tear-filled eyes. He tasted the salt of her tears. He kissed her gently on the lips, then a bit harder...

Kathy responded for a few heartbeats, then eased back. "W-What are you going to do, Tommy?" she cried.

"I don't know. I really don't know..."

"—Tommy. I—feel awful. I'm sorry I had to tell you. I—"

"Shhh. It's all right. Thanks for telling me." He sighed loudly. "I admit it was quite a shock, but—well, I think I expected it. I wish it hadn't happened though. Granny Parker is a staunch, stubborn old lady, but I've learn to respect her. I like her. I think I even learned to *love* her..." He snorted bitterly.

"Huh! That's funny, isn't it? Very funny."

"No! It isn't funny at all," Kathy cried heatedly. "I love her too. I mean, I did, but now she's sending you away. She's mean and hateful. I-I hate her! I *hate* her!"

"Kathy. Stop it!" He shook her hard, then held her close, thoughtful for several moments.

"You don't hate her either," he said softly. "Maybe she has her reasons. I'm not her son. She didn't adopt me, and she doesn't have to keep me. Besides, I'm clumsy and noisy and—Well, she's used to living alone all these years. I guess that's how a person gets when they live alone for a long time. They can't stand noise, or something or someone breaking up their routine."

He smiled down at her. "Besides, it isn't so terrible at the

Home. They don't beat you. They do their best with what they have, and I'm grateful to them. It's just that it's so much nicer *here*. Here I feel needed. I feel a part of something, like I belong. It's a good feeling, being a part of something. Can you understand that, Kathy?"

"I—think so."

"Good. Now, the world's not coming to an end. I'm fifteen now, and thanks to your father and Granny Parker and Ben Brown, I'm pretty handy. In a year I'll be able to go to work. And I'll buy a car. I'll drive down to see you. "

Forcing a grin, he chucked her under the chin. "I won't ever forget you, Funny Face."

Sniffling, Kathy forced a smile. "You—better not, Tommy Wayne."

They sat on the sand at the base of the seawall out of sight of all but boaters on the water. For over a half-hour they talked.

"Now, remember," Tommy cautioned. "Don't tell anyone what you told me. Act as though nothing had happened. When the men from the Home come here tomorrow, I'll go with them. But I'll write you every week. And somehow I'll get down to see you. I promise!" He stood up and brushed sand from his workpants.

"Now, I better get back to work. Granny might become suspicious."

Kathy gripped his hand tenaciously. "I want to stay with you. Please, Tommy."

"No. That's a sure giveaway. You might start crying again. Why don't you go for a sail in your pram?"

"But, I don't want—"

"Please, Kathy," he begged. "Go for a sail!"

Kathy suddenly darted forward and kissed him hard on the lips. For several seconds he held her tight, then released her. She looked up at him, then turned and ran down the sandy beach toward Conimicut Point.

Tommy watched after her until she turned right and went toward her house.

If only there was a way to preserve a kiss, he thought. He climbed the seawall and went back to his work cutting brush. He swung the hatchet effortlessly, leveling shrubs.

But there *was* a way! he realized. Kathy's parting kiss would forever remain with him, in his memory.

He was pleased Kathy had kept her word. She spent the afternoon sailing her pram.

As he worked, Tommy secretly made his plans. He wouldn't
go back. He couldn't! The sea, boating, special people—everything
here was too much a part of his life now. He couldn't cut it off like
these shrubs. Without them, and Kathy, he'd be a cripple the rest of
his life.

He'd run away. It sounded silly when he said it aloud. It
sounded juvenile. Well, he didn't care what it sounded like.

He'd wait until tonight—late. Darkness would give him a good
start. He didn't know exactly where he would go, or what he would
do, but he would worry about that later.

From the barn he got his fishing gear, packed a knife, matches,
some apples from Granny's tree. He took the hatchet too. He shook
out and folded the canvas Granny used to keep moisture off her
bags of cement. It would make a good tent.

He hid everything in the tall grass beside the pile of driftwood
lumber near the north end of the barn...

He had intended to eat a hearty supper, but couldn't.

"Air you sick, Boy?" Granny asked.

"Uh. No, mam. Just not hungry, I guess." He toyed with his
food, occasionally stealing a look at the old lady across from him.
Her wrinkled face was as inscrutable as ever.

Suddenly afraid she would read his mind and learn his plans,
he stared at his plate, his face and ears hot.

Upstairs in his room, he tried to read, but couldn't concentrate.
He tried to think of ways he had failed the old lady. He tried to
reason out her dissatisfaction with him.

What had he done wrong? Hadn't he worked hard enough?
Had he been too noisy? Did he eat too much? He had failed somehow, but how?

He knew he would never be able to sleep, but he had to try. He
changed into his pajamas and set his alarm clock for two A.M.,
placing it within arm's reach.

He lay on the bed staring at the moonlight illuminating the
cheerful wallpaper of his room.

The lines and shapes suddenly jiggled and blurred and blended together, and he rolled over on his stomach and buried his hot face into the pillow and cried like a baby.

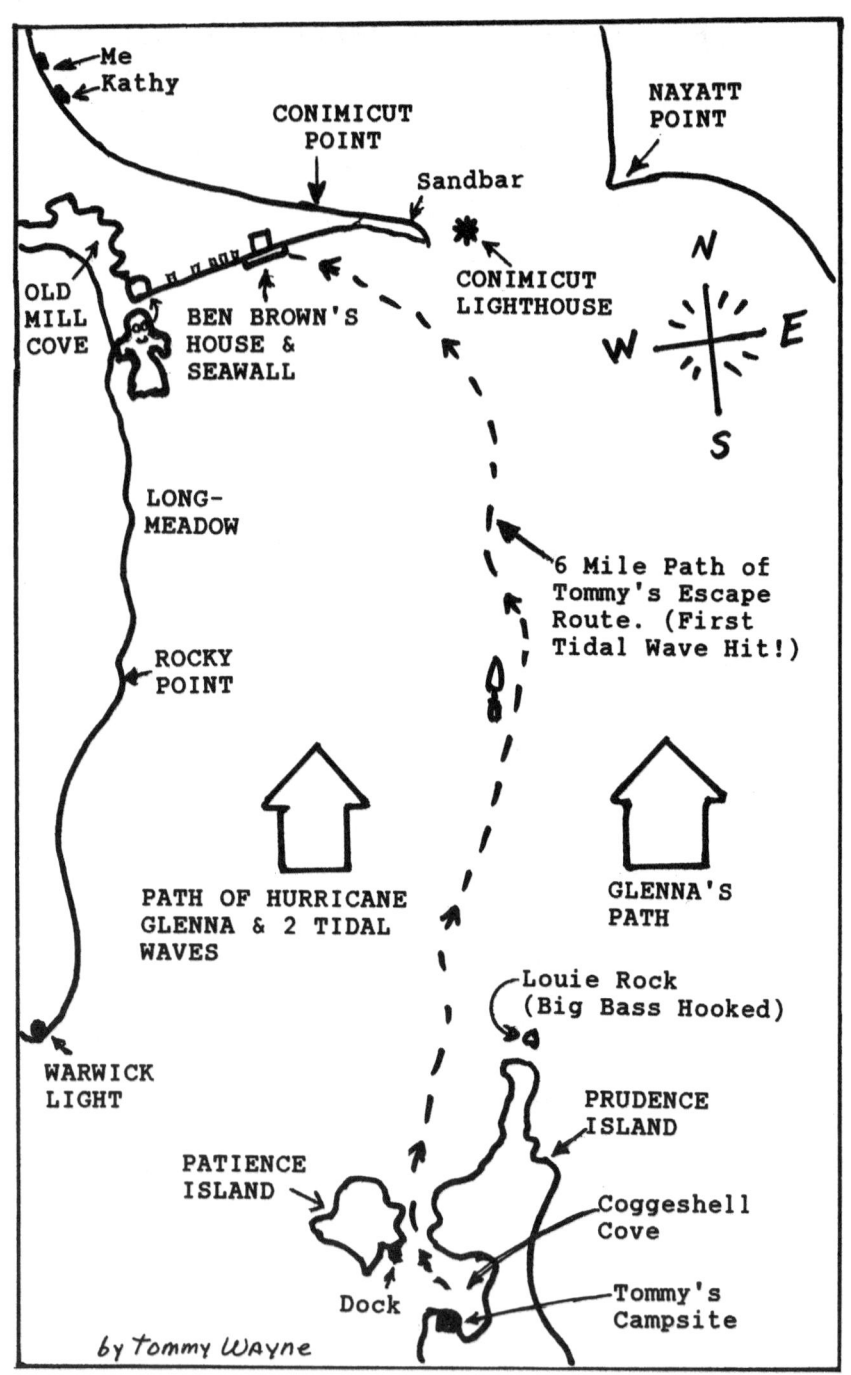

Prudence & Patience Islands, North to Conimicut Point Area

Chapter 14

Run Away Into Terror!

*L*ying abed, troubled and thoughtful, Tommy heard the clock click and instantly shut off the two A.M. alarm before the ring. The last thing he wanted was Granny Parker's awakening.

In the dim silvery light of a higher moon he dressed quickly and silently, remembering to take his savings. He packed several favorite books in his waterproofed canvas duffel bag, along with some extra clothes, a hooded red boat-shirt, some foul weather gear, a flashlight, more matches, a compass and his precious copy of Chapman's boat book.

For several minutes he gazed fondly around his room, his "home" for the past few months.

The thought of leaving it brought a hard, choking lump to his throat. He was going to miss this room, and his chair and reading lamp, his library with its home-made bookcase, the panoramic view of Narragansett Bay from the east window.

And, although she had hurt him by rejecting him, he knew he was going to miss Granny Parker too.

But most of all, there was little Kathy. At times she annoyed him and was pesty, but she had steadily crept into his life and would forever be a warm and important part of him.

Oh, who was he kidding? He would miss Kathy terribly!

Seizing the duffel bag and a warm jacket—even in Summer it was cold on the water—he silently went downstairs and into the kitchen. Risking a forty-watt light, he made a bologna sandwich lunch, six sandwiches, and wrapped them in wax paper. He slipped them into a paper bag and put it in his duffel bag.

Silently he gazed around the small kitchen, committing every-thing to memory. The clock over the sink read two-thirty. The calendar beside it read, Friday, August 30, a terrible day for Tommy.

Tightening the cord on his duffel bag, he swung it to his shoulder, picked up his jacket and opened the door. He paused, then went back to the kitchen table.

In the table drawer he found paper and a pencil. He smiled briefly at the scrawled reminder notes Granny had written to herself. Granny Parker had always preached on writing small reminders, her To-Do List, down on paper.

Writing them down, she said, made you remember double: The act of writing helped you remember better, and you always had the note to remind you.

Besides, Granny emphasized, you should not clutter up your mind with little details, things to do or buy. It was much better to use your superb mind for life's more important things.

Tommy tore off the page of notes and put it on the table. Thoughtfully, he stared at the white paper, shaping his ideas. He didn't want to say too much, such as where he was going—he didn't really know himself—but he didn't want the old lady to worry either.

He bent closer to the paper and wrote:

"Dear Granny,
  I don't want to be sent back to the home so I have gone away.
  Please do not try to find me.
  I am big enough to take care of myself. I don't need anybody anymore."

He paused and re-read what he had written. It sounded too abrupt, so he added:

"Thank you for letting me stay with you these past happy months. Good bye."

Again he paused, thoughtful, then signed it:

"Your friend,

Tommy Wayne

(PS. I used up all your balonie.)"

Nodding in approval, Tommy propped the note against the sugar bowl on the table. He wasn't sure of the spelling of bologna, but Granny would know what he meant.

He reached into his pocket for his wallet, pulled out a ten dollar bill and put it beside the note. Turning off the light, he stood for a moment in the dark, then hurried out the door. He carefully prevented the screen door from slamming.

From the barn he got his motor and gas tank, and the extra five gallons of gas he had stored there. He got his hidden fishing equipment by the wood pile.

Carrying everything to the skiff took almost another half-hour, but finally he was ready to shove off.

Tommy felt excited, yet apprehensive. This was his first time in a boat at night. Somehow, darkness made everything seem very different.

He rowed far out into the bay, not daring to start the motor for fear the sound would awaken Granny or one of the neighbors. Or maybe even Kathy, three houses down.

Overhead, the southerly moon was bright and full, ringed with three faint halos. It was near high tide, Tommy noted, abnormally high, as with all full-moon tides. Yes, today was August 30, full-moon tide, Tommy recalled, rowing slowly. Friday, August 30th. The end of summer. The end of everything...

A night bird called, a lonely, echoing shriek. Baitfish winnowed in the mirror-black water. Everything was terribly still...

As Tommy rowed, the horizon slowly lowered, and Kathy's moored pram blended in with the white of the Turner's seawall so it was no longer visible.

From this distance, Granny Parker's old seawall wasn't a mass of patches anymore. It was white, and long, and strong and durable. He was glad he had at least finished work on the wall.

Finally, he shipped the oars, storing them under the thwarts on the deck. He swung the motor down into the water, connected the gas hose to the fitting, and pumped the primer bulb on the hose. He reached for the starter cord, but suddenly stopped.

The air was oppressive and still, making it hard to breathe. Sitting down to rest, drifting slightly southeast in the black tide, he wiped his sweaty brow and gazed wistfully and sadly at the shore.

He could no longer see Granny Parker's house, or Kathy's, or Pete Bender's big dark house.

Night and distance had combined houses, land, trees—everything—into a band of grays, pinpointed by occasional firefly-like streetlights. Now the shoreline resembled a huge, long, dark hedge that badly needed trimming.

The sudden splashing of water near his skiff startled him. He grinned as the silvery baitfish fled from larger prey. But why was he grinning? It seemed everything was fleeing from something else. Everyone was running away from something. He was—

Annoyed at his negative thinking, he yanked at the starter cord and the motor rumbled softly. After a brief warm-up, he shifted into forward speed and the skiff nosed around and sliced through the smooth, inky water, like a white arrow pointing South.

Five minutes later Tommy passed Conimicut Point. He stared up, awed by the lighthouse's great silhouette. It was like a huge white ghost with one great, probing, blinking eye, searching everywhere, but never seeing.

In his boiling wake silvery phosphorescence pursued him, never quite catching up.

The night was calm and clear, oppressively hot, airless and silent.

Continuing south, Tommy finally passed the striped buoy north of Providence Point at the northern tip of Prudence Island. He recalled the great bass he and Kathy had caught. It seemed ages ago, but it had happened only a few weeks ago.

He recalled editor John Howell's excellent article in the *Warwick Beacon*. Now, he'd never be able to attend those banquets and see his mounted bass, or even get those prizes and the Penn reel that were promised him and Kathy.

As he rode across the black water, a great sense of adventure slowly filled him. He felt himself relaxing in the skiff's stern. He gazed around, curious.

Far to the right, Warwick Light winked its massive eye at him. Beyond, and slightly to the left were the hundreds of star-like lights of Potowomut and East Greenwich. Still further south, almost straight ahead, were the many colored lights of Quonset Point and Davisville with their many ships and Naval installations.

And seven miles on his left—126 degrees according to his

compass—were the arched lights of the Mount Hope Bridge, connecting Bristol with the island of Newport.

No, it wasn't Newport Island, he remembered. Newport was the name of the town or city. It was Aquidneck Island. But most people called it Newport.

He guided his skiff through the narrow gut between Prudence and Patience Islands and saw Coggeshall Cove on his port quarter.

"There's the perfect place to spend the night," he decided. "Maybe even a few days."

He could make camp and steam some clams and blue-shell crabs over an open fire. He could fish and roast them on a spit, or packed in mud. He could lie on the sun-warmed sand and relax and not have to think about the Home, or work, or anybody, or anything.

Here he could really enjoy life. It was a fantastic idea!

He beached his skiff, sinking the grapnel anchor high on the shore, then unloaded much of his equipment. Spreading the canvas over the taut anchor line, he made a low pup-tent, weighting the ends with rocks. He wished he had thought to take a blanket, but his foul weather gear would have to serve as a mattress and blanket.

Besides, he could wriggle his fanny and hips into the warm sand and be very comfortable that way.

Oh, he was going to have a wonderful time! Now he could do anything he wanted to. There was no one to boss him around, to remind him to wash, or eat when he wasn't hungry, or go to bed, or walk softer. He didn't need anyone... anyone at all.

As he stretched out under the canvas, he told himself he really had it made.

Sleep slowly crept into him like a numbing silence, but a tiny voice in his mind kept whispering, "Liar! Liar..."

It was not yet dawn when something awoke him. Yawning, he bolted up and gazed around fearfully. Remembering where he was, he exhaled in relief and laid back. But he couldn't sleep. Something was wrong.

It was the silence that had awakened him, he realized, the dead, hot, sticky silence, in which not a breath of air stirred. Even the cricket's chirping had stopped. Night birds in the marshes surrounding the north and west sides of the cove—why were they so still?

Maybe they were asleep, he decided, and closed his eyes. He rolled on his side, on his back, on his other side. Why couldn't he sleep? Why was he so restless, so terribly fidgety?

He had a faint, dull headache in the front of his head and his ears kept popping and seemed to be straining for something to hear. But all they heard was the awful silence.

The new day finally lightened his world. The late August sun, huge and bloody, popped over the marshes in the East. Already, the day was incredibly hot, a sticky, suffocating heat that drained off all energy and left a soggy purposelessness.

He felt tense and restless, conscious of the throbbing of his own heart.

Well, this just wouldn't do.

He stripped to his swimming trunks and dove into the calm water and swam around. The water was not cooling or refreshing. Instead, it felt sticky and thick, like tepid pea soup.

He treaded for quahaugs, remembering he was responsible for getting his own food, as well as cooking it. Those six bologna sandwiches wouldn't last very long, and neither would his savings if he used it for food.

That day he had caught the big fish he had told Kathy a person could live off the sea. Well, now he had his chance to prove it.

When he had enough quahaugs, he dug in the sand where the holes spouted water when he stepped near them and found a dozen fat steamer clams.

It would be an odd breakfast, steamed clams and quahaugs and a bologna sandwich, but a lot of things would be different from now on.

After eating, he searched the area for a fresh water spring, finding one a quarter-mile southeast. There were plenty of frogs in the spring pool. He had never eaten frog legs, but they were supposed to be a delicacy, weren't they?

Pleased, he returned to camp. Now he had all the necessary ingredients for survival: food, clothing and shelter. He was free as a fish with the whole ocean for a playground. He should be wonderfully happy...

Well, why wasn't he?

And why this dull headache, and this awfully odd pressure, as though someone had clamped his head in a vice and was steadily turning the screw?

He sat down on the stern of the skiff to rest. He was exhausted and perspiring, despite wearing only swimming trunks.

Yet, he couldn't sit still. He had to keep doing something, and the slightest activity exhausted him. What was wrong, anyway?

The sun continued to blaze down from a sky that was a brilliant purple-blue.

"—If only it would rain," Tommy said out loud. "Maybe it would cool things off."

He went out in his skiff and tried to fish, using cut-up quahaug for bait. He couldn't concentrate on fishing. As much as he loved it, today fishing seemed too much like distasteful work.

And then he saw it, an oily grayness on the horizon far south of him.

"Ah— Some rain *is* coming," he said. "Good!"

Suddenly a dry, sandy breeze came from nowhere. It smelled oddly of dust, and choked him. It smarted his eyes. It rippled the water, swaying tall grasses in the marshes, and rocked the tree tops.

Tommy wet his face with sea water and closed his eyes, letting the dry breeze fan and cool him. He didn't feel quite so lonely now; the breeze was almost company.

All morning the odd breeze blew steadily from the south. It gradually increased to a lusty eighteen to twenty knot wind, blowing up waves, building them into dirty whitecaps that bumped and rocked his skiff. The sky was gray all over now, and darkening.

"It won't be long before we get some real rain," he decided, and thought of Granny Parker's vegetable garden. Granny would be pleased.

"But I'm not going to think of Granny," he reminded himself. "Not any more. She didn't want me, so I don't need her. I don't need anybody!"

The southerly wind was gusty now, and he hurried back to shore to secure camp. When he saw the sea water rising, he decided he had better move to higher ground. The move took over a half-hour. When he again looked, the entire sky was a dull slate, an oily gray, and the wind was cooler and more moist. It whipped up tiny cyclones of sand from the beach, blinding his eyes, stinging his semi-nude body. He hurriedly dressed and secured his boat, dragging it up on higher land.

"Wow! We're in for a real mean thunderstorm!" he spoke aloud.

In the north were huge, dirty clouds, rolling and turning into each other. Occasional jagged slashes of lightning split open the sky. A distant thunder rolled.

Tommy ate a hasty early lunch, fearfully gazing at the sky, wincing slightly at the pink-purple flashes of heat lightning. He had never been alone like this in a bad thunderstorm, not alone on an island.

He didn't like it, but he was going to be alone a lot of time from now on, so he had better get accustomed to it. But it wasn't fun. It wasn't any fun at all.

He wondered what Granny Parker was doing right now. She was probably bustling about, taking in lawn furniture, closing her windows on the south and east sides of the house. Kathy was probably double-tying her pram at its mooring, or maybe just pulling it high on dry land, the wisest thing to do. Sudden storms like this could whip up a huge sea in a very short time.

Thoughts of home suddenly filled him with a great lonely ache that pushed a choke into his throat and burned his eyes. He wished he hadn't left the way he did, sneaking off in the night.

But what else could he have done? If he had stayed, they would have come today and taken him back to the Home. Neither choice was ideal. He had only chosen the less painful one.

Tommy gazed curiously at the dark sky. For a thunderstorm it was sure taking a long time to break. The wind was increasing, and blowing strong and steadily from the south. He hastily checked his compass.

No, it was coming more from the southeast. Lower Narragansett Bay, just beyond the mouth of his cove, was white-capped and angry, truly an ugly sea.

He noticed the sea water was higher than it should be. His little mound of land was only two feet above sea level at its highest point. But he needn't worry, he assured himself. It was only natural for the sea to rise with a strong southeast wind. It wasn't as if this part of the island was going to sink under him. No. Of course not!

The rain started as tiny drops, hardly more than a spitting mist. Within minutes a driving rain pelted him, slashing into his eyes, drenching him to the skin before he could put on his foul weather gear. Fortunately it was a cool rain, even welcome, so he didn't mind very much.

After the first heavy downpour, the rain slowed to a steady drizzle, but the gusting twenty-five knot winds sometimes turned it into a solid wall of water.

Tommy hoped Granny Parker was all right, and not worried about him. Sure, he was getting wet, and he was a little scared, but here he was perfectly safe. In an hour or two this thunderstorm would pass over, the sun would peep out and everything would rapidly dry and be sparkling fresh again.

—And cooler too!

But right now, it sure was miserable. Not fit for boy or gull. He grinned at the pun, and was glad Kathy wasn't with him.

He could hardly see the dock on neighboring Patience Island. He couldn't see Warwick Light at all, or any of the west shore of the bay, or Conimicut Lighthou—

Suddenly Tommy's body went rigid. He felt sharp terror. "Oh, No!"

He closed his eyes and shook his head, disbelieving. He had to be seeing things. Again he looked into the slashing rain. He stood up to see better.

"Oh, God, no!" he gasped.

Rounding the gut between the islands was a tiny boat, its single, white triangular sail whipping insanely on a port tack. It was a pram sailboat.

There was one person in it, struggling frantically against the mounting wind and raging seas, fighting to keep afloat.

"Kathy!" Tommy cried. "It's Kathy!"

Chapter 15

The Sinking Island!

"That crazy kid!" Tommy cried. But this was the wrong time for recriminations. Kathy was in serious trouble out there. Small, eight-foot sailing prams were not built for twenty-five knot winds and foot-high waves. It was a miracle, or exceptional sailing, or both, that she had sailed this far without capsizing.

Tommy hurriedly pulled the canvas tent from the taut line, then put the grapnel anchor into the skiff. Yanking and straining, he tugged at the heavy skiff, moving it toward the water, all the while acutely conscious of Kathy's continuing battle to keep afloat.

At times the driving rain hid her from view and he was terrified she had capsized, but when the rain pattern shifted, he again saw the white sail and sighed in relief.

The wind lashed rain into his eyes. It slashed at his hair, at his clothes. He again glanced at the gut between the islands. Kathy was still afloat, thank God, but she was not making headway. The shrieking, southerly wind seemed to be blowing her back into the open bay, away from land.

Choking, gasping, Tommy finally got the skiff into the water. He pushed it out, heedless of the fact that he was walking in water up to his knees with his clothes on.

As soon as he was in deep enough water, he swung the motor down, praying it would start quickly. He squeezed the fuel primer bulb, then pulled the starter cord, and the small outboard barked into life.

Without waiting for a warm-up, he pulled the shift lever into forward speed, swung the bow around, and raced through the white, frothy waves toward the gut and Kathy.

Once he cleared the land area, the foot-high waves slammed at his port side, knocking him off course, splashing white water into the skiff and all over him. He gunned the motor full, ignoring the pounding hull and the slapping, pitching and yawing. He thought only of getting to Kathy...

In the gut between the islands he turned a sharp right and headed due north. Kathy saw him, but had no time or opportunity to wave. She was far too busy keeping afloat in the stormy sea.

With the wind behind him, Tommy rapidly closed the distance. Kathy was struggling with the sail, trying to lower it. The tiny boat was low in the water, dangerously low. It seemed to have less than three inches of freeboard.

He raced past her and abruptly turned his bow into the wind. Varying his speed, he brought his skiff up to the foundering pram. He shifted into neutral and seized the pram's gunwale, pulling the two boats together.

"Give me your anchor!" he yelled over the wind.

Kathy stared at him, bewildered. She was kneeling in six inches of foamy, dirty water. Her denims and shirt were plastered to her body. Her sailor hat flopped soggily on her head.

"Your anchor!" he cried again, and Kathy fumbled in the water. She came up with the anchor and a tangle of line which she passed to Tommy.

"Come on. Get in the skiff. Hurry, we're drifting!"

Kathy needed no second invitation. She scampered into the skiff, rolling on her back. She got up, smiled briefly, and tried to help by holding on to the pram.

It took Tommy several minutes to untangle the wet line. He made one end fast to the center thwart, and verified that the other end was tied securely to the pram's bow ring.

"Okay. Let the pram go. I'll tow it in," he yelled over the wind.

But saying it was easier than doing it. The water-filled pram seemed to have a will of its own. It jerked and yawed and burrowed into white water. Tommy increased his speed. The quarter-inch nylon line stretched taut, snapping off spray as the trailing pram, like an obstinate puppy, jerked to be free.

He saw Kathy was trembling with cold, but there was nothing he could do about that. First things first, and he had to get them back to the protection of the cove.

White water broke over the starboard side as he made the turn.

The bulky, water-choked sailboat jerked his stern off course, He steered to compensate for the heavy drag stern-wise.

As they neared the land, the waves slowly diminished. Finally, they were in the lee of the island and the pram towed docilely behind, splashing like a half-sunken white log.

"Whew!" Tommy was exhausted. And relieved.

He steered his skiff toward the rapidly-disappearing beach. Most of the sand bar area of Coggeshall Cove was now gone, covered by wind-whipped water.

He shut off his motor and swung it up, then jumped into the thigh-deep water and pulled the skiff up to shore. He sunk the anchor high on the beach. Kathy helped him pull the skiff to higher ground. Together they tackled the pram.

Working swiftly and silently, they lowered the sail, tied it to the boom, disconnected the boom and unstepped the mast.

"Put the centerboard and rudder in the skiff, under the stern seat," Tommy yelled, conscious of the fact that he now had to almost scream to be heard. What kind of a crazy thunderstorm was this?

He gave brief orders, yelling close to Kathy's ear. They tied the mast and boom together and fastened them on the skiff.

"Help me pull the pram up on land," he shouted. "We'll turn it over for a windbreak."

Once the water was emptied out, the pram was much lighter, but they now had to struggle to prevent the wind from blowing it out of their hands.

Together, they sunk one side into the sand to break the wind. Using the centerboard as a wedge, they lowered the pram against it. Now they had both a windbreak and protection from the heavy rain.

Tommy carefully moved his canvas duffel bag and gear inside.

"Come on, get in." He waited until Kathy crawled under the boat, then crawled in after her.

Kathy flung her arms around his neck. "Oh, Tommy. I was so scared for you!"

"You little nut!" Tommy cried. "Look at you. You're drenched. You'll catch cold." He rummaged through his duffel bag, pulling out a red hooded boat-shirt and dry denims.

"Here. Put these on."

"But—"

"This is no time for modesty." He unbuttoned her blouse and pulled the soggy material from her richly tanned shoulders.

Kathy flushed. She wore a white bra that wasn't much different than the top of her red bathing suit. Using a dry shirt, Tommy dried her shoulders, back and arms, then helped her into his boat shirt.

"Oh, that's much better," Kathy said, her trembling subsiding.

"Now your denims," Tommy said, and tactfully turned away.

When Kathy had changed, she touched his shoulder. He rubbed her hair with a dry undershirt, then rummaged into his duffel bag for a comb, grateful his bag was waterproofed.

For several minutes he watched her, acutely conscious of the howling wind outside, wincing occasionally as the wind-pelted rain slammed against the thin plywood bottom of the pram.

Kathy gave him the comb. "Thanks. I feel much better."

"Why were you sailing in weather like this?" he demanded.

"—I came after you."

"After me? How did you know I was here? I—Oh, never mind. As soon as this storm is over, you're going back."

"No! I want to go with you, Tommy."

"That's out." He was almost abrupt. "I don't know where I'm going, or what I'm going to do."

"I don't care," Kathy cried. A second later, she added, "I saw Granny Parker this morning and she told me you ran away. She's worried, Tommy. You *must* go back."

Tommy snorted. "Huh! I can just bet she's worried. Were those two men from the Home worrying with her?"

"She *is* worried, Tommy! And she was crying too. I never saw her crying before. Never!"

Tommy was thoughtful for several seconds. "I—don't believe you." Bitterness was a distasteful thing, very hard to swallow.

"Granny Parker doesn't care about me. She never did. All I was was two hands to work for her. Not once did she ever tell me she liked me. Not once!"

Kathy loudly slapped her fist into the palm of her hand. Her young face was flushed in anger.

"Did you ever tell her you liked her?"

Tommy felt his face grow hot. "N-No. —But I do, Kathy."

"Why didn't you tell her you liked her? Why, Tommy?"

"I-I don't know. She's not the easiest person to talk to."

"And neither are you, sometimes!" Kathy said heatedly. "You're both nice persons, but you're both loners. And you're both stubborn. That's your trouble, stubborn. I think you ought to go back."

"Well, I'm not! And I'm not stubborn. I can tell when I'm not wanted."

"But I think you are wanted," Kathy insisted. "I think Granny Parker loves you, and I know you love her, even if you are too pigheaded stubborn to admit it. Please, Tommy. You've got to go back. Now!"

For several seconds Tommy said nothing. Finally he shook his head.

"I'll go back only to take you home. I'm not going to be sent back to the orphanage. Just as soon as this thunderstorm is over, I'll take you back to Conimicut Point."

Kathy's eyes widened. "*Thunderstorm!*" She seized his hand, demanding his full attention.

"—Tommy... This isn't a thunderstorm. This is a *hurricane!*"

"A-A hurricane!" Tommy gasped, horrified. The word sent a frozen chill through him.

"But—"

"It is. It is!" Kathy insisted. "It's Hurricane Glenna. She's huge! She has steady winds up to 120 miles per hour, and higher, and she's heading right for Rhode Island. Part of her is already here."

After several minutes of numbed silence, Tommy again found his voice. "But—How? When?"

Kathy's eyes were still wide, her breath coming from between open lips. Behind them, the hurricane winds slammed and shook the tilted pram, driving the centerboard deeper into the sand.

"I didn't know about it either," Kathy explained. "Not until late last night when I heard on television it may come here. Hurricane Glenna had been hanging out to sea for over two weeks. Daddy said it was waiting for a low front, or something...

"Anyway, it suddenly moved up the coast, and last night it suddenly turned in and is racing for Rhode Island and Connecticut. It's a bad one, Daddy said. But the winds weren't supposed to start until later tonight. It's moving this way *very fast!*"

"You *knew* it was coming?" Tommy gasped. "You knew, and yet you sailed all the way down here in your pram? Why?" He squeezed her hand.

Wincing, Kathy pulled away. "B-Because somebody had to warn you," she cried.

"But the wind wasn't bad when I started four hours ago. I thought I could make it and we could get back before the hurricane came. It—It just came *much faster* than they said it would..."

Tommy looked at her in the dim light under the overturned pram. He felt a lump swell in his throat. His eyes burned from the sting of sudden, grateful tears. He remembered her tiny boat caught in the raging sea, the terror in her eyes. Kathy had sailed all the way down here, over seven dangerous miles, to warn him. She cared about him...

He felt deeply grateful, and very ashamed for the mean things he had said earlier.

"D-Do your folks know you came?" he asked finally.

"Oh, goodness, no. I didn't dare tell them."

"Does Granny Parker know?"

Kathy shook her head.

The rain drummed hollowly on their makeshift windbreak. The pram shifted and Tommy put his weight on the low side, pushing it deeper into the wet sand. It seemed to help.

"Oh—" He groaned. "What a mess I got you into." He looked deep into her green eyes.

"...Kathy. I'm sorry."

"It wasn't your fault. It was— Well, it wasn't your fault," Kathy said.

All the time they talked, the winds of Hurricane Glenna had steadily increased to whole gale force. Shrieking and moaning, it blew shrubs and dead branches all around. Several times it worked under the low edge of the pram, jerking it up, and almost carrying it away.

When Kathy finally spoke, her voice trembled: "Tommy. W-What are we going to do?"

"I—don't know. Wait it out here, I guess."

Several minutes of silence passed. Each had private, frightening thoughts.

Kathy suddenly cried out, her voice shrill, edged in panic:

"Tommy!" She seized his arm, her eyes wide in terror. "Look. Sea water at my feet. The island is sinking! It's sinking!"

Tommy turned to look, releasing his hold on the pram. The wind lifted it, flipped it around, and blew it several yards away, correct side up, into the water.

Tommy raced into the water, seized the floating pram's anchor line, and tied it to the skiff's stern thwart.

The wind and rain pelted them unmercifully. Tommy gave Kathy his foul weather gear and shrugged into his wet jacket. The back billowed out like a spinnaker. He leaned into the wind to keep from being blown backwards into the water.

"It's *sinking!*" Kathy screamed. "Oh, God. What are we going to do?"

In mounting terror, Tommy stared into the slashing, wind-whipped rain. He could see only a few yards ahead, but most of the land was gone.

He knew the island wasn't sinking. Instead, the entire Atlantic Ocean was being blown into Narragansett Bay, flooding everything. From what little he could see, there was only a tiny bit of this part of the island left, and they were standing on it.

"We have to go back!" Tommy yelled over the wind. He crawled about, collecting his gear, and shoved it under the skiff's stern thwart with the pram's centerboard and tiller.

"But we can't go back," Kathy screamed. "The sea's too rough!"

Tommy stared at the pounding, slashing sea a few hundred yards west of them. He again looked around at the rapidly-disappearing island.

Practically all of the northern end of Prudence Island was now underwater. The sea was rising rapidly. They couldn't stay here. To do so meant certain death.

He caught Kathy's hand and pulled her toward the rolling skiff.

"No! No!" Kathy was terrified.

"Come on! We can't stay here."

"But we can't go back," Kathy screamed in horror. "We'll be drowned. We'll be *drowned!*"

Chapter 16

Lost In A Hurricane Sea!

(The First Tidal Wave!)

What Kathy said was very true: They *could* be drowned!

But staying on the sinking island was suicide, Tommy realized. At least they had a slim chance on the water.

"If we stay here we'll certainly be drowned," Tommy said. "The whole island may go under. We've got to go back!"

More fearful than he acted, he looked about at the rapidly-rising water. In the past few minutes it had risen over two inches. West of them, little Patience Island had decreased to less than one-third its normal size.

The long, high dock on the northeast side was almost awash. He estimated the tide was already well over five to seven feet above normal high tide. And the water was swiftly rising...

"Come on. Let's go, Kathy."

But Kathy only stared at him. A sudden gust of wind caught her from behind, knocking her down. It rolled her several feet.

Running, Tommy caught her. He helped her to her feet and into the skiff. She was now too frightened to protest.

He quickly put his orange life jacket on Kathy and tied it securely. In her rush to warn him of the coming hurricane, Kathy had forgotten to take her own life jacket.

In the skiff's stern he pumped the gas tank bulb and lowered the motor into the water. Kathy's pram was floating ten feet behind the skiff at the end of the nylon anchor line he had given her for her birthday. For several seconds he debated, then pulled at the knot.

Kathy bolted up. "What are you doing? No. You're not leaving my pram here. Tommy, no!"

Tommy shouldered her aside. "I've got to. It will be in the way. It's light. The wind will blow it into us."

Kneeling beside him, Kathy jerked at his hands. "No. Please!"

Despising himself, Tommy eased her aside. The knot was wet and difficult to untie. He'd have to cut it.

"Please, Tommy," Kathy begged. "Don't leave my boat." She was crying now. "It will be destroyed. Take it with us, please!"

Tommy continued working at the knot, acutely conscious of the great anguish on Kathy's face. He felt like a child-beater. Finally he sat back on his legs.

"Okay," he said. "We'll take it. I can't get the silly knot untied anyway. But I'm warning you now, if it causes trouble, I'll have to cut the line." His voice softened as he faced her.

"Gee, Kathy, I don't want to. But our lives are more important than your pram. *Or* my skiff, as much as we love them. Understand?"

Nodding, Kathy's pretty mouth was a grim, white line. "—Yes."

"Okay. Remember, now," Tommy warned her.

For several seconds he studied the bobbing pram. It floated high and light. On the open water it would surely ram them unless— He climbed out of the skiff and caught the pram's side. Leaning heavily on it, he allowed the sea water to spill over the side and partly fill the pram. Satisfied at less freeboard, he started to climb back into the skiff, but stopped.

He quickly transferred the pram's mast and boom from the skiff to the pram, tying them securely atop the middle of the smaller boat.

"That's better," he yelled into Kathy's ear. "Half full of water your pram's much heavier. She might even give us a drag, and in a following sea I think we're going to need a drag."

Kathy nodded mutely, content her pram was coming with them.

Tommy started his outboard motor and pulled up the anchor. The roaring southerly wind immediately caught the skiff, shoving the bow around, and swiftly blew them into the deepening cove.

Tommy turned the throttle, increasing speed, and slowly made headway. The pram dragged behind, yanking at the towline.

Once they cleared the protection of land, great waves slammed into the skiff's port side, showering them with spray and soapy foam. Wind and rain lashed them unmercifully. The rain swept in over the water almost horizontally.

As Tommy made the right turn to pass through the gut between the islands, he saw the high dock on Patience Island was almost under water. The whole of Patience Island had shrunk to a twenty-foot plot of land. All around them the waves peaked and bobbed, their foamy whitecaps flying in spindrift.

Heading due North, Tommy saw waves breaking over the skiff's low transom and prayed the salt water wouldn't work into the motor housing and short out the sparkplugs. If that should happen, they'd be helpless.

He speeded up slightly and less water came inside the boat. Thank God for that, he thought.

Wind-driven waves caused them to pitch and roll violently. Waves pounded at the small boat. The skiff suddenly raced ahead as it sped down a huge trough, threatening to capsize them.

To compensate, Tommy frantically varied the motor speed. Faster—slower—faster—slower... It was essential that he keep the skiff's stern to the sea and try to move forward at the same speed as the waves. That way, he lessened the chance of pitch-poling into a trough.

He glanced behind him. Already they were out of sight of land. Now they were alone—very much alone—in a hurricane-battered sea!

"Oh, dear God, help us," Tommy prayed, conscious the words were Granny Parker's.

After ten minutes frantic piloting, Tommy was grateful for the pram's drag behind them. Half-filled with water and heavy, the pram's weight was preventing their stern from being knocked sideways by the waves. Without the drag, they could easily roll over between successive waves in a broach.

The wind was higher now, shrieking steadily as Hurricane Glenna moved closer. Kathy had said its forward speed was over fifty miles an hour and Glenna packed winds over 100 miles per hour, with gusts over 130 miles an hour. Glenna was huge and vicious!

Tommy shuddered at the thought, afraid to think even one second ahead.

Soon he lost all track of time. He guessed they had travelled over one mile—maybe two—propelled more by the furious, southerly wind than the motor.

But they still had over three or four miles to go to reach Conimicut Point. Once there, if they got there, they had to go around the Point and head west to shore.

If they could...

Tommy shuddered uncontrollably. He didn't see how they could make it. But he was going to try. And try he did!

At times, maintaining a straight course was impossible. He had to tack like a sailboat, head slightly northeast for a while, then northwest, and back again to northeast. Good thing he had a compass.

All around them the bay was fuming mad, white and frothy, spitting and hissing. The tiny skiff leaped high. It slammed down again and again, with violent, sickening regularity. It pitched and rolled and bobbed and lurched.

Kathy sat huddled on the bow deck, her young face whiter than the wind-driven foam.

Sitting on the stern thwart was suicide, so Tommy also sat low on the deck, holding on to the gunwale with his other hand.

He glanced ahead, then astern, then to the left and to the right, constantly changing course, varying motor speed to compensate for the ever-changing patterns of the sea.

Every so often he stole a glance at his compass. As close as possible, he kept on an eighteen-degree heading, allowing for a port drift. If he increased his heading to twenty or twenty-five degrees, he might miss Conimicut Point entirely.

Visibility was less than ten feet. Actually, most of the time he couldn't see a thing. As far as he and Kathy were concerned, Hurricane Glenna had swallowed up the world.

But by heading north and maintaining that course as well as possible, Tommy knew land was some place a few miles on his left. That would be Warwick Neck, Rocky Point, River View, or Long Meadow, all—like Conimicut Point—extremely vulnerable to a southeasterly wind and hurricane sea.

Every so often a dark outline would appear in the water. Sometimes it was bits of wood, leaves, small trees, floating debris. Later, he saw long timbers, then floating bollards from broken docks, huge telephone poles, parts of destroyed shore-front homes from low-lying districts.

Several times he saw drowned human bodies...

The awesome sights were terrifying, and growing progressively worse. He did not mention the dead bodies to Kathy who was hovering on the deck, her eyes closed tight against the slashing wind and rain, her lips moving in silent prayer.

—He didn't dare mention them.

To Tommy, it seemed hours had passed. His body ached. His eyes burned fiercely. His lungs felt as if they were filled with salt water. Breathing was very difficult.

Suddenly their small skiff lurched and leaped like a thing alive. Water poured over the sides and low transom as a new danger arose. Tommy noticed they had slowed down, despite his running at near-full throttle.

He saw the following sea was now catching up and passing them. It slammed hard against their stern, drenching him, as streams of green water poured into the skiff, wave after wave.

Frightened, he increased speed to maximum. They still lost headway. Why? Then he noticed the six inches of water sloshing inside the skiff.

"Oh, God, No!" They were sinking!

He yelled to Kathy in the skiff's bow. She opened her eyes and looked dully up at him.

"Bail out the boat, Kathy," he cried. "Hurry!"

But Kathy made no movement at all.

He pulled the plastic bailer from under the stern thwart and shoved it into her hand.

"Bail! Please, Kathy."

Kathy dropped the bailer. She seemed like a sleepwalker, too terrified to fully realize what was happening to them. The skiff slowed still more, despite his going full throttle.

Huge waves slammed over the stern. Tommy couldn't leave the motor for a second. He couldn't steer and bail. Somehow, he had to snap Kathy out of her lethargy.

"Kathy," he screamed. "We're sinking! You've got to bail!"

The terrifying words worked almost immediately. Kathy's eyes widened in horror. She saw the six inches of water she had been sitting in. She scrambled to her knees and furiously shoveled out the water. Much of it came back in, blown by the wind.

"No. Throw it out the other side," Tommy yelled. He turned

the skiff slightly to the left.

Moving around, Kathy bailed the water over the starboard gunwale. The tearing, screeching wind carried it high into the air. For ten minutes she bailed furiously, until she dropped, exhausted, to the deck, sobbing and choking. Then, remembering, she straightened up and continued to bail.

Soon the skiff was lighter. Their forward speed slowly increased so Tommy was able to keep even with the waves' forward speed. Less water splashed in over the transom. They seemed to be flying...

"Good girl. You're doing fine," Tommy yelled encouragement. "You can slow down, but keep bailing."

Kathy's white lips parted slightly. She grimly returned to her task.

Their world was a drenching grayness, the color of soot. All around was a constant, howling wind and white, boiling seas.

Tommy strained to see ahead. Where was the land? They should be seeing land now. Or hearing surf. He was suddenly afraid, his heart hammering in his chest.

Suppose he had made an error? According to his compass, the wind seemed more from the east now. Was his compass correct? Or had the metal objects in the skiff affected the compass reading, giving him a wrong heading?

Oh, God! They should be sighting land. But they weren't! For an instant Tommy thought he saw it, but he was wrong. Instead, it was a heavy concentration of wind-driven rain on his port side.

The soapy water was now heavily littered with debris, parts of peoples' homes, a porch chair, a splintered dock, a half-sunken inboard boat, a man's stove-in dream.

Tommy frequently had to vary his course to avoid the debris. If his propeller hit a submerged object, it would snap his shear pin, and without power they'd be helpless. The hurricane wind would take over, either quickly capsizing them, or driving them against the windward shore, destroying them on the deadly, barnacle-encrusted rocks.

As he fought against wind and waves, Tommy thought of Granny Parker and her patched seawall. Would it hold? Was her old house high enough to be safe from the rising water? Or would the angry sea grasp it and pull it to pieces with wet, dripping fingers?

He thought of old Ben Brown, and of his great seawall facing south. Ben's wall was really getting a pounding. Tommy prayed it would hold together and protect the old man's beloved seaside home.

And he thought of Kathy's folks. They were probably worried sick. They wouldn't know where Kathy was, but they'd probably notice her sailing pram was missing and they'd know she was somewhere lost in a hurricane sea. They'd be frantic with concern.

And it was all his fault!

His thoughts were bitter, accusing. Yes, everything was his fault. If he hadn't run away, Kathy wouldn't have tried to find him to warn him of the impending hurricane. She would be home, safe and dry. She wouldn't be kneeling in the bottom of a pitching and yawing skiff, bailing until her little hands were raw and bloody...

Everything was his fault... His fault...

It was then Tommy heard the roaring behind him. It quickly grew louder. Risking being blown overboard by the violent winds, he quickly stood up and looked south into the slashing, horizontal rain.

He saw a great wall of water racing toward them. It looked exactly like what old Ben Brown had told them about—a tidal wave!

The words terrified him. He looked again. It was a tidal wave, a monstrous wall of gray water bearing down upon them in their tiny skiff!

Within minutes the massive tidal wave would slam into them. There was no escape. It would kill them both!

"*Forgive me, Kathy,*" he yelled over the shrieking wind. "I didn't mean for it to happen this way."

"W-What do you mean?" White-faced, her green eyes great in new fear, Kathy stared at him sitting in the stern of the skiff.

Suddenly Kathy's eyes widened still more, and she shouted, her shrill voice rousing Tommy from his terrified thoughts.

"Tommy!" Kathy pointed behind him. "Tommy, look! The ocean's coming at us. It's a tidal wave. A TIDAL WAVE!"

She screamed it again and again.

Tommy glanced around and up. He saw the huge wave racing

closer. Oh, God! It was much higher than before. It was massive, a mountain-high wall of water, boiling and frothing. The top seemed fifty, sixty feet high! And it was bearing down upon them.

Closer...closer... There was nothing they could do.

"A tidal wave!" Tommy thought bitterly. "And it's all my fault. Now everything is *ending* with a wave..."

* * *

"Oh, no, no, nononono!" Tommy screamed in defiance. Yet, his brave words changed nothing. The great wave raced closer. Closer...

"Kathy, hold *tight* to the sides of the skiff!" Tommy yelled. He knew this was the end, but couldn't tell that to Kathy. He knew the great tidal wave would slam down into their skiff, instantly killing them. Only bits of driftwood and their dead bodies would remain.

"I'm sorry, Kathy. I'm— sorry..."

He caught her hand and closed his eyes, waiting to die...

But the great wave didn't slam down upon them. Instead, the skiff abruptly leaped high into the air and the outboard motor screamed as the propeller spun free of water.

Higher and higher the skiff raised. Up. Up. Up. Higher. Higher! It seemed they would never stop.

Suddenly Tommy felt himself falling forward. He held Kathy tighter, protecting her with his own body. He braced for the thunderous crash of millions of tons of salt water which would crush them both, and splinter their skiff and pram.

But the crash *didn't* come! Instead, the skiff abruptly lurched. It tilted, stern down. It dropped abruptly, swiftly, as though in a falling elevator. Down. Down. Down...so fast Tommy felt his ears pop and his heart leap into his throat.

Gallons of frothy water poured over the stern into the skiff. The boat's propeller suddenly bit into solid water. The skiff leaped forward again.

Stunned, Tommy looked around in amazement.

The tidal wave had passed them! It *hadn't* sunk them!

But—How? Why?...

And then he knew: The tidal wave had occurred in deep water. It had not crested like a wave crashing on the beach. Instead, it was a great, rolling movement in the water, a massive, one or two mile-long, wind-blown tidal surge, and they had miraculously ridden up, and over it like a tiny stick.

Kathy's trailing pram, now filled with water, had kept the skiff's stern from swinging around.

Without that wonderful drag from her beautiful little pram they would have rolled over in a broach. They both would have been drowned by millions of tons of water!

Kathy's pram had saved their lives!

"Thank You, God," Tommy breathed, crying softly. "Thank You!"

Fifteen minutes later Kathy paused in her frantic bailing. She pointed off the port bow.

"Tommy. Is—that land over there?"

Tommy shaded his eyes against the driven rain.

"Yes! It *is* land!" He shouted excitedly. He smiled as he saw the long, gray outline of Conimicut Point. The view filled him with joy. Giddy, laughing and crying, he thanked God, tears of gratitude running down his cheeks.

Straining to see ahead in the drenching, wind-driven rain, he could barely make out Ben Brown's great house. But the seawall was gone. It had been destroyed.

Tommy stood up briefly, refusing to believe the great wall had been destroyed. No, Mr. Brown's seawall was still standing. It was mostly covered by the flood and leaping waves, but was still a mighty bulwark against the fury of Hurricane Glenna.

Great, white plumes of spray shot thirty feet into the air as the incoming surf pounded mercilessly against the hidden wall. Again and again the water geysered up, then fell, as though in slow motion. Even higher geysers appeared at Conimicut Lighthouse to the right, and at the high seawall and rocks at Nayatt Point, further on the right.

Tommy saw the entire Conimicut Point area was now completely covered by the boiling sea, so Ben Brown's great house seemed to be resting in the ocean.

It was then he realized that most of the other houses on the Point, smaller summer cottages, were smashed, many gone, floated off their foundations and destroyed by the wind and tidal wave of Hurricane Glenna.

Several brick chimneys remained, gaunt reminders of Glenna's visit.

Cautiously, Tommy brought his skiff closer to land. No, they couldn't go around the Point as he had thought. It was too dangerous. The underwater sandbar was building up monstrous ten and twelve-foot waves that crested and slammed down, churning the entire Point area into a frothy, swirling nightmare.

It was impossible for them to make it around the Point. Somehow, they had to land on the windward side. But that also was suicide.

They were now several hundred feet off shore, closer to the big, three-story house.

Varying his motor speed, Tommy anxiously searched for a low spot where the water did not leap as high into the sky as it hit rocks or the top of Ben Brown's seawall. A low spot meant deeper water.

He finally saw a place on his left, close to the old house. But could they make it? Or would the raging wind behind them, and the leaping seas all about them, smash them against hidden rocks, killing them?

He had no choice. He had to try...

"Hold very tight, Kathy," he cried and gunned the motor. He quickly turned the skiff into the fierce southerly wind, almost capsizing in the process. He held his position until the trailing pram was astern of him. The skiff's bow leaped and pounded sickeningly with each passing wave.

For several seconds he recalled everything he had studied in Chapman's book on surf seamanship. It would be impossible to go in bow first. Those waves would whip his stern around and roll them over, or else smash them against the house or submerged seawall.

No, he would have to keep control of the skiff. But how?

Like it or not, he had to go in stern first. —And pray!

Maintaining just enough forward speed to keep the skiff's bow into the wind and oncoming sea, Tommy let the waves and wind steadily push both boats backward, closer to the house. As a huge wave approached, suddenly lifting them high, he speeded up the motor, then suddenly slowed it as the wave passed them.

Each time the skiff streaked down into a trough, white water splashed from under the skiff's bow. It was seized by the wind, drenching them, but most of it falling astern of them.

Faster and slower he varied the motor speed. All the while the wind and waves steadily inched them closer to the west side of the old house. Now they were fifty feet away. Now, forty...

Kathy watched, terrified, yet fascinated, unable to tear her eyes from the boiling scene. Each time a new wave approached, she winced momentarily, but she didn't close her eyes.

Now they were twenty feet away... Now ten... five...

"Help us. Protect us!" Tommy prayed aloud.

After several seconds of panic, he saw they were going to make it. The skiff moved closer to the big house. He could see the curtains inside. Maybe Mr. Brown was watching them. The skiff moved still closer.

Suddenly the outboard motor screamed as the churning propeller hit a hidden rock or the seawall. The shear pin had broken! The motor was useless!

The wind and waves seized the small skiff and swung it around, jerking and bobbing it violently. They were trapped, helpless in a trough!

Kathy screamed as the skiff rolled dangerously close to capsizing. They were being pulled past the old house, back into the raging sea. They were helpless!

"No!" Tommy cried. No, no, no!"

Suddenly a voice called out loud and clear. Looking up, Tommy saw Ben Brown in the upstairs west window. The old man leaned out and flung a line .

But the throw was too high, the line too far away. There was no time for a second chance. They were doomed!

But Tommy hadn't counted on the wind, whereas the old man had. The line whipped and lashed toward them like a thing alive. It was Kathy in the skiff's bow who caught it. She passed it to Tommy and quickly moved out of his way.

Gasping, Tommy hurriedly looped the line around the skiff's bow cleat, cinching it, and the two boats abruptly jerked to a stop, then swung in toward the house. They slammed hard against the front porch.

Moving swiftly, Tommy made the line tight to the railing. He helped Kathy on to the first-floor porch, now fully awash with foam, bits of debris, grass and scum.

Kathy clung to the porch railing, sobbing in relief. "Oh, God, thank You, God. Thank You..."

The front door opened and Ben Brown waded out, joining them. He helped Tommy secure both boats to the porch columns. They were in the lee of the house, and safe. As safe as anything else.

Tommy stared gratefully at the old man. For several moments he hugged him tight. They had made it! It was a miracle. They had made it!

Still without speaking a word, Ben Brown helped them inside the house. He pushed the heavy oak door closed against the storm. Tommy dropped to the floor beside Kathy, exhausted.

"We're safe," he choked. "We're safe!"

The old man nodded and finally spoke. "Yep, Tommy, Kathy. You're safe. So long as my old house holds together."

He sighed wearily, and helped both of them to their feet. His ruddy face seemed ancient, so tired and defeated.

"—Just as long as she holds together..."

Chapter 17

Trapped In The Island House

(The Second Tidal Wave!)

Ben Brown helped them into the kitchen where he had hot coffee on the gas stove.

The electricity had failed, and the light of several kerosene lamps filled the darkened room with eerie shadows that darted about each time the great house shuddered in sudden blasts of wind. The north windows were open, Tommy noted, and wondered why.

Ben Brown poured the hot, black coffee into them, insisting they drink it. Trembling from cold and exposure, they obeyed willingly.

Inside the old house was cold and drafty. The water had risen so some of it was now bubbling under the first-floor door. It streamed across the polished oak floors.

Tommy watched it, fascinated.

After Ben Brown lighted the gas oven, he closed the north window and soon the small kitchen warmed. The heat was welcome and most comforting. Ben Brown insisted they both strip off their wet clothes.

Noting Kathy's concern, he handed her a blanket and directed her into the pantry adjoining the kitchen.

"Take off everything," he ordered. He waited until the door closed, then faced Tommy.

"You too, Son." He draped a blanket over Tommy's shoulders.

A few minutes later Kathy returned to the kitchen, her face flushed. She gave her dripping clothes to the old man.

He rinsed them in fresh water, then wrung them out and hung them on the back of a chair which he placed close to the open oven door. He did the same with Tommy's clothes.

Soon the warmth and hot coffee did their work. The curl slowly returned to Kathy's hair. Her cheeks colored. A faint smile found her lips. Suddenly she made a gasping sound in her throat.

"Oh! My folks. They'll be worried sick. I've got to go home."

The old man shook his head. "Sorry, Kathy, but you ain't goin' anyplace with this hurricane outside. Not for quite a spell. We're surrounded by floodwater, ten, twelve feet deep. Maybe more. I'm sorry."

"But— Oh, what will I do? They must be terribly worried!"

Tommy's thoughts turned to Granny Parker. She'd be worried too. He listened to the howling wind outside, the incessant drumming of rain against the windows, and was suddenly afraid for Granny Parker's safety.

If the water was this high here at Conimicut Point—over ten feet above normal high tide—it must be over Granny's seawall. Maybe it was even inside her house!

A horrible feeling of desolation filled him.

"Granny!" he cried. "I've got to find out if she's all right." He got up, clutching at the blanket.

"Do you have a telephone? Is it still working?"

Kathy also leaped up, almost losing her blanket and her modesty. She seized the edges and wrapped them tightly around her.

"Where's your 'phone?" she asked. "I'll call home and have Daddy check Granny Parker."

The old man led them into the parlor. It was a huge room facing south, and completely empty of furniture. It was very cold, damp and drafty, and Tommy saw the west windows were slightly open. Other windows looked like they were broken. He saw the telephone was on the windowsill.

"W-Water," Kathy gasped. "On the floor."

The old man looked at the inch of water covering the oak floor. He shrugged.

"Nothing I can do about that now," he said sadly.

"But where's all your furniture?" Tommy asked him.

"Upstairs. Everything I could carry."

Kathy seized the telephone and waited a full three minutes for a dial tone. She grinned triumphantly as she dialed. She waited. The line was busy. She hung up, biting on her lower lip, deeply worried. She dialed again. Still busy.

A third time she dialed. She heard the telephone ringing. No answer. She let it ring, silently praying her folks were home. At the seventh ring, the telephone clicked.

"Mommy? Oh, Mommy! Mommy... It's me, Kathy. I'm all right. Tommy is with me. He's all right too. Is Granny Parker all right? She's with you? Oh, that's good. Yes. Yes..."

For five minutes she talked on the black, rotary telephone, explaining, apologizing for both her and Tommy, answering and asking many questions. She saw Tommy was waiting anxiously.

"Mommy. Let Granny Parker talk, will you? Tommy wants to talk to her."

For several heartbeats Tommy stared at the telephone. What could he say to her? He felt ashamed for what he had done. He was grateful she was all right. What could he say? He heard the thin, tremulous voice:

"...Hello. Hello, Tommy. Is that you?..."

Swallowing painfully, Tommy felt himself filling up. Uncontrolled tears coursed down his cheeks. His voice choked.

"G-Granny? You're all right? Oh, I was so worried. Yes, I'm okay. We're in Ben Brown's house on Conimicut Point... No, we can't get home... Not yet. We're—cut off from the mainland... Yes, Mr. Brown says the house is safe... It's been through five or six bad hurricanes... Oh, Granny. Granny... I'm sorry."

He talked for several minutes more, then gave the telephone back to Kathy. In her excitement, her blanket slipped briefly off her right shoulder and Tommy saw that Kathy was a woman, undeniably a woman.

Embarrassed, he glanced away, angry at himself for looking, but at the same time strangely and secretly pleased.

"Oh, I feel so much better now," Kathy said as she finally hung up. "I wanted to talk more, but the operator said to limit the call. It seems everyone is checking on friends, and they don't know how long the telephone lines will continue to work."

Back in the kitchen Kathy haltingly told them what her father had told her: Hurricane Glenna had almost reached its full fury. In another hour or so the 130-135-miles-per-hour sustained winds would hit the state.

Her father had told her Hurricane Glenna's eye was expected to hit west of Rhode Island, the worst possible location for the Ocean State.

The meteorologist on her father's portable radio also said Glenna's vicious southerly winds averaged 135 miles per hour, with gusts up to 157 miles per hour. He said Glenna was blowing the Atlantic Ocean directly up Narragansett Bay, producing an incredibly massive storm surge, over 18½ feet.

Glenna was a huge storm, class five, and it was now racing forward at sixty miles an hour, directly toward southern Connecticut.

Many Providence streets were already flooded with well-over eight feet of water, her father had said, with more flooding expected. Trees were uprooted everywhere. No one had power or lights.

The police had blocked off all severely vulnerable areas such as Conimicut Village, Riverside, Oakland Beach, and others. They had evacuated just about everyone who would go before the storm hit...

"Why didn't you go?" Kathy asked Ben Brown.

The old man shrugged, avoiding her curious eyes.

"Leave my home?" he said finally. "Never! Too many things to do. I've been through five or six bad hurricanes here. I couldn't run away and leave. I'd be wonderin' what happened to you and—" His wrinkled face darkened and he rubbed his nose. Kathy moved closer to him, staring up into his eyes.

"Me? —And Tommy? You—saw us? You *knew* we were out there?"

The old man nodded gently. " 'Taint much I miss with these old eyes and my binoculars." He glanced at Tommy, explaining.

"They're night glasses, Tom. When I can't sleep, I spend a lot of time at my east window. I recognized your skiff in the moonlight. And early this mornin' I saw Kathy's sailin' dinghy headin' south.

"'Course, I didn't know about Glenna's sudden speed-up and change in course, and when I did learn about it, it was too late to do anything about you kids. Except wait. I figured maybe you'd stay on the island."

"But why didn't you call my folks and tell them?" Kathy

cried.

"And Granny Parker, too."

The old man sighed and examined his work-creased hands. "I thought of that, young one. Many times..." He glanced up.

"But you tell me what good it would have done? They would have been worried half to death knowin' for sure you two were caught out in a boat in the middle of a hurricane. By not tellin', they could only guess."

He sighed deeply, and was thoughtful for several moments. Finally, he glanced at them both.

"—So I waited for you to come back. I kept that line by my side just waitin' and prayin'."

He grinned widely. Now, I'm right glad I did."

"And so am I." Kathy flung her arms around the old man's leathery neck and loudly kissed him on the cheek. She clutched at her blanket, flushing.

Tommy's face was blood-red.

Ben Brown grinned at him. "'Guess maybe you two better get dressed before we have another accident."

He felt their clothes hanging on the back of chairs. "Yep. Guess they're dry enough for wearin'."

His clothes were slightly damp, but Tommy was glad to put them on and get rid of that treacherous and itchy blanket. When Kathy joined them, she had combed her hair. It was filled with russet highlights.

Talking in hushed whispers, peeking out windows and sipping coffee, the three friends waited out the hurricane in the warm kitchen.

Kathy suddenly pointed. "Water! Look. It's pouring under the closed door!"

Ben Brown nodded as if he had expected the water. "Uh huh."

"But aren't you worried?" Tommy asked him. "Outside, the water's still rising. It must be."

Ben glanced out the east window toward the Point. "It is still rising. And I'm mighty worried, if that helps any. But I kind of expected this."

"But—The water's coming inside the house!" Kathy cried, her eyes saucer-wide in fear.

"We'll be drowned!"

"No we won't! When it gets deep, we'll go upstairs," the old man assured her.

"But— But—" Tommy faltered.

"—Eh?"

"—Will the house hold together?" Tommy managed to say.

"I surely hope so. She took that giant tidal wave a-wile back."

Tommy paused, thoughtful, then said, "But—You don't *know*?"

"No. No one knows, Tommy. You just got to *believe* it will. You must have faith!"

"Oh!—" What else could he possibly say? Tommy drew a deep breath.

"But how come your house hasn't floated away like so many of the other houses on the Point, the little summer homes?" he asked in a small voice.

The old man winked. "Maybe 'cause I don't fight the sea. My home is bolted to the heavy cement foundation, and everything is strongly reinforced. Besides—"

He seemed to be taking special pleasure in explaining his foresight.

"—Besides, the cellar foundation has two huge breaks on the south and north sides. You remember that lattice-work for my roses?"

Tommy nodded, and the old man continued: "Behind that lattice are six large cellar windows. Before Glenna came I removed them all, and the other six windows on the north end. The sea is goin' right through my cellar and out the other side, sort of like a big bridge. An' like those five stilt houses on steel poles just west of us."

He grinned. "Works pretty good, so far, wouldn't you say?"

For several minutes Tommy was thoughtful. Finally, he said, "But the water is higher now. It's hitting the back wall of the house. Hear it? What are you going to do to stop it from coming in?"

"Yes," Kathy cried, chewing on her lower lip.

"I'm not doin' anything. I'm lettin' it come in if it wants to. A lot of it already did come in...in and out again when that giant wave hit a while back. It did a lot of damage, but my house is still standing!"

The two young people gasped. They looked at each other, then at the old man in stunned silence...

The water on the kitchen floor was now over three inches deep and still rising. Kathy stared at it bubbling under the closed kitchen door, fascinated, horrified.

The old man saw her growing fear and slowly got up from his chair. He blew out the two kerosene lamps and stored them atop the high cupboard.

"Guess we better leave now." He shut off the gas main behind the stove. He stacked the two kitchen chairs, motioning Tommy to do the same. "We'll bring these five chairs upstairs with us."

When Ben brown opened the door leading to the parlor, a foot-high wall of water rolled in, increasing the level five more inches.

Fearfully, Tommy and Kathy looked around the big room, appalled at the eight to ten inches of salt water covering the entire downstairs floor area.

Again Tommy noticed the broken windows on the south side of the room. He saw all the wallpaper was still wet, even torn off the walls in places. The south parlor had already been flooded.

"Well, let's go." The old man splashed toward the stairway. He went through the parlor and upstairs with the chairs. When he returned, he took Kathy's chair. Tommy followed him with his two chairs.

"What about the table?" Tommy asked, amazed at the old man's calmness.

"She's okay. She's old and strong. Salt water won't hurt much."

Ben Brown beckoned to Kathy who was staring at the water on the oak floors. Salt water didn't belong in houses!

Outside, the wind was howling and shrieking, shouting defiance. Wave after thunderous wave pounded against the south side of the old house, trembling it. The noise was terrifying: the repeated poundings of a massive giant seeking admission.

"You stay on the stairs, Kathy," Ben Brown ordered. "Tommy, you help me." He paused at one south window, looked sadly at it, and suddenly raised his foot and kicked out the glass.

The hurricane wind and rain roared in. Kathy screamed.

"It's all right," the old man yelled over the wind. "You stay there. The windows are nailed shut. I forgot to remove them."

He motioned Tommy to do the same with the other south windows facing the hurricane. Tommy did, and the hurricane wind and water streaked in, loud and fierce.

The giant was now inside the house!

Outside, the waves were half-way up to the windowsills, foam and debris sloshing over the oak sills. The thick foam was an ugly yellow-gray color.

As Tommy watched in amazement, the old man hurried through the downstairs rooms, opening all doors and windows, including the heavy back door facing north.

Out of breath, he rejoined them in the parlor. His wrinkled face was weary and flushed, and a tragic sadness showed in his deep blue eyes.

"One final door!" he said. He pointed to the huge mahogany door facing south, the one being incessantly pounded by waves seeking to enter the house.

"You better get up on the stairs too, Tommy. This one's goin' to be messy."

Obeying, Tommy splashed through the knee-deep water covered with a floating film of yellow scum, bits of eelgrass, wallpaper, sticks and seaweed. He and Kathy watched from halfway up the stairs. Kathy moved closer to him and clutched on to his hand.

They watched as Ben Brown moved closer to the door. He paused behind the heavy door, his right hand on the knob. Outside, the waves pounded incessantly, shaking the door in fury, cursing in thunderous wave after wave.

The old man suddenly threw the bolt, turned the handle, and leaped away. The heavy door swung open instantly. A monstrous wall of white water spewed through the opening. Kathy screamed, terrified.

Ben Brown splashed his way to the stairs. Within seconds, the water level in the room rose another foot to two feet, then to three feet. Water continued to stream through the open doorway. Kathy hid her eyes and sobbed piteously as Tommy tried to comfort her.

The water rose still another foot...then six inches. It seemed to taper off. The horrible pounding noise lessened...

Sitting beside Tommy on the stairs, Ben Brown puffed out his cheeks and exhaled.

"Whew! Come all of a sudden, didn't she?" He touched Kathy on the shoulder and she slowly looked around at him.

"It's all right now, Missie. See?" He pointed below. "The sea's runnin' right through my house—in one way and out the other. It's all right." His voice was gentle, soothing.

Tommy stared in fascination. The water was coming in easier now. It bubbled only with each great wave entering the house. White water occasionally splashed through the open windows. Below his feet, the water lapped at the seventh step.

The house looked a wreck, but Ben Brown kept insisting everything was all right. It had been like this before. It and the sea were old and familiar acquaintances.

After several minutes, the old man beckoned them upstairs among the clutter and jumble of his hastily-stored furniture and possessions. For five minutes they moved furniture about, making a path to all the many second-floor windows.

The high, isolated house gave them a perfect vantage point throughout all four points of the compass. From the upstairs second and third-floor windows they saw a horribly mutilated world...

All of Conimicut Point was under water. Shawomet Avenue was a sea as far northwest as Symonds Avenue, a half-mile inland. Old Mill Cove had vanished. In its place was a huge, strange sea. Southwest of them stood Marshall's Mansion, another island house, once again inundated by the hurricane sea.

Those five stilt-houses, so odd and ungainly in normal times, stood one or two feet higher than the slashing waves, safe and protected, as the storm seas rushed under them.

The sky was lighter now, and the rain had diminished somewhat, improving visibility. Hurricane Glenna's winds were at their worst, and the flood waters at their highest. All around was destruction, and directly below them the sea was a twisting, tormented thing.

As they watched, they saw many smashed boats float by, furniture, a chair, a sofa, a bathtub with a gray cat in it floating high and ridiculous. They saw personal possessions and clothes. Great parts of peoples' homes swept past Conimicut Point, heading north, and even entire floating houses, completely intact. The sights were terrifying...

As they stared, helpless, a huge white house floated closer, from the south. The storm tides steadily moved it toward Conimicut Point where it suddenly shuddered as it struck the hidden sandbar. Within minutes the huge waves slammed at it, and a man's lifetime dream disintegrated into timbers and scrap lumber.

"Oh, no..." Kathy gasped and turned away. It was a horrible thing to see. Kathy couldn't bear to look anymore. She sat numbly on the bed.

Later, Tommy saw several more human bodies floating by. He said nothing to Kathy. When he privately informed the old man, Ben nodded solemnly.

"You did right, Son. Don't say anything to her. She's scared enough already."

Boat after broken boat floated by, torn from their moorings, propelled by the vicious southerly hurricane winds, their sides stove in. Through Ben Brown's binoculars Tommy saw other boats splinter into kindling against the underwater rocks southeast of the house.

Several great trees floated north, toward Providence, their roots leading, like huge battering rams. One struck a small yellow cottage caught on the sandbar. Pushed by the wind and great tidal surge, the tree plowed through the house walls, carrying the impaled house further north and west into Occupasstuxet Cove, a mile and a half away.

The view north was appalling. Green's Island was gone, and so was Mark Rock, and several hundred feet of the eastern tip of Gaspee Point.

Using Ben Brown's binoculars, Tommy saw Occupasstuxet Cove had turned into a huge bottleneck, a dumping place for destroyed homes, boats, debris, poles, docks and trees.

It was a sickening, awesome sight.

Tommy swept the glasses closer, along the west shore of Narragansett bay toward home. He saw Pete Bender's house. The leaping waves had steadily nibbled at the green lawn, undermining the Bender's porch so it now hung free, fifteen feet above the water. Jenison's strong dock was gone.

Looking closer through the glasses, Tommy could see Granny Parker's back yard was a cluttered, debris-strewn beach. The seawall he had worked so hard to repair was now several feet under water. He hoped it hadn't collapsed from the force of the waves and undertow.

His heart thumping in his chest, he saw the water was almost up to Granny's back porch, over 12-15 feet above mean high tide. He was deeply grateful Granny was with the Turners and safe. If she had stayed home, the determined old lady probably would have tried to fight the encroaching hurricane seas as her own personal enemy.

He let his gaze drop to Kathy's house. Her back yard was also a tangled beach, but the water was still, several yards away from the high cellar foundation of the house.

Still closer, he saw great caverns in the manicured lawns of those seaside homes that did not have a high, protective seawall. Tons of rich topsoil had eroded within hours into the turbulent sea.

As he watched, a huge, crescent-shaped slice of lawn and loam crumbled and dissolved into the yellow water. Immediately, new waves rushed in to nibble hungrily at the unprotected land, and another massive crescent toppled into the angry sea.

Feeling slightly ill, Tommy sat back on his legs, thoughtful.

Kathy knelt at the window beside him. He gave her the binoculars. For several minutes he watched her, noting the horrified expression on her pretty face. Kathy put the glasses down. There were tears in her dark eyes.

"It's—awful. I can't look. It's too awful," she choked...

Further north, beyond their range of vision, the rapidly-rising ocean water backed up into sewer lines. Salt water spewed from catchbasins and flooded downtown Providence streets, eventually increasing to well-over 14.5-feet of ocean water!

The crashing force of the earlier tidal wave had destroyed great parts of Providence's proud Hurricane Barrier, but sections of it still stood, and that was later credited by city fathers with saving the city.

The massive tidal wave, pushing tons of debris, smashed homes and boats, uprooted trees, telephone poles, bollards and kidnapped docks, had slammed directly into the Hurricane Barrier and its crescent of piled rocks, destroying most of it.

The great wave then socked its fist into the Point Street Bridge—also at right angles to the wind and waves—knocking the black steel structure and its roadway into the flooded Providence River below.

The savage force of the incredible 137-MPH sustained winds,

combined with the mile-long tidal wave with its millions of tons of wind-driven water and debris, then smashed into the slender upright columns of the Route 195 Providence River overpass, destroying them.

Without full support, the heavy steel, cement and macadam roadway of Route 195 toppled down into the flooded Providence River, parallel to the destroyed Point Street Bridge and Providence Hurricane Barrier.

Later, *Providence Journal-Bulletin* news articles would state, "This natural catastrophe cut the proud winding ribbon of Route 95's great National Highway for the first time in its history."

It would take many months to rebuild it.

Nearby India Point Park, just being built, and the Point Street overpass area became boiling lakes.

In a great rolling, destructive, wind-blown wall of water, the following ocean surge streamed up Narragansett Bay, up into the neck of the funnel that led to Providence, Rhode Island. The massive surge with its tons of floating debris slammed into, over and around the smashed Hurricane Barrier, damaging it still further.

The tidal surge boiled over the Crawford Street Bridge, the widest in the world. It raced over the flooded highways, ripping, tearing, smashing, pounding everything in its path.

It crashed into automobiles, overturning them like toys.

The wind-driven ocean water streamed over parked cars, flooding them, short-circuiting their batteries, causing their headlights to come on and their horns to cry piteously for help, until the batteries finally died.

The vicious flood waters chased workers to the second floors of buildings, trapping many for days. It rolled department store goods into a jumbled, useless mess. It flooded downtown businesses and banks, stores and homes, smashing, slamming, crushing, drowning...

Throughout Rhode Island, Hurricane Glenna's Class-5 winds uprooted thousands of trees, slamming them down on homes, on cars, on people. It tore homes apart. The sudden drop in air pressure exploded tightly-sealed homes, leveling them as swiftly as a bomb.

And that was why Ben Brown had kept his house windows

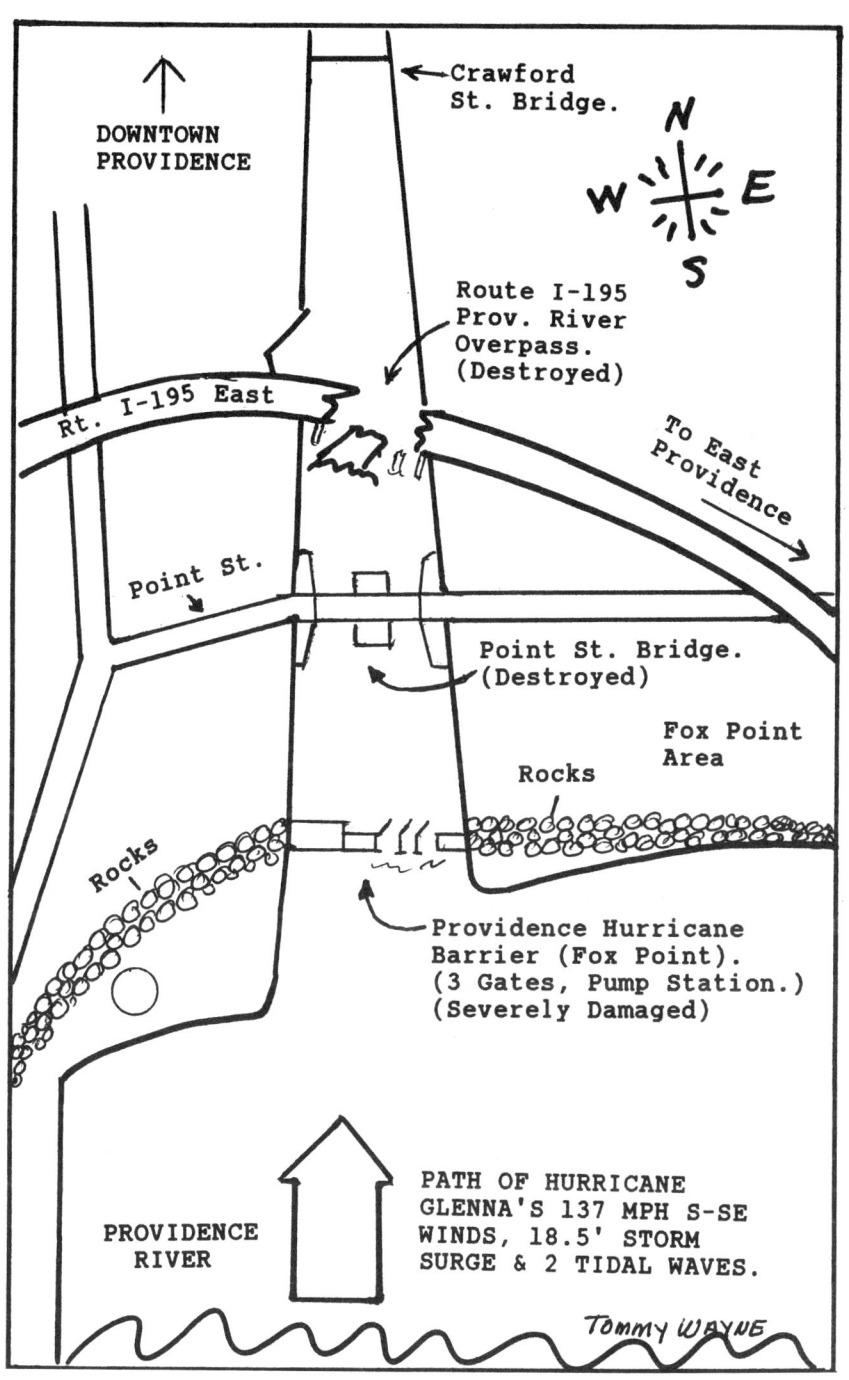

City of Providence Area: Hurricane Dam, Point Street Bridge,
Route I-195 Providence River Overpass

open, Tommy realized. To prevent air pressure explosion.

All along the shore-front, boats snapped their mooring lines. They plowed into other boats, and the entire mess was finally thrown high and jumbled on the shore, like so many child's toys strewn about.

Great docks broke up, the timbers tossed about by leaping waves, becoming massive javelins, impaling boats and shore-front homes and buildings.

There was nothing anybody could do. The entire state, and most of Connecticut and parts of nearby Massachusetts, and every person therein, was at the impartial destruction of the shrieking hurricane winds and violent seas.

And why?

Because, at long last, that capricious lady, Hurricane Glenna, had made up her mind: She had decided to visit Rhode Island!

"Oh, it's horrible," Kathy cried. "Horrible!"

From the northwest window on the other side of the house, Tommy saw most of the summer cottages dotting Conimicut Point were gone. Only their chimneys remained, like giant tombstones, pointing bleakly to the sky.

By cramming his neck, Tommy saw his skiff below the flat porch roof. He was grateful it was still safe, although more than half-filled with water and debris. He wished he had thought to bring in his outboard motor and gear. He hoped the skiff's timbers continued to have enough natural flotation to prevent his boat from sinking, drowning his motor.

He saw Kathy's pram tugging obstinately at its bow line fastened to the skiff's stern. It was now almost completely filled with water, but seemed all right otherwise. He wasn't sure because the distance was too far, but the pram's bowline seemed frayed where it had rubbed on the skiff's transom.

Well, he needn't mention that to Kathy. She'd only worry about it. He'd check it when he got the binoculars back from Kathy.

Tired of standing, he knelt at the second floor window. He winced in pain as his knee cut into something. It was a coil of rope. For several seconds he wondered what it was doing there on the floor. He moved it aside.

And then he remembered: Ben Brown had told them he had carried lengths of line with him while he was waiting for their return. And it was a good thing he had, too. Otherwise, he and Kathy would— Brrr. Tommy shuddered at the thought.

Kathy joined him at the window, kneeling beside him and peering out. Her small face was white and bloodless. Her eyes seemed huge and dark. He slipped his arm around her, holding her protectively, and she leaned slightly against him.

"It shouldn't last too much longer," he said, hoping he was right. He felt her trembling and desperately wished he could say something more comforting. Instead, he held her closer, saying nothing...

They heard Ben Brown yelling from the south room: "Tommy! Kathy! Come here. Hurry!"

They glanced at each other and jumped up. Tommy was suddenly conscious of heavy rain slamming on the old roof. The screaming wind shook the house vengefully.

Tommy seized Kathy's hand, and ran with her into the south bedroom. Ben Brown was gesturing frantically toward the window.

"What is it?" Kathy cried.

Tommy ran beside the old man, to the window overlooking the southern part of Narragansett Bay. He looked out. His voice strangled in his throat.

Several hundred yards away the whole southern sea was one massive, continuous, rolling, churning, black wall of water racing toward them. It seemed a thousand miles high!

"Oh, no!" Tommy cried. "No!"

Kathy, beside him, screamed in terror.

"It's a second tidal wave!" Ben Brown cried. "God, protect us!"

Chapter 18

Kathy Falls Into The Hurricane Sea!

Petrified, the three friends watched the tidal wave approaching. Within seconds it towered high above them. Ben Brown suddenly seized them both and pulled them to the floor.

The huge wave's leading edge slammed against the hidden seawall. Spray and foam shot high into the air.

The violent wind caught it and flung it against the house, smashing the upstairs windows, like so many rocks. Kathy screamed.

A second later the monstrous wave hit. The house shrieked in pain, like a thing alive. It jumped and lurched sickeningly as the solid mass of dirty green water poured through the downstairs windows and open doors, flooding every downstairs room in the house.

At the same time a solid mass of white water streamed through the broken upstairs windows. It violently rolled Tommy, Kathy and Ben Brown across the floor and slammed them against the opposite wall.

Several moments later the crushing water level dropped, then raced across the floors and fled downstairs in a hundred massive, cascading waterfalls.

As suddenly as it had appeared, the great wave moved on. The remaining water rolled and rumbled downstairs and out the open doors and windows, back into the frothy sea, rushing toward Providence...

The south windows on both floors were smashed completely. The casements were gone from most of them.

Silence!

It was Ben Brown who first moaned and moved. Painfully, he struggled to his feet. He carefully checked Tommy and Kathy. He saw they were drenched, dazed, cut a bit and bruised, but they too seemed okay! Incredible!

He slowly helped them to their feet, talking gently, reassuringly. He kept patting their backs to help them cough up swallowed salt water.

A few minutes later the three survivors gazed around the room, unbelieving.

A great, gay grin suddenly split the old man's tired face.

"She held, by golly!" he cried. "Thank the good Lord, my old house did hold together!" He laughed shrilly in delight.

Or was it relief?

Tommy didn't know which, and he didn't care either. He also began laughing.

Joyous, relieved tears rolled down his wet cheeks as he hugged Kathy.

She stared at him, then at the old man as if they both had gone stark, raving mad.

"Don't you see, Kathy, we're safe!" Ben Brown explained. He danced Kathy around the room, still covered with several patches of salt water, seaweed, reeds, broken glass and debris.

"The wind and the sea have done their worst, Kathy. We're safe!"

Puffing, the old man sat on the edge of the bed, also soaked. He fumbled in his pockets for his pipe and tobacco. The tobacco was wet; the matches useless. Shrugging, he sucked at his pipe, sea water dripping from his chin, a serene expression on his gentle face.

"Yes... God is good. God is *very* good!"

Tommy smiled secretly. He had never heard a more eloquent prayer in his life.

"Amen to that," he added softly.

While the old man walked about checking his house and possessions for damage, Tommy and Kathy examined themselves and each other for cuts and bruises. Some minor injuries were sore, but none really serious. It was a miracle!

Together they looked out the different windows to check the storm's progress. Tommy wasn't sure, but the water seemed to have stopped rising.

On the stairs, they counted the steps down to the ocean water inside the house. Despite the great flood from the tidal wave of several minutes ago, the actual water level hadn't risen above the fourth step from the top. Tommy grinned triumphantly.

"It's stopped rising, Kathy." His words were almost a benediction.

He saw Kathy finally understood his meaning. Despite being soaked and bruised, her hair plastered to her head, Kathy's relieved smile was the most beautiful he had ever seen.

He hugged her tight. She was safe!

Together they walked about the second floor rooms, around cluttered, wet furniture, looking out different windows.

From the corner window overlooking the north porch they saw piles of driftwood and broken boats on the highest points of land.

There was something strange about them, Tommy thought. And then he knew!

"They're not *moving!*" he cried loudly. "The water's *receding*, Kathy! It's going down." He had to tell Ben Brown.

"Be right back." He left Kathy at the northwest window and hurried to tell the good news to the old man.

"That's wonderful!" Ben Brown said, and puffed at his dead pipe. For a few seconds he gazed around at the cluttered bedroom, at the shiny, damp oak floors, the soaked furniture, the wet and stained wallpaper, much of it torn off the walls. His lips moved silently and tears were streaming down his lined cheeks.

He was praying, thanking God, Tommy realized. He said nothing.

The old man finally sighed and shook his head. "I have a whole winter's work ahead of me rightin' things, Tommy."

Tommy greatly admired and loved the old man. He was unbeatable!

"I'd like to help you, Sir," he said. "But I—don't think I can. I might be going away."

Afraid to elaborate for fear he would break into tears, Tommy returned to the northwest room and Kathy.

But Kathy wasn't at the window!

Tommy looked for her, calling her name, checking adjoining rooms. She wasn't there either. Very concerned, he called louder.

Finally, he ran back and told Ben Brown Kathy was missing.

They both searched for her.

But Kathy had vanished!

"She has to be here someplace!" Tommy cried. He looked into closets, under furniture, even downstairs, although the water was still many feet deep.

Acutely concerned, he returned to the second floor northwest window where he had last seen her. Joining him, the old man shook his head. Tommy was suddenly very afraid.

"But where is she?" he cried. After all they had gone through together, Kathy couldn't be hurt or—missing now. The thought of anything more serious sent an icy tremor through him.

"Kathy! Kathy!" he yelled. "Where are you?"

He heard only the shrieking of the wind, the pounding of the waves...

Then he heard something different. It was Kathy's voice, and she was calling his name. She seemed very far away.

He looked at the old man. Together, they ran to the open window.

"Oh, no!" Tommy gasped. Kathy was outside in the hurricane. She had crawled out on the near-flat roof of the back porch and had somehow worked her way down the column into his half-sunken skiff. She was struggling with the bow line holding her sunken pram.

Kathy also had noticed the frayed line, and now she was risking her young life to save her beloved sailboat.

She called again. "Help me, Tommy. My boat."

Hurricane winds from Glenna were more from the direct West now. The sea all around was a confused jumble of white-crested peaks and valleys, constantly changing location.

Tommy noted both boats had shifted slightly toward the northwest. His skiff was more than half-filled with water and debris, and Kathy's additional weight in the stern had raised the bow so high the water-logged boat slapped and rolled dangerously with each oncoming wave.

But Kathy was too intent on securing her pram to realize her own danger.

"I've got to help her," Tommy cried and climbed out the window. The violent wind jerked him down to his hands and knees. Ben Brown caught his arm and pulled him back. Tommy tried to pull away.

"Let me go. I've got to help her!"

"Wait!" The old man held him tight with his strong right arm while he picked up the coil of anchor line from the floor.

"Tie this around you first," he ordered.

Tommy slipped the line around his waist and tied the fastest bowline knot of his life.

He again climbed out the window and, this time huddled low against the driving westerly wind, he worked his way along the slippery roof.

A strong wind gust caught him and knocked him off balance. He rolled several feet toward the edge of the roof. His arms flailed, fingers caught shingles. For several seconds he lay motionless, momentarily stunned. He heard Ben Brown yelling at him.

"Hurry, Tommy! Kathy fell into the sea!"

Scrambling to his knees, Tommy looked below. Kathy was gone!

"Kathy! Oh, dear God, no! Not Kathy!"

Bitter tears stung his eyes, choking him. He frantically searched the violent, swirling, debris-strewn water. He couldn't see her. She was gone...

His fists clenched until white and numb. His pleading eyes stared at the gray heavens. "Oh, please, Lord..."

Without Kathy, his life was ended. He didn't want to live...

The old man's shout seemed from another world. "Tommy! There she is, beside the house. Hurry. She's going under again!" He pointed almost directly below the window on the *west* side of the house.

But Kathy couldn't be closer to the house, Tommy thought. The old man had to be seeing things. The fierce currents would take Kathy out beyond the two boats, and...

Tommy shaded his eyes against the driving salt-water spray and looked where the old man pointed. He saw a dark object in the water.

Ben Brown was right! Somehow, the fierce, whirlpooling currents had swept Kathy from the north side of the house, around the porch front and into the protected lee of the house on the west. Tommy didn't know how it happened, and he didn't care.

"Thank You, God," he cried.

Without regard for his own safety, he jumped feet first into the water. The swirling black sea swallowed him. It twisted him upside-down. It clawed at him, spun him around.

His lungs bursting for air, he struggled to find the surface, finally breaking through.

Choking and confused, he looked about. He saw Kathy struggling to keep afloat. She was several yards away.

Summoning all his strength, Tommy swam toward her. But the more he swam, the further away she seemed. He realized the strong eddy-currents had caught her and were now sweeping her along, another piece of debris to end up lifeless on Conimicut beach...

Choking, half-blinded from the gray, oily scum, he swam faster, his thoughts intent only upon one thing: to reach Kathy before she vanished forever, another of Glenna's victims!

"Jesus, help me!" he screamed.

His flailing hand suddenly hit something. He looked up into Kathy's terrified face. He seized her by the hair and pulled her closer, then caught her around the waist.

She struggled in panic, pulling them both underwater. He surfaced and screamed her name. She recognized him, and her body relaxed.

He moved behind her and slipped his left arm under her left shoulder and across her chest, his hand gripping her right armpit. He swam with his right arm, kicking furiously, as Ben Brown pulled on the rope, dragging them both back toward the house.

They were a few feet from safety when the force of the water slammed Tommy into the porch railing.

He screamed in pain. His right hand clutched at the porch, holding tight. His left shoulder was afire in agony. He couldn't move another inch.

A few moments later Ben Brown waded out on the porch to help them. The water was up to his upper chest.

He seized them both, pulled them over the railing, and helped them inside the flooded house. On the stairs he briefly checked Tommy who said he was all right, to take care of Kathy.

Ben Brown carried Kathy upstairs. She was crying, a deep, convulsive sound...

A few minutes later, Tommy was able to wearily climb the stairs. He rested on the second floor landing, coughing up sea water.

He untied the line still around his waist, deeply thankful for it. Once again Ben Brown had come to their rescue. Once again the old man's preparedness and quick action had saved both their lives...

He heard Kathy's sobbing. Painfully, he got up and joined them in the near room.

Kathy was violently ill, vomiting swallowed salt water, choking and wheezing. She protested artificial respiration, but the old man insisted.

After several minutes, Ben Brown had worked most of the water from her lungs. She felt slightly better. A tint of color returned to her chalky face. Her eyes lost that hollow, glassy look. Soon she was able to sit up without choking.

Several minutes later she was breathing easier, occasionally coughing, a hacking, convulsive sound. They wrapped her in several reasonably-dry blankets.

"You sure you're all right, Son?" Ben again asked Tommy.

Nodding, Tommy rubbed his painful left shoulder. He had badly bruised it when he had slammed into the porch. He removed his wet shirt and saw the skin was discolored and bloody. The wound was intensely painful. He worked his arm slowly.

"—Nothing broken," he said. "Just cut and sore. It's—all right."

He saw Kathy watching him. Her lips trembled and she suddenly burst into tears.

"I did that... I caused that!"

"No. No, stop it, Kathy," Tommy soothed. He knelt beside her and held her close. He lightly kissed her face and hair. She tasted salty. He silently thanked God for sparing her life.

Without heat, Ben Brown could do little about drying clothes, so he rummaged through bureau drawers for something dry. Tommy dressed in a damp pair of the old man's khaki trousers, several sizes too large, and an old red sport shirt.

They helped Kathy into one of the dry beds on the north side of the house and Ben insisted she undress while under the covers. She did, and her trembling finally subsided as her body warmed.

While still under the covers she put on a pair of khaki trousers and a checkered blue-and-white sport shirt belonging to the old man. She pulled the covers aside and sat on the edge of the bed, momentarily dizzy. Presently, she smiled.

Ben Brown gave her a gaudy, red, polkadotted necktie.

"For a belt," he explained, grinning at her. "That's about all it's good for."

Smiling, Kathy threaded it through the loops and tied it around her slim waist. She rolled the trouser cuffs several times and pulled up the sleeves of her shirt.

When she stood up, Tommy laughed. Kathy made a face at him and smiled warmly.

"You look funny too," she said.

Tommy glanced down at himself and laughed still louder. Kathy joined him.

"Yes, I guess I do," Tommy said.

Their thoughts returned to Hurricane Glenna outside. It seemed quieter; that tremendous, continuing roar was gone. At the windows, they noticed the wind had diminished considerably.

Hurricane Glenna was finally moving further north, toward Canada. Her deadly visit to Rhode Island was ending. She would forever be remembered, but never be mourned.

The old house shuddered less often now, and only in the more severe blasts of wind. The drumming rain had lessened to a heavy drizzle, and the slate sky was brightening in the East.

"Storm's passin'."

Ben Brown spoke without turning from the southeast window. "Glenna's done her worse, an' now she's leavin' us."

Huddled together, their arms around each other, the three friends watched the water recede. It dropped much faster than it had come in. They saw a cellar foundation appear, then a second... a third...

The long brown sandbar of Conimicut Point was now faintly visible under the dark, turbulent sea. The great white lighthouse near its tip still stood proud and defiant atop its base of granite rocks.

The time was near five-thirty o'clock in the afternoon.

The marooned friends moved to the northwest window facing Shawomet Avenue. It didn't look like a street anymore, but they all knew Shawomet Avenue was there under the frothy, dirty water.

Through the binoculars they saw automobiles in the distance, the red-and-blue dome flashers of Warwick Police cruisers, the brilliant red of a Conimicut Village fire engine. They saw people moving about.

Through the binoculars Kathy saw two yellow raincoated and booted policemen pushing a white skiff up the flooded street. As the water deepened, the police got into the boat and started rowing up Shawomet Avenue toward Ben Brown's house, almost a half-mile away.

A great, wide smile brightened Kathy's weary face.

"They're coming!" she cried excitedly, and hugged them both.

"A boat is coming to take us home!"

Chapter 19

The Sweet Happiness Of Reunion

*B*y the time the skiff arrived, the floodwater level was even with the porch floor. The three friends watched excitedly as the policemen guided their boat beside Tommy's partly-sunken skiff and Kathy's pram.

The frayed nylon anchor line hadn't snapped, after all, Tommy noticed happily as he waited for the shorter policeman in the bow to heave him a line.

He caught the tossed line and pulled the boat closer to the house, making the line fast to the porch railing.

The policeman nodded in greeting and stepped aboard the house.

"Everyone here all right?" The taller man glanced curiously at their oversize clothes. He offered no comment. Hurricane Glenna day was a day of make-do and improvisation.

"Yep," Ben Brown said. "There's just the three of us and we're all right."

The policemen entered the old house, their boots clumping loudly. A long, low whistle escaped from one of them.

"Man, you were lucky!" the shorter man said.

"Amen to that," Ben Brown said. His blue eyes were pained as he surveyed the waterlogged downstairs rooms of his cherished home. Strewn about the puddled floors were great mounds of debris, broken glass, silt, mud, seaweed, bits of wood, and long slivers of torn wallpaper.

Several oak floorboards had already swelled and buckled. They would require refitting and nailing. Scattered bits of window-glass were everywhere, making shoes or sneakers essential. Most of the windows were broken or missing, and several casements had been torn out by the force of the two tidal waves and wind.

Sometime during the storm a long, thin oak board had been hurled like a javelin through the inside parlor wall. Its other end protruded eight inches into the kitchen.

Later, Ben Brown would cut off both ends of the board, leaving a foot-long section of wood in his wall, a grisly reminder of Hurricane Glenna's vicious visit.

Tommy gazed around solemnly. The old house would need washing with fresh water, drying, airing, wallpapering, painting, repairing... a thousand tasks. He wished he could stay to help the old man, even for a few weeks. It was the least he could do for the man who had saved their lives.

But those two men from the Children's' Home were probably still waiting to take him back. And if Hurricane Glenna had prevented their arrival, they would probably come tomorrow or Monday.

Now that the danger of Glenna had passed, the thought of leaving the seashore and Kathy was uppermost on Tommy's mind. It filled him with a growing dread and choking desperation.

"—Yes. You all were mighty lucky," the short policeman repeated. "Most of the houses on the southern shore of Conimicut Point and Mill Cove are gone, as you've seen. Vanished." He beckoned to his tall partner.

"Well, let's go, Steve."

To Tommy, he said, "We'll take you ashore. We have lots of lost and stranded people to locate." He nodded to Ben Brown.

"—And most of them weren't so lucky."

The short policeman's insistence on luck annoyed Tommy. It wasn't all luck that the house had survived. God helped too. And so did Ben Brown. Ben had *prepared!*

He had a good seawall to break the force of the waves. He had not tried to prevent the hurricane sea from entering, an impossible thing to do. No, he had *allowed* it to enter!

Ben Brown's knowledge and experience had helped save the old house in a hundred different ways:

There was that open cellar foundation on the north and south sides—

"A bridge for the sea", Ben had vividly described it.

Tommy recalled the open doors and windows on the leeward

side to prevent explosion from the sudden drop in air pressure. And most of the furniture had been moved upstairs. And all of it would have kept perfectly dry except for that fantastic second tidal wave.

Most of the other homes on Conimicut Point had floated, or been knocked off, their cement foundations. Ben's house hadn't, but that was no accident either. Ben had reinforced his home and rigidly bolted it to the high and thick, heavily-reinforced cement foundation.

No. It wasn't luck at all. It was God and man working together, as they should do!

Thoughtful, Tommy stepped into the skiff and sat beside Kathy. He saw the water level had dropped another couple of inches. The wind had diminished to less than thirty knots, practically a breeze, from the northwest now. The rain had stopped completely.

In the western sky several patches of blue showed through the rolling gray clouds.

Tommy looked up and saw Ben Brown waving from the porch.

"But aren't you coming with us?" Kathy asked, deeply concerned.

The old man shook his head. "Not now, Kathy. Got too much work to do here. But I'll see you two again when you come to pick up your boats." His wide smile included them both.

"Thank you, Mr. Brown," Tommy said. "For *everything!*"

He stood up and reached over to shake the old man's hand. It was a good hand, capable, dependable, the most important hand in the world—the hand of a good friend!

And it was also the dear hand of a man who had saved his and Kathy's lives. —Twice!

Suddenly choking up, Tommy stepped out of the boat on to the porch and hugged the old man fiercely.

"I love you!" he whispered, and held him tight. A few seconds later he returned to the skiff and sat down slowly, fighting tears. Would he ever see the wonderful old man again?

He saw Kathy smiling at him and at Ben Brown. She understood...

The shorter policeman untied the bow line and pushed the skiff back away from the front porch.

"Stop! Our boats," Kathy cried.

"They'll be safe where they are," Ben Brown soothed her. "I'll keep my eye on them. You can come and get them tomorrow."

For several seconds Kathy was hesitant. Finally she nodded in agreement. She'd trust her precious pram with Mr. Brown.

That was a remarkable concession, Tommy thought, pleased.

He wondered what was going to happen to his own boat and motor. Granny Parker would probably sell them and send him the money. She would never keep it herself. He saw Ben Brown waving at them.

"Bye, Kathy, Tommy..."

They both waved back. "Good-bye, Ben, old friend," Tommy choked.

Once free of the protection of the house, the skiff bobbed in the choppy water. The taller policeman, Steve, rowed smoothly toward high ground while his partner moved aside floating logs and debris with a long stick. On impulse he tentatively probed the bottom, then held up the stick, grinning widely.

"Hey, Steve. Look at this!"

The water under the boat was now less than three feet deep. If necessary, they could have walked ashore, although the footing would have been treacherous, and the force of the outgoing tide and floodwater would have made the going difficult.

The boat slowly moved up the street toward loved ones.

Tommy gazed around in horrified fascination. It was an odd sensation to be rowed up Shawomet Avenue, a familiar street that wasn't a street.

Instead, it was now a salt-water pond filled with partly-submerged telephone poles, uprooted trees, houses, and cars caught in the storm. All around was a bleak scene of desolation and destruction.

Near the Point area, many small summer cottages had vanished. Others had toppled over, thrown helter-skelter, and abandoned like a child's building blocks. Others were smashed apart, torn open, or crumbled into painted kindling.

Floating about were numerous items of household furniture, packaged goods, sofa cushions, pillows, books—thousands of lost items.

Tommy knew the scenes were the same at all vulnerable, low-lying areas: Oakland Beach, Long Meadow, Rocky Point, Potowomut, Nayatt Point, Bristol, Barrington, Riverside, Apponaug, Cranston, Providence...

Their small boat moved past several abandoned autos, now dripping with seaweed and mud, their windows smashed by debris, engines flooded with salt water, batteries short-circuited and dead.

Some later model cars would be salvaged and reconditioned at great expense, but most of them would never travel the highways again. Salt and ocean chemicals would silently rust and corrode in ten-thousand hidden places, turning metal and fabric into oxide and dust.

As the skiff moved closer to higher land and loved ones, Tommy saw Kathy's parents anxiously waiting. Several dozen persons had collected near Shawomet and Symonds Avenue. The crowd was held back by policemen and uniformed soldiers of the Rhode Island National Guard.

Tommy saw other skiffs being rowed about, searching for survivors. When he again looked at the crowd he noticed the policemen and National Guard soldiers were heavily armed.

"Looters!" he suspected. "Parasites of tragedy!"

He searched the faces of the crowd, but Granny Parker wasn't among them. He hadn't really expected her to be, but he had hoped...

"Look! There's Mommy and Daddy!" Kathy cried, and excitedly ran her fingers through her tangled hair. She stood up and hastily straightened Ben Brown's borrowed tent-like trousers.

"Better sit down, young lady," the tall policeman cautioned. "I'm afraid you'll have to wait a few minutes more."

Kathy sat heavily, rocking the skiff. "Oh. Gee..."

The policeman smiled. They rowed past gaunt trees, many uprooted, or broken by the vicious hurricane winds. Many of the trees still standing were now denuded of leaves by Hurricane Glenna.

This year they would have an early Fall season, Tommy knew, and the windburned and salt-coated leaves of maples and oaks—usually the most brilliantly-painted by late Fall—would not appear this year. Instead, the muddy, wounded leaves would continue to blacken.

Soon they would drop silently, unnoticed, to the ground. This year it would be a Fall season without color. They would step from Summer into Winter...

When they were a few dozen feet from dry ground, the oars scraped the macadam street.

"Guess this is it, kids." Steve stepped into the shallow water and held the boat steady for them.

"Now you may go, young lady," he informed Kathy.

Her young face beaming in pleasure, Kathy leaped out. "Oh, thank you!"

She splashed through the filthy, scummy water, almost tripping on debris in her great eagerness to rejoin her parents.

Tommy followed, hoping to share in the sweet happiness of reunion.

The police-and-soldier-barrier opened briefly, allowing the Turners through. Kathy ran into her father's open arms. He swept her high, hugging and kissing her. Mrs. Turner embraced her daughter. She was laughing and crying. She looked at Kathy's oversize clothes and hugged and kissed her again.

"Oh, thank God. Thank God!"

Tommy watched from several feet away. He stood silently in ankle-deep water and absorbed the happy scene with a mixed feeling of joy and envy.

Mr. Turner saw him. He splashed up to him and seized his hand. Without saying a word, he pulled Tommy close and hugged him very tight for several precious seconds, then practically dragged him to the others.

To Tommy's surprise, Mrs. Turner kissed him. She hugged them both, her attractive face now streaked with grateful tears.

"You're both all right?" Kathy asked. "Our house is all right?"

"Yes. Yes! A few leaks. A little seepage water is in the basement. The lawn is a mess. We lost one maple tree. Yes, we're all right."

For the first time, Tommy spoke: "G-Granny Parker. How is she?"

"She's fine, Tommy." Mrs. Turner said. "She stayed with us all through Glenna. She's in the car, waiting. Jim insisted she stay there. Go to her, Tom. She's terribly worried." She pointed up Shawomet Avenue.

His heart pounding, Tommy ran up the debris-strewn street, squishing water from his sneakers. The police let him through. Curious spectators opened a path and stared after him. He raced on, around huge uprooted trees, over broken limbs and power lines.

Granny Parker saw him coming. She got out of the car.

A foot away from her Tommy stopped abruptly. A warm, overpowering sensation of joy, love and gratitude suddenly swept through him. But there was a hint of fear too, the fear of rejection. He took a hesitant step forward...

"Tommy. Oh, Tommy..." Granny Parker held out her arms.

Love was triumphant!

"Granny!" Tommy ran to her and flung his arms around her and held her close for a long time. At long last he felt loved and wanted. It was an emotion sweeter than anything he had ever known in his entire life!

The old lady kissed him on the face, then started to cry. He tried to comfort her, insisting they both were all right. He said a hundred things, but none of them made much sense except that he was so relieved she was safe, and he was sorry for what he had done, and he loved her very much. Yes, he loved her.

To his great surprise, the old lady began scolding him. But she kissed him to make up for it. She scolded him again, and all the while she was sobbing softly in relief, the sound like the whisper of a gentle breeze among the swaying eel grasses.

Kathy ran up and hugged the old lady around the waist. She was excitedly chattering like a magpie, clutching at her oversize clothes, laughing, giddy, tripping over her words as often as she tripped over her long trouser cuffs.

Mr. Turner opened the car doors. "Let's go home. There's spaghetti and meatballs waiting. You kids must be starved. I know I am. —Now!"

He helped Granny Parker into the car, then faced Tommy and Kathy.

"I want to hear all about it at home. And later I want to go out and thank Ben Brown." He nodded at his wife and at Granny Parker.

"—Ben may be a stranger to me, but we owe him a lot."

"Oh, he's wonderful, Daddy," Kathy said. "You'll like him too." She sat on the rear seat beside Granny Parker.

"He sure is," Tommy said, and sat on the other side of the old lady. "Not only did he help us and show us how to do a lot of things, but—" His voice trailed off.

"—He...saved our lives!"

Almost as he spoke, a sudden thought flashed through Tommy's mind: Wouldn't it be wonderful if Ben Brown and Granny Parker— No, that was too fantastic! Granny was older than Mr. Brown. Besides, they were old people and old people didn't fall in—

But why was it so fantastic? Love wasn't reserved for the young. There are ten thousand, wonderful kinds of love. Love was for everybody!

As Kathy had told him, "Love was a gift from God to everyone!"

Tommy grinned secretly to himself: Granny Parker and Ben Brown. What a wonderful, happy thought!...

He was still blissfully entertaining the idea as Mr. Turner drove a long, round-about route up Shawomet Avenue, left up Stokes Street to West Shore Road. He drove a few hundred feet north on West Shore Road, then finally turned right on Beach Avenue, back to Bellman, bypassing downed powerlines, uprooted trees, damaged cars, fallen branches and flooded streets.

The Turner car finally stopped before Granny Parker's house on Bellman Avenue.

Suddenly, Tommy's happy dream popped like a pricked soap bubble, bringing a sharp sting to his eyes. Parked before Granny's house was a shiny black car with out-of-state registration plates. No one was in it now, but Tommy knew who owned the car. He should. He had seen it often enough.

"Oh, gracious!" Granny Parker exclaimed. "Those two men. I forgot all about them."

A suffocating, choking sensation shook Tommy so he trembled like a pennant in the wind. He felt cold and empty. His breath gasped in his throat.

In the sudden joy of reunion, he had forgotten about everything else. Now he remembered everything. Now he realized that Granny Parker didn't really love him. She was relieved he was safe, that's all.

Now she could discharge her duties and be free of him.
That black car belonged to the two men from the Home.
Despite Hurricane Glenna, they had come to take him back!

Chapter 20

The Delightful Decision

Mr. Turner got out of the car and opened the doors for Granny Parker and Tommy.

"Remember. As soon as you clean up and change, come over to our house for dinner. Both of you."

Tommy nodded solemnly. As he watched, Mr. Turner cautiously backed out of the dirt driveway and into the treebranch-cluttered street, avoiding the shiny black car parked in front of Granny Parker's house.

As her father drove up Bellman Avenue, Kathy waved from the back seat.

For several minutes Tommy stared after the Turner's car. He tried to avoid looking at the shiny, black, out-of-state car as he turned toward the house. He didn't know where those two men were, but they were around some place.

He saw Granny Parker waiting for him at the door. She beckoned impatiently. He hurried to join her.

"You get out of those wet clothes before you catch your death," Granny ordered as she pushed open the door. "I'll make you some hot cocoa."

"—Yes, mam."

Tommy was glad to escape upstairs to his room. Deeply troubled, he removed his borrowed clothes, then gazed at them on the floor, watching a small puddle form.

With those two men here to take him back—wherever they were—he wouldn't even be able to return Ben Brown's clothes. Granny Parker would probably ask Kathy to do it. He felt himself growing bitter and resentful, and strongly resisted the negative emotions.

Slipping on his robe, he walked to the east window and looked out over a still-angry flood tide at a greatly changed Narragansett Bay. He didn't recognize it anymore. It looked cold, abandoned, destroyed...

He noticed the cluttered back yards and the badly-eroded beach areas. Granny had lost a lot of topsoil, he noticed. The back lawn needed cleaning, filling, raking and re-seeding.

Despite the still-high flood waters, he could see the top of Granny Parker's seawall, It was still intact. A pleased smile briefly found his tired face.

The old seawall had held! His hundreds of hours of cementing, piling rocks, back-filling—it all paid off! The old wall did not fall outwards during the hurricane sea's massive incoming and ebbing tides.

It was odd how that gave him a sense of deep satisfaction, but it did.

He gazed around his own room and a great, hot lump formed in his throat and pushed hot tears to his eyes. He had not expected to be here again. The familiar chair seemed to beckon to him to sit and relax. The loved books in the bookcase seemed especially inviting, warmly comfortable and secure...

"No!" he cried aloud.

He resisted their invitations. This room wasn't for him anymore. It was a room full of ghosts of happy memories. It had to be locked tight in his past, and best forgotten.

He showered and scrubbed his body and hair, lathering them several times before he was able to remove all the scum, grime and oil of Hurricane Glenna.

Thoroughly drying off, he carefully cleaned, disinfected and Band-Aided the wound on his left shoulder. It had looked much worse than it was, and was still stiff and painful, but it felt a bit better now. He would forever have an inch-long scar.

He quickly dressed, then applied a dab of Vaseline into his hair and combed it. Satisfied at the reflection in the mirror, he went downstairs.

Granny Parker had cocoa waiting for him. He sat at the table, avoiding her eyes. When he noticed his note to her was still where he had left it, a sudden flush heated his face.

Granny Parker sat opposite him. Her soft voice was startling.

"Why did you run away, Tommy?"

The question was direct and pointed. There was nothing subtle about Granny. He was still unable to look at her.

"I— You saw my note? It's—right there on the t-table."

"Yes. I saw it." She forced him to look at her. Her eyes were moist. "But I thought you *liked* living here, living with me," she said softly.

"I-I do, Granny. I do!" His voice lowered to a whisper. "I do like it very much. I—"

"And so you ran away."

He was suddenly defensive. "Yes. I had to. Don't you see? I didn't want to be sent back to the Home. "I'm sorry if I made you worry. I didn't mean to hurt you, or cause you trouble."

"But you *did* hurt me, Tommy. You did!"

The old lady was silent for a moment. Presently, she said, "Besides, who said I was sending you back? I didn't."

Tommy flushed and felt like a traitor.

"K-Kathy did," he finally admitted. "She overheard you on their telephone. She told me those two men were coming today to take me back. I *made* her tell me!"

He glared accusingly. Bitter, uncontrolled words flooded out.

"I mean those two men who came in that big car out front! And they *did* come, didn't they, Granny? Not even Hurricane Glenna could stop them. Oh, you sure wanted to get rid of me in a hurry, didn't you?"

The old lady gasped. She slumped back in her chair as though he had slapped her across the face. He saw tears forming in her eyes. He despised himself.

"I-I'm sorry, Granny. Forgive me..."

"Kathy heard wrong," the old lady said haltingly. "Those men didn't come to take you back. They are lawyers from the Home. They came because they had to talk to you. They needed your consent..." She leaned forward, placing her thin, wrinkled hand on his.

"Tommy. I want you to *stay* with me. I want to legally make you my son. I— Oh, Tommy... Tommy... Don't you understand? I love you. I want you to stay with me. For *always!*"

For several long, silent minutes Tommy sat, stunned. Suddenly, as though regaining his ability to move, he bolted out of his chair and knelt beside the old lady. He touched her arm gently.

"Granny. You're— You're not—fooling? You really want me to stay? I—I can live here? With you? For always? You're—not fooling?"

The old lady looked down at him and he saw her eyes were red and swollen, tears streaming down her cheeks. He had never seen her cry before. He didn't want her to cry. Never again.

"No. I'm not fooling," the old lady finally replied. "I—guess I should have told you my plans, but I was saving it for a surprise."

"It's a wonderful surprise!" Tommy cried and hugged her so hard she gasped. He apologized and she laughed, then he laughed with her, and hugged her again, but gentler.

He kissed her on the cheek. Grinning widely, he stood up and gazed around the old, familiar house he had come to love so deeply. His first real home!

Oh, there was so much he could do to fix it up for Granny Parker. And now he had the time!

Yes, and he could even help Ben Brown make repairs to his damaged house. The whole south porch and much of the siding, and the windows were destroyed, plus all the damage inside the house and to the property.

And next week, or a few weeks later because of the hurricane damage all over, he could go to school, like Kathy.

—Yes, Kathy. Wonderful little Kathy. They could stay together. Oh, this was fantastic!

"At last!" he thought joyfully. "At last I have a home!" All he had to do was say yes, and sign some papers.

He recalled Ben Brown's simple but very eloquent prayer: "God is good!"

"Oh, God is very good!" he shouted out loud, and impulsively kissed Granny Parker on the forehead.

"I never told you before, Granny, but I'll say it *often* from now on. I love you. Very, very much!"

The old lady's smile was the sweetest thing he had ever seen.

"Oh, this is fantastic news!" Tommy cried, giddy with happiness. But he also realized everything wasn't going to be perfection. He had to make changes and adjustments. Except for the past three-and-one-half months when he had lived with her, Granny Parker was accustomed to living alone. His presence wasn't going to break habits of thirty-years standing.

No, he was the one who was going to have to make adjustments and changes to accommodate her. He grinned widely.

He guessed they *both* were going to have to learn to live with each other, to understand, to grow, to share...

But that's what life was all about, wasn't it? Understanding, sharing!

Oh, but the effort was worth it...

At long last, he belonged to someone! He was loved. He had a home, his own home!

"Oh, wow!" he cried aloud. "Wait until I tell Kathy the wonderful news!"

Almost at the same moment, there was a loud thump on the door. Tommy turned the handle and Kathy stood before him. Despite her harrowing experiences of the terrifying day, she looked radiant!

She was clean and sweet and beautiful, smelling of soap and Granny's toilet water. Her chestnut-colored hair was washed and combed loose so it brushed her shoulders. She was wearing her new red dress and was the most beautiful girl in the whole world!

Tommy seized her hand and pulled her inside. "Kathy, wait until—"

"Come on, slowpoke!" Kathy interrupted. She caught Granny Parker's hand.

"Please come with us. Mom and Dad have dinner waiting. It's going to be by candlelight." She giggled.

"No electricity, you know. No telephones either." Turning back to Tommy, she caught his hand and pulled him toward the door.

Kathy's invasion left Tommy speechless. He looked at Granny Parker, at a loss what to do. The old lady smiled and waved him on.

"You go, Son. Tell them I'll be there in five minutes."

"Whee! Let's go!" Kathy jerked him outside and practically dragged him the short distance to her house.

Tommy was very anxious to tell her the good news, but Kathy was so full of bubbling enthusiasm she didn't give him the time, or the opportunity, to slip in a single word. She pushed open the screen door of her home.

"Here he is, Mom and Dad."

Mr. Turner strode across the kitchen floor and shook Tommy's hand. He glanced outside.

"Where's Granny Parker?"

"She'll be here in a few minutes," Kathy told him.

"Fine." He motioned Tommy into a chair. "Sit down, Tom. We all have a lot to say to you and not much time to say it."

Tommy sat. Kathy and her mother stood behind Mr. Turner's chair, looking at Tommy. He felt self-conscious and suddenly guilty. He was in for it now. They were going to reprimand him, probably forbid him to see Kathy again. Well, he wouldn't lie and make excuses for his behavior. The entire mess really was his fault.

He looked at Mr. Turner, waiting for the verbal barrage.

Mr. Turner took a deep breath.

"Tom, Kathy's told us everything—about the telephone calls and the Home, and your running away because you didn't want to be sent back. She also told us how you dove into the water and saved her life, and a lot of other things too, private, personal things." He paused several seconds.

"Fortunately, you're both safe, so we won't go into the hurricane business now." He glanced briefly at his wife and Kathy, then continued:

"What we *do* want to talk about is you. We don't want you to go away either. We *all* have come to love and respect you."

The announcement brought a surprised gasp from Tommy. Mr. Turner resumed:

"Yes, Tom. We all have learned to love you. Beth and I have discussed this many times. And today we mentioned it to Kathy. She agrees. Right, honey?"

Kathy nodded vigorously. "Uh huh!"

"Anyway, to make this short, Tom, we want to adopt you. That is, if that's agreeable with you."

The surprise announcement stunned Tommy. He felt glued to the chair. His voice squeaked:

"A—Adopt me?"

Mr. Turner held up his hand. "You don't have to say yes or no. Just think about it, Son. That's all we ask. But remember one thing: we do want you to stay with us. Very much!"

After several moments Tommy somehow found his voice.

"But— I don't have to think about it," he said. "I'd like nothing better, but—"

"But what, Son?"

Tommy blushed furiously, his face hotter than the spaghetti bubbling on the gas stove. His tongue seemed to swell in his throat. He looked up at Kathy, sweet and lovely Kathy, and felt weak and watery inside. He knew she would someday mean so much more to him, more than a sister.

"—Well?" Mr. Turner was persistent.

"Yes. Please explain yourself, Tom," Mrs. Turner said. "We'd love to have you as our son."

Tommy stood up and awkwardly cleared his throat. Somehow it was filled with cotton.

"I—I'd be proud to be your son..." He struggled to hold back tears. Crying made him feel ashamed and unmanly, but he could not help himself.

Mrs. Turner sensed his discomfort. She placed a gentle hand on his shoulder and pulled him close. Tommy felt the physical comfort of a person who loved him. It was the most precious thing in the whole, wide world, to be loved... and to love!

He gently eased away and faced them all.

"I—I don't want Kathy for a sister!" he cried. He saw their shocked expressions and immediately regretted his choice of words. He had hurt them. They didn't understand. Somehow, he had to make them understand.

Kathy suddenly stood in front of him. She caught his hand and he saw in her eyes that she understood and approved. She faced her parents, her cheeks pink.

"Mommy...Daddy... Someday, when Tommy and I are older, we—" She paused and mouthed several soundless words.

"—Well, I think Tommy's wonderful, and very special!" she cried defensively. "But I don't want him for a brother, either. Not a *real* brother, Daddy, because—well, I—"

Kathy's pretty face colored almost to the shade of her vivid red dress. She spun around and hid her face against Tommy's chest.

Her eyes misty, Mrs. Turner hugged them both. "I—think I understand," she whispered.

She glanced briefly at her husband, and then smiled warmly at Tommy.

"—Because brothers and sisters don't fall in love. Isn't that it?"

Acutely embarrassed, Tommy nodded. Mrs. Turner was wonderfully understanding, he thought.

"I think Kathy's very special too," he replied simply.

But to Mr. Turner this new thought was startling. It seemed incredible that his little Kathy was growing up so fast. His expression told them that this thought was going to take some getting used to.

He clasped Tommy on the shoulder. "Huh! I guess I almost goofed! Okay, you can be our foster son, legally and all, but you won't have to be Kathy's brother. Now, how about it?"

Tommy delighted in the proposal. It was fantastic! First, he had no family, and now he had offers of two families!

"I—I—" he stammered, and was deeply grateful for the soft knock on the kitchen door.

Tommy hurried across the room to let Granny Parker into the house. She was dressed in her Sunday best. She looked so tiny and fragile, something he had never really noticed before.

As he helped her into a chair, Tommy realized for the first time that Granny Parker—despite all her hard work and fierce independence—was an *elderly woman*.

And she not only wanted him to live with her as her son, but she actually *needed him*... as much as he needed her.

Tommy faced the others and took a deep breath and exhaled. He spoke slowly and thoughtfully, carefully selecting each word.

"Kathy. Just before you came into the house, Granny Parker told me she wasn't planning to send me away. It was a mistake. She wants to *adopt* me!"

He saw their surprised faces and forced himself to continue.

"She said she didn't tell me before because she wanted it to be a surprise. Those men from the Home didn't come to take me back. They brought papers for me to sign, and—"

There was so much more he wanted to say, but his voice choked...

For several minutes no one spoke. Mrs. Turner finally walked over to the gas stove. She drained the noodles into the sink, dumping them from the colander into a deep bowl which she placed on the table. Next, she poured the savory spaghetti sauce and meatballs and Italian sausage into another bowl and put it on the table.

She motioned to them all to sit at the table.

"Well—" Mr. Turner seemed to shake himself awake. He lighted the two candles on the table.

His face unbearably hot, Tommy stared at the floor. He knew they were confused, even hurt. He finally sat down and Kathy slipped into the seat next to him, her hand lightly brushing his own.

Swallowing painfully, Tommy cleared his throat and continued:

"Please understand, Mr. Turner. Mrs. Turner. Kathy. You're all wonderful and I do appreciate your offer of adoption—"

He heard Granny Parker's gasp and saw the astonished look on her face. He saw the pain come to her eyes.

Oh, he was doing everything wrong, and it was so very important that he do it right. These four people, and Ben Brown, were the most wonderful he had ever known. He didn't want to hurt any of them.

He prayed they all would understand his decision.

"I—I've decided to stay with Granny Parker," he blurted out.

He knew he sounded abrupt.

"Oh, please don't be angry! I love you all, but I—I—" The words died in his throat.

Mr. Turner suddenly stood up and seized his hand in a crushing grip.

"Tom, we understand now." His glance included his family. "And we all think it's wonderful that you will be Mrs. Parker's son! We're all delighted with your decision. It shows real intelligence and maturity."

"It—does?" Tommy grinned feebly, very relieved.

"Yes, it sure does."

"Oh, I'm so very happy for you, Tommy," Mrs. Turner said, and wiped her eyes.

"Me—e too—o!" Kathy was bawling, unashamed. "Oh, Tommy, how wonderful!" She suddenly hugged him, then ran around the kitchen table and kissed Granny Parker who was making little, soft, happy sounds deep in her throat.

"Me and my surprises," Granny Parker said. She dabbed at her eyes with a pink lace handkerchief. "At my age, I should have known better."

She gazed proudly at Tommy and reached across the table to squeeze his hand.

"Thank you, Son. Thank you."

Tommy flushed happily. All this sudden attention was very nice, but it was kind of embarrassing too. He had only decided what he felt was right. After all, Granny Parker needed him. And he really needed her too.

Besides, his thoughts added, feeling the way he did about Kathy, his living in the same house wouldn't be such a good idea, after all.

Mr. Turner loudly cleared a froggy throat. "Hem! Well, let's eat!"

"That's a good idea," Kathy agreed. "I'm starved!"

The candlelight seemed much brighter now, for the west kitchen had darkened to dusk. They all sat around the table excitedly talking and laughing, a happy end to a terrifying visit by Hurricane Glenna, the state's worst hurricane.

They were one. They were a family!

As Mrs. Turner served the macaroni onto Granny Parker's plate, Kathy stood up, her expression horrified.

"Oh, goodness. I almost forgot. Mr. Brown's still out on Conimicut Point. He must be starved too. Daddy. Mommy..."

"I already thought of that," her mother said. "I have a heaping plate of spaghetti and meatballs, and some Italian bread, put away for him. After supper we'll re-heat it and bring it out to him. All of us!"

"That's for sure," Mr. Turner agreed. "Old Ben Brown's one of the family now. Besides, I have a great debt of gratitude to pay."

Visibly relieved, Kathy sat down again.

She nudged Tommy gently with her elbow. Her left hand slipped under the table. So did Tommy's right hand. Hidden from view, their fingers met and entwined...

The Turner family had a good, old-fashioned custom: They said Grace before meals. At Mr. Turner's signal, they all bowed their heads.

"Lord, we thank Thee..."

Tommy glanced from face to face in the warm candlelight. These were *his* family now: Granny Parker, Mr. and Mrs. Turner, Ben Brown who wasn't physically present, and Kathy...

Yes, the sweetest and most important of all was Kathy!

Tommy's heart was full, almost bursting in happiness. He

humbly and gratefully bowed his head. Aloud, he said:
"Dear Lord, I thank Thee..."
Never in his entire life did he thank the Almighty with deeper and greater fervor.

* * * * *

CONIMICUT HURRICANE
The End... But a new beginning—

(Be on the lookout for further adventures of Tommy and Kathy in **CONIMICUT HURRICANE**, Book II.)

You've Enjoyed The Novel...
Now Meet and Hear the Author!

Don Vieweg is a resident of Conimicut Village in Warwick, Rhode Island. He is President of DON VIEWEG COMMUNICA-TIONS, a company that focuses on motivating, speaking and training, and on building confidence and self-esteem through seminars, workshops and consultation.

A much-in-demand speaker, seminar leader and trainer, Don is the author of the exciting, best-selling inspirational novel, *Conimicut Hurricane*. He publishes fiction and motivational articles in national magazines, such as Norman Vincent Peale's *Guideposts*, and Full Gospel Business Men's *Voice*.

A Brown University graduate, Don is a U.S. Navy veteran who lived through eleven land-based hurricanes, and survived four Pacific typhoons aboard U.S. Navy Destroyers. He is still an avid lover of boats, fishing and beautiful Narragansett Bay.

A professional speaker and motivator, Don is a member of the *New England* and *National Speakers Associations*.

To have Don Vieweg SPEAK at your business, group or convention, call or write him today at the address below.

To PURCHASE GIFT COPIES of *Conimicut Hurricane*, please copy and use the information on the next page. Thank you.

MEMBER

NATIONAL
SPEAKERS
ASSOCIATION

Don Vieweg
210 Bellman Avenue
Warwick, RI 02889-2833
Telephone: (401) 737-2058

The Perfect Gift!

CONIMICUT HURRICANE, The Adventure Novel for the entire family!
by Don Vieweg

Conimicut Hurricane makes the perfect gift...for the young, such as Tommy and Kathy...and the young-at-heart, like Granny Parker and old Ben Brown—everyone nine to ninety who loves an exciting, warm, family-oriented adventure story that grabs your interest and keeps you reading and cheering, and reading again!

ORDER YOUR COPIES TODAY!
(Copy the information below and mail today!)

YES! I want _____ Gift Copies at $14.95 each
(Please add $2.00 postage and handling.)

Enclosed is my check for $_____, payable to **Bellman Publishing Co.** (RI residents add 7% sales tax) Allow 2-4 weeks for delivery.

Send my copies of CONIMICUT HURRICANE, The Adventure Novel to:

(Print Your Name) _____

Address _____

City _____ State _____ Zip _____

Please Mail Your Order to:
Bellman Publishing Co.
P.O. Box 9118
Warwick, RI 02889-0118 USA
Telephone: (401) 737-2058

Thank you...